CHASING PAIGE

Washington Guardians
Hockey ~ Book #2

By Ellen Devlin

Chasing Paige

Limitless Publishing, LLC
Kailua, HI 96734
www.limitlesspublishing.com

Formatting: Limitless Publishing

ISBN-13: 978-1-64034-620-8
ISBN-10: 1-64034-620-1

Dedication

To Kelly
(she's kind of a big deal)

Chapter One

"You gotta help me, Micky. I'm losing my shit."

"You need me to hop on a plane and come beat the crap out of someone? I got your back, Becks."

"No, no. I met someone."

Tom (Micky) McCullin paused before answering. "And there's some sort of problem with that? That sounds like a good thing."

Chris Beckman paced around his apartment, talking on the phone with his best friend. "A woman. I met a woman."

Micky laughed. "I figured that part out. I still don't understand the problem."

"I don't know what to do."

"Seriously, Becks? I thought we had this conversation when we were fourteen or so. I know you don't get much action, but did you forget how things work? I can send you links to some very helpful educational videos. 'Tab A goes into Slot B…'"

"Shut up, Mick. I'm serious." Chris took a breath. "She's fucking gorgeous. And I can't stop

1

thinking about her."

Micky left off his teasing. "What's the deal? Have you gone out already, or did you just meet her?"

Chris stopped pacing and sat down. "I just met her. I have her number, but I don't know if I should call."

Micky laughed again. "Dude, if she gave you her number, you should definitely call her. What the fuck's gotten into you?"

"She didn't give it to me. Her friend did." He paused. "This feels weird. But I think I'm going to lose my fucking mind if I don't see her again."

"Damn. Okay, that does sound weird. And you already sound like you're losing your mind. Elaborate. How did you meet her? How did you get her number?"

"It was at a fan event."

"No shit." Micky was surprised. "You're losing your mind over a puck bunny?"

Chris and Micky were both pro hockey players. Chris was in his second season of a long-term contract as a winger with the Washington Guardians, and his best friend was a defenseman with the Montreal Lynx.

"No. Jesus, Mick." He took a breath and rubbed his free hand on the back of his neck. "I was working a fan event, and I looked across the room and saw this…shit, I don't even know how to describe her. She's fucking gorgeous."

"You mentioned that." Micky had a small smile on his face, amused to hear Chris so flustered. This was something new.

"She's like, five-foot-two, tiny, brown hair, the nicest curves you can possibly imagine…anyway, I look over and see her, and I just can't stop staring." He paused again to take another breath. "I must have stared at her on and off for like a half-hour. When I finally thought to look to see if she was there with someone, I noticed that she's with another woman, and I accidentally catch *that* woman's eye because she's totally looking at me. And then she smiles and starts heading straight for me."

"Shit."

"I know, right? I'm thinking I'm screwed. How do you tell someone, 'Hey, you're cute and everything, but I really only want to talk to your friend,' and not come off like a total dick?"

He stood up and started pacing again. "So, the woman comes up to me and introduces herself, says she's a huge Guards fan, was glad to see me traded here, a few other things. Her friend is just standing with her, kind of looking around, and I'm trying not to blatantly stare at her friend while this woman is talking to me. I have no idea what I said."

Chris stopped pacing and sat on the couch again. "And then, so help me God I am not making this up, the woman says, 'This is my friend, Paige. She doesn't know anything about hockey. I think you could probably explain the basics to her better than I could.' And then she smiled and winked and started to walk off, leaving me standing there with this tiny goddess."

"You are fucking kidding me." Micky was fascinated. "What happened?"

"The goddess—I mean Paige—looked stunned and started to say something, but her friend said, 'I'll be back in a few minutes, just gotta go check something out.'" Chris leaned his head back against the cushion. "I'm not sure what I said. I think I introduced myself...and maybe made small talk? Shit. I don't know. I think I tried to explain something about hockey. Fuck, Micky. I was a mess."

Micky started laughing. "So how did you end up with her phone number?"

"Her friend came back after a little while, and the three of us talked. That was easier, somehow. And then, when they were going to move on, her friend shook my hand again and handed me a piece of paper that said, 'Here's her number in case you forgot to ask for it.'"

"Holy shit!"

"Micky, I had totally forgotten to ask for her number." His voice reflected how potentially devastating that would have been. "She would have walked away and I never would have seen her again."

"So why haven't you called her?" Chris just sat there, staring at the ceiling, long enough to make Micky wonder if they had been disconnected. "Becks. Why the fuck did you pick up the phone and dial my number instead of hers?"

There was a pause before Chris replied in a hollow voice, "I don't know."

Micky chuckled. "I think you're scared shitless. Hang up the phone and call her, you idiot."

"Okay."

***

Paige Smith and her roommate, Liz Williams, were having dinner in their apartment when Paige's phone rang.

"Huh, that's not a number I recognize." Paige picked up the phone and said hello, and there was a rather deep male voice on the other end.

"May I please speak to Paige?"

"Speaking. Can I help you?"

Liz watched Paige with interest while continuing to eat her dinner. She had a suspicion as to who was on the other end of the line. If she was right, it was surprising it had taken him this long to call—she hadn't seen anyone so obviously, utterly smitten in a long time.

"Um, this is Chris Beckman. From the Guardians. I don't know if you remember, but we, uh, we met at the fan event the other day."

Paige's eyes were huge, and she turned to stare daggers at Liz, who simply smiled in return.

"Yes, I remember you. I'm wondering how you got my number, though."

Chris's heart was racing, and he was sweating. "Your friend gave it to me. I hope that was okay." He paused, rubbing the back of his neck. "I meant to ask you for it, but I didn't manage to. I mean, I didn't remember to, but I wanted to, and…" *Shit, shit, shit, stop talking.* "…she gave it to me before you guys left." Deep breath. "I hope that's okay." He had the vague idea that he had started repeating himself.

Paige was glaring at Liz but found the corner of

her mouth turning up listening to the man on the other end of the phone. He sounded completely flustered. It was rather sweet.

"It's fine. I will kill her later."

Chris breathed a sigh of relief and then hoped she hadn't heard it. He suspected she had.

"So, Chris Beckman from the Guardians, can I help you with something?"

He realized that he hadn't said anything. "I, uh...I was wondering..." *Shit, get it together, Beckman.* Deep breath. "I was wondering if I could take you out to dinner sometime."

"Oh. Well, I mean, all right." She was still staring at Liz but now simply blinked rather than glared. "Sure," she said. "I guess."

Liz looked at her curiously, lifted an eyebrow, and mouthed, *"I guess?"* at her. Paige shrugged, eyes wide. Liz put her hands over her eyes and shook her head.

Chris froze at her response. She had said yes to a date, but on the other hand, he couldn't tell if she was interested or was just agreeing to placate him. "Um, okay, how about Friday night?"

"This Friday? I, uh..." Paige was faltering.

Liz sighed and shook her head. She looked at Paige and exaggeratedly nodded, mouthing, *"Say yes."*

"Yes, that would be fine." Paige's eyes were wide and she shrugged again.

"Okay, great." Chris felt panic gripping him, realizing he didn't know where to take her, where she lived, what kind of food she liked. So many logistics to address and he suddenly didn't have any idea how to do any of this. Even his palms were sweating. *Jesus, Beckman, get a grip!* "Is seven-thirty a good time?"

"That would be fine."

"Okay." He paused. "Then I will make reservations and will pick you up Friday night." Another pause. "I guess I need to get your address. Unless you would feel better meeting me there. In that case, I will tell you where I make reservations and we can just meet. But I don't mind picking you up, if that would be all right with you. But only if that won't make you uncomfortable." *Holy shit, shut the fuck up.*

"No, that would be fine with me. I will text you my address, and I will see you at seven-thirty on Friday."

Chris breathed out in relief. "Great. Good. That sounds good. I will see you then."

Paige looked at Liz after the phone disconnected.

"What. The. Fuck? Why did you give him my number?"

Liz laughed. "Paige, I told you, I don't think I have ever seen anyone look at another person the way he was looking at you. I think the only reason he looked over at me was to see if I was your boyfriend. He was looking at you like you were water in the desert. You just can't ignore things like that."

Paige shook her head. "He sounded really nervous on the phone." Her lips quirked into a small smile. "It was kinda cute."

"And he's more than just kinda cute."

"I'll admit that there's nothing wrong with the

7

way he looks."

"'*Nothing wrong?*'" Liz asked, incredulous. "Paige, please." Paige's smile was much bigger this time. "Yeah, I thought so. He's a great-looking guy with the body of a pro athlete. He's handsome. And hot. Perfect combination."

"Shut up."

"You're welcome."

***

Chris hung up the phone and texted Micky.

Chris: Date Friday holy shit.

Micky responded with a few emojis. Some appropriate for the situation, some less so. Chris laughed and tried to relax a little, still feeling a bit sweaty, his heart still racing. He had never been particularly smooth-talking or super confident with women, but he was pretty sure he hadn't sounded that awkward since he really was fourteen years old and his voice was cracking.

Chapter Two

"What do you think? Too much?" Paige turned to show Liz her outfit for the evening. She was wearing tailored slacks with a sleeveless silk blouse. The look was completed with heeled sandals, a nice belt, and classically tasteful pearl jewelry. Her makeup was perfect. As usual.

"Probably not, but where are you going?"

Fussing with her hair, Paige answered, "DiNatali Brothers in Old Town. Have you heard of it?"

"Ooooh, yes! That place is supposed to be fantastic! And very nice, so no, you are not overdressed. But you might want to take a light sweater in case it's cold in the restaurant."

"Yeah, I have one that I'll bring with me that goes well with this."

Liz chuckled. "I still don't understand how you always look so completely put together." Liz was sprawled out across their large armchair, her legs draped over one of the arms, wearing worn jeans and a faded t-shirt.

Paige responded, "I just get classic stuff that

9

won't go out of style and then add an accent piece here or there to jazz things up." Looking over at Liz, she rolled her eyes and said, "This isn't rocket science, Liz. You could do this if you wanted to."

"Who has that kind of time?"

Making a "tsk" noise as she continued to fuss with her hair, Paige said, "Everyone has a few minutes. You just choose jeans."

Liz smiled. "True. But to be fair, I do wear cute shirts and shoes. Sometimes, anyway."

"You're very cute."

"Yeah, well. You are gorgeous." Liz watched Paige twist her hair up in the back and added, "No, leave your hair down. It looks great down."

Paige released her hair and fluffed it back out again, pacing nervously for a moment before sitting down on the couch.

Liz asked, "What's wrong? You're going to have a good time tonight."

Sighing, sliding back into the couch, Paige responded, "I know, you're probably right. It should be fine. But it's been a long time since I had a real first date with someone I didn't already know. And I don't know this guy *at all*. That feels a little weird."

Thinking for a moment, Liz said, "Oh, wow, that's right. The last time would have been…Fred?"

Paige laughed. "Oh yeah! Fred. It's been quite a while since I've thought about him."

"Boniest dude I've ever met."

Paige hit her with a throw pillow from the couch. "He was very nice."

"Sure, he was very nice. But he was the most

10

angular guy I've ever seen in my life." Paige was laughing. "Seriously, he was a very nice bag o' antlers." Changing the topic, Liz said, with a small smirk, "A few 'accent pieces' to jazz up your wardrobe? Does that include hot pink five-inch heels?"

"Oh my God, I *knew* you wouldn't let that comment go by. One tequila-fueled ill-advised fashion decision. You're never going to let me live that down, are you?"

"Nope. Never."

"I did end up wearing them. Once."

"Yeah, when you dressed up as a hooker for Halloween."

"Shut up." They were both laughing as Paige got up. "I'm going to go finish getting ready."

The doorbell rang a few moments after Paige closed her bedroom door.

***

Liz found Chris standing outside the door. "Oh, hi!" she said. "Wait, you're Chris Beckman, right? We met at the fan event last week. What brings you to my door?" She tried not to smile at the horrified look on his face.

"Oh, for God's sake, Liz, would you please just let him in?" Chris exhaled in visible relief as he heard Paige's voice from inside the apartment.

Liz's eyes were twinkling as she let him in. She said, "Sorry, it was too good an opportunity to miss. Paige is my roommate. I'm Liz. Please have a seat. She'll be ready in a minute." She gestured him over to their couch. "Can I get you anything? Water? Coffee? Something to restart your heart, perhaps?"

Chris sat down and said, "No, thank you, I'm fine." He looked over at Liz with a little smile and said, "That was mean."

She sat down at the other end of the couch and grinned. "Yeah, but I figure I've gotta have a little bit of credit banked with you already. Thought I'd go ahead and use some right away."

Paige came out of her room, and Chris stood up and stared. "Hi, Chris. Sorry about my roommate. She's...challenging."

"You mispronounced 'amazingly fun and wonderful,'" Liz corrected.

"Riiight." She drew the word out in response.

Paige looked over at Chris and smiled at him. He really was a very handsome man. Tall, she was guessing around six-foot-one, with short, very dark hair. He was sharply dressed too, wearing suit pants and a crisp white button-down shirt open at the collar and rolled at the sleeves. When you added his athletic physique, he could easily have stepped out of a high-end menswear catalog. His dark brown eyes were currently looking at her with something akin to awe—the look was so admiring she was almost uncomfortable.

Chris knew he was staring but was temporarily unable to help himself. Paige was...beautiful. Exquisite. He had no idea what to say. He drank in the sight of her...thick, wavy, shoulder-length chestnut brown hair, green and gold eyes, stunning smile, and all those perfect, petite, curves.

"You look lovely." It wasn't quite a croak. Yay

for him.

"Thank you." She paused for a few seconds, not sure what to say to this man who was looking at her as if she were a work of art.

Liz stood up, intentionally breaking this spell, and said, "Okay, kids, have a nice time." She turned to Chris, who had been startled but appeared to appreciate the interruption. "Don't keep her out past curfew." She turned to Paige and said, "Don't do anything I wouldn't do." Paige rolled her eyes and laughed. Liz turned back to Chris and added, "Don't worry, that actually sets very few limits." Then she winked at him and walked off to her room.

Chris laughed—a warm, rich sound that Paige liked instantly—and turned to Paige. "Are you ready? I hope you're hungry. DiNatali Brothers' pasta is amazing."

He didn't know what had changed, but he felt a little more comfortable and less like he was at a middle school dance.

Paige responded, "I have never been, but I hear that it's fantastic. And I'm definitely hungry." Chris smiled and offered his arm to her. She took his arm, smiled back, and they set out.

***

"So, you know what I do for a living. What about you?" Chris sipped a glass of wine as they waited for their entrees. He finally felt like he was mostly in control of himself talking to her.

"I'm a high school English teacher."

"Really?"

"You seem surprised. Why is that?" People always seemed surprised to learn that she taught high school.

"You're just...I mean...you're..." *Shit.* "You're tiny. High school guys can be huge. And jerks."

Paige laughed. She had suspected that was what he was going to say. "Teaching has a lot to do with self-confidence. Or at least the ability to fake it. Being able to control a class is an important part of being able to teach, and that's true whether you're five-foot-two or six-foot-one. Besides, I might be short, but I can be fierce." She gave him her intimidating teacher look. "They only mess with me once."

Chris was impressed. "I was just transported back to high school. Yikes." He continued his questions. "English, though? I'm doubly impressed. Where did you go to school?"

"I got my bachelor's degree from George Mason University. I keep thinking I'll go back for my master's degree, but I haven't done it yet." She looked at him and asked, "How about you? I know nothing about how hockey works. Did you go to college, or did you start playing right out of high school?"

"I went to the University of Minnesota. I was drafted by the Columbus Union when I was eighteen and then started playing for them as soon as I graduated from U of M."

"What was your major? I'm assuming that 'Hockey' isn't one of the options, right?"

Chris smiled. "I was a business major."

Paige was impressed. This guy was definitely no

14

dumb jock. "So, how did you end up here?"

"I was traded by Columbus to Washington a year ago. This is my second season with the Guardians." He looked at her curiously and said, "So, do you really know nothing about hockey?"

Paige laughed and said, "Really. Nothing. Well, I know that there's a puck and sticks and ice skates and the general idea is to get the puck into the net. But that's where my knowledge ends. Liz is the hockey fan." She paused and added thoughtfully, "You would think that I would have absorbed more knowledge simply from living with her, because she watches every game. I should have learned by osmosis at this point."

Dinner had arrived, so conversation died down some while they ate. The restaurant was known for its homemade pasta dishes, and the ravioli Paige had ordered did not disappoint.

"Oh my God, this food is amazing. This was a great idea, Chris. Thank you."

Chris felt a little pang in his chest, so pleased that she was enjoying herself. "I'm really glad you like it. Some of my teammates have been coming here for years and introduced me to this place. It's been my favorite ever since."

He sat back in his chair and watched her. Paige looked up to see him gazing at her, and he flushed a little, embarrassed. "Sorry, I'm not trying to make you feel uncomfortable." He took a breath. "I'm finding it difficult not to stare. Sorry about that."

Paige blushed a little herself. "That's okay. You've been a perfect gentleman, and I've had a lovely dinner."

"Do you want to stay for coffee? Maybe dessert?" Chris was silently begging her to say yes.

"Would you mind terribly if I passed on that offer?" Paige looked a little sheepish. "I'm actually quite full, and I'm getting sleepy. I know that sounds utterly lame, but during the school year, I'm on a much earlier schedule, and I end up going to bed at old-person times, I'm afraid. We're right at the beginning of the school year, and I'm still adjusting." Seeing the look on Chris's face, she added hastily, "I'm having a wonderful time. I swear this has nothing to do with the company. I'm just afraid that I'll turn into a pumpkin or fall asleep on you."

Chris's brain froze on the idea of her falling asleep while leaning against his chest, with his arms around her, and he suddenly had no idea what to say. His heart was racing, and all the blood was heading south in his body. He gave his head a quick shake, trying to rid himself of the oh-so-attractive image that idea had formed.

"No, no. Not at all. I'm sorry, I didn't think about that." He flagged down their waiter and asked for the bill. "Our games usually don't start until seven at night, sometimes later, so I'm kind of on the opposite schedule. We will have a morning skate before games, but most things aren't scheduled very early in the morning."

They left the restaurant and strolled back to his car. Paige didn't particularly want to hurry, even though she was the one cutting the evening short. They chatted a bit more as they walked, enjoying the quaint area and the lovely weather.

"So what are you teaching right now?" Chris asked. "I mean, English, obviously, but, like, any specific book that I might know?"

Paige was pleasantly surprised that he would ask. "Well, each grade has a different curriculum, but right now I've got the senior class working on some British poetry."

"Oh, that's cool," Chris responded. "Like Yeats?" Paige was surprised to the point where she stopped walking briefly and looked at him. "I mean," Chris continued, "I know that he's Irish, but I thought that maybe…"

"Yes, as a matter of fact." She started walking again but looked at him curiously.

"What? Is that weird or something?"

Paige replied, "No, no. Not weird. I'm just surprised. Yeats isn't particularly mainstream, I guess. He's a little obscure, and I don't meet many people that mention Yeats first off when thinking about British poetry."

Chris gave her a little smile and said, "Well, in the interest of full disclosure, when I was in high school, I was really into a girl who liked poetry…"

Paige started laughing, and the sound was so genuine and free that Chris felt an immediate reaction in his chest—the warmth, the glow, the sheer pleasure of her laughter was like a physical touch.

He started laughing too but talked over her to say, "No, wait! It started that way, but I really ended up liking poetry." She turned to him, eyes bright. "Really! It started for her, but I kept reading it for me."

"Uh huh," she teased. "Sure you did."

"Really, Paige," he insisted as their laughter died down. "My favorite poem is *'He Wishes for the Cloths of Heaven.'*"

They had reached his car by this time. Paige cocked her head to the side slightly and said, "'Had I the heavens' embroidered cloths, / Enwrought with golden and silver light...'"

Chris quirked a little smile and continued, "'The blue and the dim and the dark cloths / Of night and light and the half light, / I would spread the cloths under your feet: / But I, being poor, have only my dreams; / I have spread my dreams under your feet...'"

His voice was soft and warm, and he spoke the poem in a way that showed his familiarity and appreciation of the verse, rather than just a recitation of the words.

Paige felt a flutter in her chest, and she finished quietly, "'Tread softly because you tread on my dreams.'"

The moment stretched between them, strung along the lines of the poem, until Paige finally blinked and reached for the door handle.

Chris started out of the moment and reached past her, saying, "Please, Paige, let me," as he opened her door.

"Thank you," she replied, taking another moment to look at him as he got into the driver's seat. So much about him was surprising and unexpected, and she was impressed.

When they arrived at the apartment complex, he opened the car door for her and walked her to the door of her apartment.

"I had a really nice time tonight, Chris. I'm glad you called." He felt her smile like he was standing on a beach, all fresh air and sunshine.

"Me too." He breathed out, looking at her a little sideways. "I almost didn't." She looked surprised. "I'm not sure if you could tell, but I've been more than a little nervous about this whole thing." He rubbed his hand on the back of his neck and gave her a small smile.

She smiled back, feeling that flutter in her chest again. He was disarmingly sweet, and this admission was kind of adorable. "I might have noticed. A little. I'm not sure I understand why, though. I try to only intimidate my students," she teased. Chris looked genuinely surprised. "What?" she asked.

"You really don't know why I'm nervous?" She shook her head. He felt his heart speed up, feeling slightly as if he was about to step off the edge of a cliff. He took a breath, looked into her eyes, and said, "Because you are the most beautiful woman I have ever seen in my entire life."

He looked up for a moment and breathed out. When he looked back down at her, Paige's expression was rather unreadable. "Thank you for coming to dinner with me tonight, Paige. I would very much like to see you again. May I call you?"

Paige stared at him, stunned, trying to process what he had said. She hadn't realized that she was taking a long time to respond to his question until Chris said, "I understand. You have my number if you change your mind. I really did enjoy tonight," and then turned to walk away.

"Wait." Paige reached for his arm. "Wait, please. I'm still stuck on your earlier comment. I didn't mean to stand here not answering." She took a deep breath against the butterflies and said, "I would like to see you again. Yes, please do call me." She smiled at him a little shyly. "And thank you. I've never had anyone say anything like that to me before."

"Really?" Chris's heart was racing. His voice got a little husky as he said, "I find that hard to believe."

His smile was a little shy and a little sexy, and the butterflies in her chest migrated lower.

"Really." Her voice had gotten husky too. "And you're quite easy on the eyes, yourself." She could hear her heartbeat in her ears.

"I will call you, then." He looked at her, put his hands in his pockets to keep them from shaking, leaned over, and kissed her. Gently, sweetly, softly, his lips pressed against hers. "Good night, Paige."

"Good night." Her voice was a whisper, and she watched him as he walked back to his car. He turned, gave her a little smile that made her insides flip, and she went in and closed the apartment door, standing with her back against it.

Chapter Three

Liz was sitting curled up on the couch reading a book and looked up when Paige walked in. She opened her mouth to ask how things went but then closed it again when she saw the look on Paige's face as she leaned back against the door.

Paige turned and looked at her. Her eyes were wide, and she just shook her head a little and then walked over and sat down on the other end of the couch.

She finally just said, "Wow."

Liz smiled.

***

Chris sat in his car and put his head back, willing his heart rate to slow down. Then he grinned to himself, started the car, and set off back to his apartment. On the way, he called Micky.

"Hey, Becks, what's up?" It sounded like Micky was in the locker room—Chris looked at the clock and realized his game must have only just finished.

21

"Micky, sorry, man, I can call back."

"No worries. I'm all finished. Just leaving now."

"Did you win?"

Micky scoffed. "Of course we won, you asshole. Now, why did you call? Oh, shit, it's Friday. What happened? Wait, why are you not still out with her? Did it bomb?"

"No, no, it was great. Amazing, actually. She's a high school teacher, so she normally goes to bed really early during the school year, so I took her home right after dinner."

Micky chuckled. "And that ranks as amazing in your book?"

Chris got serious. "It was fucking amazing, Micky. And she said she wants to see me again."

"Well, that's a good start, then." Micky was amused by the intensity. This woman was obviously under Chris's skin already. "Did you kiss her good night at least?" He couldn't resist asking the teasing question and was surprised by Chris's answer.

"Yeah," Chris breathed out. "One kiss. One fucking amazing kiss that felt like a goddamn bolt of lightning." He paused for a second. "Shit, Micky."

"Shit is right, my friend. It sounds like you are well and truly fucked." He chuckled to himself. "Or definitely that you want to be."

Chris laughed, and the tension was broken. "Shut the fuck up." And then he added, "Thanks, Mick. This is some crazy shit."

"No worries, my brother. It will be fine. You're a good guy. You deserve to find someone. It's about fucking time."

"Take care, man. Talk to you later."

"Sounds good. Hey, Becks, let me know what happens. And if she has a sister. Preferably one that lives in Montreal. You know, all the important stuff."

***

Liz waited while Paige gathered her thoughts.

"Dinner was lovely. Delicious food—that place lives up to the hype—and engaging and interesting conversation." She looked at Liz. "He's the same age as we are and was a business major at the University of Minnesota."

Liz looked amused and asked, "Why are you home so early, Paige? If you were having fun, why not stay out a while?"

"I don't know. I told him that I go to bed really early during the school year."

"Okay, well, that's true, but not on Friday nights usually." Liz pressed a little harder. "Not this early, anyway. What gives?"

"I'm not sure. He was so…admiring. It was a little unnerving." At Liz's questioning look, she added with a smile, "Not in a psychopath way. I wasn't frightened or worried or anything like that. It just felt…I don't know, intense."

Liz kept looking at her. Her look kept changing slightly, as if she was asking specific questions.

Paige said, "Just intense!"

Another look from Liz.

"Stop that. I don't know."

One more questioning look.

"Okay, I am really attracted to him! There, I've said it. I'm very attracted to him, and I made him take me home early because it's kind of freaking me out."

Liz smiled. "Now we're getting somewhere. So," she continued, "tell me why you looked completely overwhelmed when you came in the door."

Paige blushed. "He kissed me."

Liz's eyebrows climbed up her forehead, at the blush as much as the comment. She waited for Paige to continue, but nothing more appeared to be forthcoming. "Are you saying you're blushing like that because he *kissed* you? Just how much kissing are we talking about?"

Paige looked at her best friend and said, "One kiss. Just one small kiss." Liz looked surprised, and Paige added, "It was amazing. I think I understand now the concept of sparks between people. It felt like…electricity. Like touching a live wire."

"Please tell me that you're going out with him again."

It was Paige's turn to smile.

***

Chris lay in bed looking at the ceiling, vaguely wondering how soon was too soon to call her again. He wasn't sure he cared, though. He felt himself grin, knowing that he would probably call her tomorrow.

He was trying to sleep, but his mind just wouldn't go more than a few minutes without thinking about kissing her. He hadn't been kidding when he told Micky it felt like lightning. It had shot straight through his entire body, igniting every nerve ending.

At some point he just gave up, realizing that he was never going to get to sleep without some additional assistance. There was just too much going on in his head, and that was sending too many signals south of his belt. Since he couldn't stop thinking about her, he just gave in. He reached down, thought about that kiss, stroked himself, finishing much faster than he thought he would, and easily fell asleep soon after.

***

The game the next day was at three in the afternoon, so there had been no morning skate. Chris was warming up with the team but having some trouble focusing. This did not go unnoticed by his line-mate, Jakob Zimmerman.

"What's with your head, Becks?" Zee asked after Chris shanked an easy shot.

"Shit, Zee." He took a breath and focused. This was not the time to let outside thoughts wander in his head, no matter how gorgeous those outside thoughts were. "Sorry, man. Having trouble with focus. I'll get it together."

Zee looked at him oddly but let it go. Zee played right-wing to Chris's left-wing. They played well together and were usually paired on the same line. There was a bit of an age difference—Chris was twenty-eight and Zee was twenty-two—but they had both joined the Guardians last season, and their playing styles had meshed well right away.

The first period came and went, ending with the Carolina Tempest up one-nothing. In the locker room during the first intermission, Zee asked Chris again what was going on. "You're not all there, Becks. What the fuck is up?"

Chris looked at the younger player, shook his head, and said, "So help me God, Zee, if you give me shit about this, I will kill you slowly, but I met someone, and I can't stop thinking about her."

Zee's face registered total shock. "Are you fucking kidding me?" He laughed out loud, hard enough that some of the other players looked over. "Shit, man." He clapped Chris on the back. "That's fantastic. Does she have a sister?" Chris stared daggers at him, and he laughed again. "Okay, okay. So, old man, call her after the game."

"What?"

"You heard me. Decide now to call her after the game. That way you can get your head out of your ass and fucking play while we're on the ice."

Chris blinked, laughed, and said, "Every once in a while, you say something that isn't impossibly stupid."

"And for that comment, you get moved up to the top of my 'next to prank' list."

The team played well for the rest of the game, but it wasn't enough to win, and the Guardians went down in a tough three-two loss.

Zee met up with Chris on their way out of the locker room and asked, "Did you call her yet?"

"What? Oh. No, I didn't."

"So, call. Right now." Chris just looked at him.

"Seriously, Becks? This girl has you tied up in knots. Would you just fucking call her? Look, let's go out for drinks. Call her and ask her if she wants to join us. There. I just gave you a reason." When Chris sighed in response, Zee threatened with, "Don't make me take your phone and do it myself. You know I will."

"Shit." He would. Zee had no concept of boundaries when it came to that sort of thing. Chris got out his phone and called Paige's number, while Zee stood by, supervising.

***

Liz saw the phone ring on the kitchen table and saw Chris's name pop up. Paige called from her bedroom, asking who it was, but Liz simply picked up the call.

"Hey, Chris! It's Liz. Paige has her hands full right now, but I knew she wouldn't want your call to go through to voice mail." Paige had run out to her as soon as she heard Liz start talking. She had a look of horror on her face. "Yeah, I saw the game. That was a tough one." A pause. Paige had her hands out, trying to take the phone from Liz, who kept turning and pushing her away, using the advantage of being seven inches taller to make things difficult. "Really? That sounds great. No, we're both free. We can meet you there in about thirty minutes or so. See you, Chris." And then she hung up the phone.

"What did you just do?"

"We're going to meet Chris and at least one of

27

his teammates for drinks in thirty minutes." Paige stared at her. "It's gonna be fun, and you're gonna thank me."

"I hate you."

"I know."

"Why do you do this?" Liz looked at her with a small smile on her face. Paige's shoulders slumped. "I know why." Liz's smile got bigger. "I still hate you."

"I know. Now go cute-ify yourself. You have like ten minutes."

Chapter Four

The guys were already waiting seated at a booth when Liz and Paige walked in.

"Shit, Chris. You weren't kidding."

Chris looked over at him and said, "For the love of God, Zee, do not fuck this up for me."

Zee laughed and gave his best, "Who, me?" look. Chris glared, which just made Zee laugh harder.

They both stood up to welcome the women. Liz gave Chris a big hug. "I'm a hugger," she explained. "You get one handshake, and then you get hugs." She turned to Zee, who grabbed her in a huge bear hug, making her laugh. "Or we skip the handshake altogether. That works too."

"Jake Zimmerman, but please call me Zee."

The introductions between Paige and Zee were calmer.

Paige and Chris greeted one another almost shyly. Zee and Liz looked at each other, recognizing kindred spirits, and Zee took the lead and squished the four of them together in one big hug. Liz couldn't stop laughing.

"Shit, please stop encouraging him. You'll only make it worse." Chris was smiling as he said it, though, and so was Paige, so mission accomplished. "Oh, sorry about the language. It's hard to leave the locker room vocabulary behind after a game, sometimes, especially after a loss. And especially if I'm still hanging around with this idiot."

It was Paige's turn to smile. "Please, don't worry." She looked at Liz, who was grinning broadly. "You have no idea what I hear from my roommate on a daily basis. I'm fairly certain nothing you could say would shock me."

Zee looked at Liz, wide eyed, looked over to Chris and Paige, and said, "I think I'm in love."

"Shut the fuck up, you asshole." Liz thought about making it even more colorful but decided to stick with the basics. Zee threw back his head and laughed.

Paige looked at Chris and said with a smirk, "I'm finding this combination frightening." Chris grinned at her, and her insides flipped over again. It was probably the first easy-going, genuine, completely non-nervous look he had given her, and she liked it. A lot.

He was clean-shaven, and his thick, dark hair was still damp from a post-game shower. Once again he was wearing slacks and a button-down shirt, open at the collar, looking unreasonably like a photo from the cover of a magazine.

Paige and Chris sat down on opposite sides of the booth. Liz and Zee were still standing and talking.

"Well, in good news, if he's occupied with Liz,

he will be less of a pain in the ass to us." He looked at Paige and smiled warmly in a way that crinkled the corners of his eyes and made the butterflies zoom around again. "I'm really glad you could come out tonight on short notice." His voice lowered a bit as he added, "It's really great to see you again." Her heart was beating a little faster.

"You too." Paige's voice was a little breathy, and she cleared her throat. "So, I watched the game with Liz today." Chris looked so pleased that she blushed. "She's trying to explain things to me. Some are easier to understand than others."

"Like what?" Chris looked thrilled by this development. "Anything I can help explain?"

"I think the hardest one was icing. Oh, and offsides. You guys are always skating all over the place, so I don't understand how there can be such a thing as 'offsides.'"

Chris chuckled and said, "That's a good point. Let's start with offsides, then." He was in his element now and took the time to explain the basics, using menus and utensils and condiments to demonstrate. He was calm and clear, and an excellent teacher, making sure she understood what he was talking about before he moved on to the next point, without ever sounding condescending. Seeing him like this, confident and knowledgeable, was more attractive to her than pretty much anything else he could have done.

They had all ordered drinks by this time. When Chris finished teaching Paige about offsides, he realized that she was staring at him with a small smile on her face. He felt his chest squeeze and noticed an increasing need to adjust the front of his pants as he smiled back at her.

"So, how did you like your first hockey lesson?" He tried to keep his voice from sounding like he was thinking about sex. He was only moderately successful.

"Very educational." She smiled at him again. Neither one of them had noticed that Liz and Zee had left the table to play pool a while ago. She looked at him from under her lashes and said with another small blush, "So does that mean there will be more lessons? I still need to learn about icing."

Chris closed his eyes briefly and willed himself to calm down. He opened his eyes, reached across the table, and took her hand. Electricity. He thought she must have felt it too, because her eyes got wide suddenly. "There can be as many hockey lessons as you want, Paige."

Paige's heart was beating too fast, and she felt the color flooding her face. The feel of him holding her hand had sent little sparks shooting up her arm, spreading to the rest of her. "I'd like that." Her voice was rough. She cleared her throat again and took a drink. His eyes were deep, dark, and gorgeous. They looked a little playful right now, and she was having trouble thinking, especially while he was holding her hand.

Zee and Liz reappeared, and it was a sudden, boisterous, laughing distraction. Paige breathed a bit easier. Chris sat back but didn't let go of her hand. Zee and Liz both noticed and raised eyebrows to each other but said nothing.

"She's a pool shark, Chris. Do *not* play pool with

her." Zee pointed at Liz, who was laughing at him.

"Did you bet with her?" Paige asked. "Because that's never a good idea."

"Now you tell me. Thanks ever so much for that heads-up. Of course I did." Chris and Paige were both laughing now.

Chris asked Liz, "What did you win?"

"Game tickets. Of course." Liz grinned and finished her drink. "What else?"

"She kept making me laugh when it was my shot. Cheating."

"Really?" Chris was impressed. "Usually he's the one doing that to other people."

"Ah ha! I knew it!" Liz crowed, and Zee glowered jokingly.

"All right. Fine. But you have to give me your phone number." Liz looked at him curiously. He was twenty-two, and that was a little too young for her. Seeing her hesitation, he added, "You're my new post-bad-game person. I will call you after a bad game, and you have to tell me something funny." Liz laughed. "Deal?"

"Deal." She put out her hand to shake his. Then she grabbed a pen from a passing waiter and wrote her phone number on a napkin, laughing the whole time. "I will gladly pay you in funny stories."

She then looked at Chris and Paige, paused for just a moment, and said, "Hey, Zee and I settled the tab so far, and we're going to head over to another bar. Chris, would you mind giving Paige a ride home?"

Paige put her hand over her eyes. "Jesus, Liz." Chris smiled broadly. Paige uncovered her face, which was now a rather impressive shade of red.

"I might be a while. I'll text before I come home. Say, a half hour before I will be home." She winked and blew a kiss to Chris and reached over to give Paige a hug.

"I hate you."

"I know."

Chris couldn't stop smiling.

***

Zee looked at her as they headed for the exit. "What the fuck, Williams!" He was laughing. "Not that I mind heading out to another bar with you, but where the hell did that come from?"

"Their date needed a shove in the right direction, and I'm a pain in the ass," she said as she was settling their tab with the server. She turned to look at him. "I thought you would have figured that out by now. It usually doesn't take very long." She winked at him, and he laughed.

"Oh, we're gonna be good friends. I can tell." He put his arm around her shoulder as they made their way out the door.

Chapter Five

Chris looked at Paige, thinking that the deep blush made her look, if possible, even more beautiful. He simply couldn't help the smile on his face.

"She's a pain in the ass." Paige looked at him. "Sorry about that."

"You're kidding, right? She's one of my very favorite people in the world already."

Paige sighed and shook her head. "Yeah. She does that." She smiled at him, and he felt it, physically. In his chest, in his gut, in his groin.

"So, do you want to stay a little longer," he asked, his eyes beginning to smolder, "or would you like me to take you home now?"

Paige's heart was racing from the heat in his eyes. She wasn't sure how to answer. "I…" She took a breath and tried to steady herself. Chris had started gently rubbing his thumb on her hand in a slow caress, and it was systematically disconnecting her brain cells. She put her other hand on top of his to stop the movement so she could focus. "I believe

I would like you to take me home, please, Chris."

She smiled at him, and he was fairly certain his heart stopped.

He flagged down their waiter and found out that Liz and Zee had, indeed, paid the entire tab. Chris didn't want to pull his hand from between hers, but she had just asked him to drive her home, and at the very least he felt confident that he would have the opportunity to kiss her goodnight again; the thought of that was enough to drive almost every other thought from his mind. He smiled at her, stood up, and offered her his hand, which she took.

They walked slowly to his car, holding hands, with Chris continuing a gentle caress with his thumb. He opened her door and took her hand again immediately after starting the car. He wanted to maintain contact with her as long as possible. The drive to her apartment was quiet, but comfortably so, and the times when Chris glanced over at Paige, she was looking at him.

"What?" he asked finally, with a smile at her.

She simply answered, "It's my turn to stare."

His heart started beating much more rapidly again, and he felt blood racing around his body. A good amount of that was headed south, and he was suddenly glad he hadn't asked earlier. They were close to her apartment now; if she had flustered him this much ten minutes earlier, he would have gotten lost. Or driven off the road.

Chris walked her to the door of her apartment, and they stood there for a moment. Then, once again with his hands in his pockets, he leaned down to kiss her.

Electricity.

Sparks.

His lips touched hers in a soft kiss, and the feel of it sent shocks through her body, just like the first time. She brought her hand up and placed it on his cheek, not wanting him to move away after one kiss as he had the night before.

Her hand on his cheek was a multiplication of the sparks between them, and he leaned into their gentle kiss, trying to control his breathing. She slid her hand up along his jaw and gently stroked the short hair on the back of his neck, feeling the softness against her fingertips.

He shivered, broke away from the kiss to lean his forehead against hers, and whispered, "Please tell me you feel this too." He still had his hands in his pockets. Not because he thought they would shake, but because he was afraid to touch her.

"It feels like lightning," she whispered in return, stroking his neck gently.

"Yes." He kissed her again. "I'm almost afraid to touch you." He looked at her and smiled in that shy, sexy way. "I'm glad you feel it too. I would hate it if I felt this and you didn't."

Paige looked at him, her heart twisting in a way that shouldn't be possible with someone she just met. "Me too. I was afraid that I was somehow imagining this." She took a breath. "I feel like my heart is going to beat out of my chest." She smiled, took another breath, and stepped back from him. He smiled and tilted his head a little, questioningly. "Would you like to come in?"

"I would love to." The rough sound of his voice

sent shivers down her spine.

Chris followed Paige into the apartment. She invited him to sit on the couch and then sat down next to him and then remembered manners and started to ask him if she could get him anything, but he captured her mouth with a kiss before she finished the sentence.

Chris cupped her face gently with his hand and gave himself up to the sparks between them. He softly cradled her face in his large hands and parted his lips to gently touch hers with his tongue. The small sound she made at this contact caused a surge to his groin that was almost painful. He was unbelievably aroused, and they had barely kissed.

Paige was drowning in sensations. She parted her lips when she felt his tongue touch them and put her hand on his chest, feeling his heart beating, feeling the heat and strength of him. She touched his tongue with hers and felt him slide his hand behind her neck and into her hair as his other hand moved to hold her gently around her waist. The hand behind her neck held her as he shifted to deepen the kiss, their tongues now moving together in a sliding dance. Paige felt his hand move up her side and graze her breast, and she gasped.

Chris still held his hand at the back of her neck but moved his lips so they were resting against her cheek and said, "I'm sorry. I don't want to move too fast. I'm afraid to touch you, but I don't want to stop touching you."

"No, it's okay. I just…this is intense." He chuckled, and she smiled, pushing back from him just slightly to look at his face. "I don't want to stop touching you, either." Her voice was quiet and breathy, and Chris felt a new surge of arousal.

Paige was wondering how much of this she was going to be able to take and how she was going to be able to stop. Because she didn't want to stop. This was just their second date, but every nerve ending in her body was ready for her to do a lot more with this man than sit on her couch and kiss him. When his hand grazed her breast, she felt such a rush; her nipples contracted, and she was already slick with desire. She wanted him to touch her. She wanted to know what the electricity between them would feel like if he slid his hand between her legs. The thought made her shudder.

Desire was starting to overwhelm her senses. She took Chris's hand, placed it on her breast, and whispered, "Touch me."

Chris moaned quietly, closed his eyes, and gently squeezed her breast, running his palm across the stiffness of her peak through her shirt, shifting to capture and roll it gently in his fingers, listening to her gasps and sighs. He shifted his other hand to slide under her shirt, reveling in the softness of her skin, and then moved both his hands up under her shirt. He captured her mouth again as he fondled her breasts through her bra.

Slipping his hands behind her, Chris unhooked her bra and slid his hand back underneath to finally touch her breasts directly. Her reaction was immediate; the feeling of his fingers playing with her nipples made her gasp loudly. She looked at Chris, wide-eyed, and he kissed her. Harder this time, with more heat and less sweetness, still fondling her, gently tugging. Paige made a sound of sheer desire and grabbed his thigh.

Everything short circuited in Chris's brain when he felt her fingers on the inside of his thigh, even on top of the fabric. His groan was deep, and he released Paige's breasts and moved his hands back to her face, cupping her jaw as he tried desperately to find a way to disengage from the kiss while simultaneously continuing to kiss her. He finally held her face a few inches from his own, breathing hard. Her hand was still on his thigh. He was trying to think.

She moved her hand, sliding it up his thigh another inch. "Wait." She stopped and looked at him. She was flushed and breathing hard, and he almost forgot what he was trying to say. She squeezed his thigh, and he remembered. "Oh God, Paige, you need to stop, because if you don't, I don't think I will be able to." Paige laughed, a low sound that made it even more difficult for him to think, and he looked at her and smiled, asking, "What?"

She sat back, leaving her hand on his thigh, and said, "You are kind of wonderful." His heart contracted.

"I don't want to stop," he said as he kissed her, and she gave his thigh another brief squeeze, causing him to make a sound of desire and frustration. "But this...with you...is amazing. Special. I don't want to rush anything with you." With small growl, he added, "Except that, God, I want to rush everything with you."

She sighed and said, "I know what you mean.

And thank you." She looked at him under her lashes. "It is special, Chris. This, what I feel with you, it's…exceptional." He thought his heart might stop.

He stood up and pulled her into him for a hug and then laughed as she twisted away to take off her bra in the way that women could, pulling it through her sleeve. He stopped laughing when he saw that it was black lace, and his eyes got dark with desire again.

He fondled her breasts through her shirt, gently pinching her nipples, until she stopped him. "If you're going to leave tonight, you need to stop that now." He groaned and pulled her in for a hug again. She felt every inch of his desire hardened against her, and she had to fight the urge to run her hand up and down the firm ridge it formed in his pants.

"I'm going to be on a road trip for the next five days. I will call you. And when I get back, we can get together again." He looked down at her. "I've known you two days and I already don't want to be away from you."

She smiled and said, "Me too."

He kissed her again, deeply, unable to make himself stop as he moved his hands to stroke the sides of her breasts. She whimpered her desire, and he felt her press and slide herself against his erection. He groaned against her mouth, moved both his hands to her ass, and picked her up.

Paige's arms were wrapped around his neck; she now wrapped her legs around him too. She broke away from his mouth and moved her face to his neck, placing light kisses there and up under his

41

jawline. He was breathing hard, trying to remember…something. She bit his neck gently, and he shuddered and gripped her more tightly, his erection throbbing.

"Paige…" He was losing his mind. She bit him again, and he sat back down on the couch with her and kissed her as if he would never be able to stop. She straddled him, running her hands through his short hair, and he pulled her shirt over her head, freeing her breasts, pushing back so that he could look at her.

She was perfect. He stared at her with that look of wonder before he leaned over and took a nipple into his mouth. He sucked gently, swirling his tongue around her peak, feeling it get even harder in his mouth. She was gasping.

He brought his hand up to her other breast to gently roll and tug her other nipple while he continued to lick and suck at the first one. Paige moaned and moved in his lap, unable to keep still.

"Oh God, Chris."

He switched sides, shifting his mouth to her other breast, fondling the first one with his hands.

"Oh," she whispered. "Oh, yes." Her hands were still running through his hair, holding his head to her.

He dragged his lips and tongue up her body, kissing her chest and neck before capturing her mouth again. "I don't want to stop." His voice was hoarse. "I want to make you come." She made a sound of desperation and desire that fried his last brain cells. He turned and pushed her down onto the couch and reached for the button on her pants.

Paige's phone chimed with a text message.

They ignored it.

Chris unbuttoned her pants and pressed kisses into her hips. He started to pull them off her when the phone chimed again.

Paige said, "Crap." She grabbed the phone and saw Liz's message:

Liz: ETA 30 minutes.

Chris looked at her, and she held up the phone. He swore and then looked at Paige and said, "I'm pretty sure I can make you feel really amazing in thirty minutes."

Paige groaned and sat up. "I'm sure you can. And I want you to. And we shouldn't. Because we were going to stop several important steps ago, and I'm pretty sure it's my fault that we didn't." She looked at him. He was staring at her breasts, and she laughed. He looked up to her face, startled.

"Sorry. Shit, you are so fucking beautiful." He shook his head. "Sorry again. My language is terrible, and I can't think." She started to get dressed. "Oh, I don't want you to do that."

"I know." She finished putting her shirt on. "I don't want to, either." She tilted her head and smiled at him. "Thank you, Chris." She kissed him, and he stood up and offered her a hand.

"I will call you." He looked at her again and added, "And I'm going to have to try not to think about you during the games, because I might end up in the boards. Or the penalty box." He smiled at her, and her insides did a flip. "I'm going to miss you,

Paige."

"I'm going to miss you too." They kissed one more time, and he left, and she sat back on the couch, wondering what the hell she was getting herself into.

Chapter Six

"So, what happened?" Zee punched Chris in the shoulder as they were getting settled on the plane, and sat down across the aisle from him.

"What? I took her home. Beyond that, none of your business," Chris said with a smile.

"Oh, ho! I knew it. You so owe me."

Chris shook his head, unable to suppress a grin. "What are you, twelve? Besides, what happened with you? What did you do with Liz after you left?"

"Ha! She's an awesome wing-woman." He paused for a second and then added, "And possibly completely insane." Zee looked around and lowered his voice a bit. "Would you believe she bet me that she could get me laid at the next bar?"

"Are you serious?"

"As a heart attack." He looked around again for a second and then said, "She walked up to this really cute girl at the bar, talked to her for a few minutes, and then brought her back to the table with us so that I could buy the girl a drink." He chuckled for a minute and then said, "She even told the girl about the bet but introduced me as the friend of her younger brother."

Zee sat back in his seat, shaking his head.

Chris waited for more and finally asked, "So? What happened?"

With a slightly cheeky grin, Zee replied, "Well, let's just say Liz is going to be coming to a lot of games in the near future."

Chris started laughing. "Good God. I'm starting to wonder what we've gotten ourselves into with these women. Well, I guess her success in winning that bet for you would explain why she was home earlier than I expected."

"Oh, shit, did she interrupt something awkward?" Zee leaned across the aisle. "Were you and Paige getting busy?"

"Twelve. You're twelve years old, Zee. I'm not talking about this with you."

Zee settled back into his seat again, saying, "Oh, yeah. You totally owe me."

***

"What's up, Becks?" Micky was surprised to be hearing from Chris again so soon. They were as close as brothers, but their conversations were usually more like once a month rather than every few days.

"She's it. She's the one."

Micky laughed and asked, "She's the one what? And can I assume that we're talking about Paige?"

"Yes, Paige. She's the one. The One, Micky." Chris settled into the chair in his hotel room.

"Um, okay." Micky wasn't sure if Chris was kidding or if he had lost his mind. It was clearly one of the two. "Did you see her again? Or are you basing this off of Friday night's exceptionally short dinner date and one kiss?"

"I saw her again last night. And I'm serious, asshole." Chris took a breath and let it out again. "I'm gonna marry her."

"Oh." Micky took a different approach. "Does she know this yet?" At an annoyed noise from Chris, he added, "I'm just checking, man! This is all a little weird. More than a little, Becks. This actually trips over into 'fucked-up weird' territory. If you're serious." He paused briefly. "Are you really serious?"

"God damn it, yes, I'm serious." Chris calmed himself, realizing that it would be hard for Micky to understand this. "Yeah, I can see how you'd think this was fucked-up weird. And no, she doesn't know yet. But I know, Micky. I just know."

Micky started laughing. "All right, then. I'll jump on board your crazy train with this. When do I get to meet her?"

"Huh." Chris thought for a minute. "Are you going to be in Minnesota for Christmas this year?"

"Yeah."

"I'll bring her to meet you then."

Micky laughed again. "Okay, my brother, if you guys are still together at Christmas, then I will see you in Minnesota. That's good, because you know my mom is going to want to meet any woman you're planning on marrying."

Chris smiled and chuckled. "Definitely. I would

never be able to live it down otherwise. And I don't want to get on the wrong side of your mom."

Micky's voice got a little more solemn. "Becks, you know I love you, man. Just be careful, all right? Don't jump into anything that you can't jump back out of if you need to. You *just* met her, you know almost nothing about her, and I don't want to see you get screwed over. Keep your head in the game too. Don't fuck up your playing. Got it?"

Chris understood Micky's cautions. Micky had been in a long-term relationship that had ended very badly, with him catching her cheating. It had been dicey for a while if he was going to let it ruin his career too.

"Got it. I will not be a total idiot about this." He heard Micky start laughing again. "What?"

"You're off to a great start not being an idiot. Shit, Becks. Two dates." Chris heard Micky chuckle to himself.

"I know, but I'm telling you, she's the real deal. Not just beautiful, but smart and kind...the whole package."

"Hell, if she makes you happy, you know I'm with you a hundred percent."

"Thanks, Mick. You'll meet her at Christmas."

"I look forward to it."

"Later, Micky."

***

Chris called every day while he was on the road, and he and Paige talked for as long as possible, until either it was too late to talk longer or until one of them had another obligation. They talked about everything. And nothing. Considering the awkward start to the relationship, it was amazing that their conversations now seemed rather effortless.

True to his word, Zee had called Liz after the next bad game, starting the conversation with, "Hey, that game sucked. Tell me something funny." She had laughed and obliged, rather pleased he had followed through on calling her.

Liz was intrigued seeing just how much time Paige and Chris spent talking together. There was already something radically different about this relationship than any other that Paige had been in since Liz had known her. They had been best friends since college, so that covered a lot of territory.

Chris came over to their apartment the first night that the team was back in town. Liz answered the door and greeted him with a hug; when Paige came to the door, he greeted her with a kiss that looked like it could melt asphalt.

Liz was impressed; it was almost awkward to be standing there. She escaped quietly, grabbing her coat, purse, and keys to head out of the apartment for a few hours, calling friends once she was outside to see about meeting someone somewhere for dinner, or coffee, or a movie. Anything that would require *not* being in the apartment for a while.

By the time Chris released Paige from the kiss, Liz had already left. "I missed you." He looked so sincere that Paige blushed.

"I missed you too. I'm glad we got to talk while you were away. I feel like I know you better now."

"Me too." He smiled at her, already feeling a level of arousal that was threatening to unhinge his brain. "Do you want to go get dinner somewhere?"

"That sounds good." She turned to call to her roommate. "Hey, Liz, we're going to dinner." When she didn't hear an answer, she looked around and realized the missing purse, coat, and keys. She giggled and said, "Oh, wow. She left. And we missed it."

"Really?" Chris took his eyes from Paige for the first time since she walked up to him and looked around. "Huh. Either she's exceptionally stealthy, or we were very distracted." He turned his gaze toward Paige again. "Well, I know that *I* was very distracted." He placed a soft kiss on her lips. "She probably could have performed an 'I'm leaving' song and dance routine and I would have missed it."

Paige laughed and blushed again, swatting him. "She is stealthy when she wants to be." She looked at him from under her lashes and added, "But I was very distracted too. You are a distracting man, Chris Beckman."

Chris's smile was incredibly charming. "So apparently we have the apartment to ourselves. Still want to go out for dinner?" His eyes were picking up some heat as he spoke. "Or maybe we could order in?"

"Ordering in sounds good." Paige's voice had gotten a little breathy, and her heart was speeding up. The memory of where they had left off last time was causing a flood of sensations. "Are you hungry now? Or do you want to wait and order food...later?"

Holy shit. "Later. Definitely later." Chris bent to kiss her again and lifted her effortlessly. He carried her over to the couch, sat down, and had her straddle his lap, continuing the kiss. He was already hard. There was no possibility of hiding that, so he didn't try and pulled her close to him.

Paige let out a little moan against his lips when she felt the thickness of his arousal pressing against her. Chris ran his hands up under her shirt to play with her nipples, gently tweaking them into hard points through her bra, and then took off her bra and shirt so he could look at her again.

She was flushed, and he took his time to enjoy the view, gently caressing her breasts with his hands before lowering his head to capture one of her nipples in his mouth. He teased her breast, licking and swirling his tongue before gently sucking her nipple to a harder point, then flicking his tongue over it, making her gasp. He moved to her other breast and repeated his attentions, not wanting to be unfair.

She finally pulled his head back up to her mouth and between kisses said, "Take your shirt off. I want to look at you too." Chris obliged, untucking and unbuttoning his shirt and shrugging it off his shoulders.

Paige stared. "Holy cow." She looked up at him as she ran her hands over his chest. He was beautifully muscular. Broad shoulders led down to strong arms; well-defined pecs led down to gorgeous abs. And an unexpected tattoo circled his right bicep, bringing a half smile to her face.

"What's this?" she asked, drawing her fingers

along the edges of the tattoo gently. It was attractive and well done—Celtic knotwork—but almost out of character, based on what Paige knew of him so far.

"That was the result of an ill-thought-out wager in my rookie year with Columbus." He smiled a bit self-consciously. "I guess I should be thankful that they took me to a really good tattoo artist and not some hack."

Paige traced the pattern with a fingertip and murmured, "It's lovely. Quite beautifully done." She met his eyes again and said, "I like it."

A small ripple of relief flowed through Chris.

Lingering for a moment more in her tracing of the tattoo, she said quietly, "It's surprising." She turned her eyes once again to meet his and brought her hand up to his cheek. "Like a sudden edge where I expected a gentle curve," she said as she pressed a quick kiss to his lips before returning to her inspection of his muscled frame.

Chris willed himself to stay still while she explored his upper body. Every touch of her hands sent little shocks through him, and when she started tracing the trail of hair that led from his navel down into his pants, he groaned and gently took her hand to pull it away. "You have no idea what you're doing to me." His voice was low and rough.

"I have some idea." Her voice was husky, and he looked in her eyes and saw the same heat reflected back to him. Chris pulled her close so that her breasts pressed against his chest as they kissed. The skin-on-skin contact was electrifying, taut nipples against soft hair.

With another small groan, Chris pulled back

from the kiss and nuzzled into her neck. "I want you so badly I can't think straight. I don't know how far you want to take this tonight." He moved his face so that his cheek rested against hers. "I will go as slow as you want, Paige, but if you leave this up to me, I'm going to take you to bed. Right now."

Paige's breath caught. He was the sexiest man she had ever met, and everything about this relationship—because it was definitely a relationship already—was moving at light speed. But it seemed right. Everything about *him* seemed right, and while all conventional logic said to wait, this level of attraction defied all conventional logic.

She had known him for a week and already knew that he was smart, considerate, gentle, and kind. And sexy. So very, very sexy.

"My room is the second door on the right." She whispered it against his face. Her hand was stroking the short, soft hair on the back of his neck.

Chris's entire body stiffened, absolutely sure he had heard that wrong, and he moved to look at her, holding her face in his hands. "What?" he asked, eyes clouded with lust, voice rough.

"Second door on the right. My bedroom." She kissed him. "With my bed." She kissed him again, and he stood suddenly, still holding her, and she squeaked in surprise.

He put her down for just a moment and then scooped her up properly, with one arm under her knees and the other behind her back. She looked up at him and said, "Oh my God, are you romantic too?"

"Definitely."

Paige laughed softly as he took her to her bedroom and laid her gently on the bed. "You're like something out of a romance novel." Chris smiled, looking beyond pleased, and her heart melted.

"You're like something out of my dreams." He bent down to kiss her gently.

Chapter Seven

Chris paused and sat down on the edge of the bed, gazing at Paige with longing, gently touching her breasts and stomach, once again looking at her almost in reverence.

Paige sat up and put her hand on his shoulder, sliding down to feel the hard muscles of his chest, and asked, "Are you all right?"

Chris chuckled and said, "Yes. I was getting lost again in how beautiful you are. And honestly," he lifted his head and looked her in the eyes, "I was just realizing that I'm going to end up embarrassing myself the first time with you."

His eyes took on a smoky haze that was raising Paige's heart rate. At her questioning look, he added, "There is no way that I'm going to be able to last." He brought his face closer to hers and, in a voice that was gravelly with desire, said, "I'm so turned on that I might come the moment you touch me."

He kissed her deeply, running his hands along her sides, up to her breasts, trailing his thumbs across her nipples as she squirmed and moaned.

"Chris…" It was a pleading sound.

He moved his mouth to her neck, kissing down as he gently pushed her back onto the bed.

"I've only got one choice here, Paige."

His hands were fondling her breasts, his mouth joining them as he began worshiping her body. He laved his tongue across her left nipple, moving onto the bed without taking his mouth from her, trailing his tongue over to her right breast.

Moving up to kiss her mouth again, he added, "I'm going to have to make sure that you have at least one truly spectacular orgasm before we start anything else."

The sound Paige made caused a surge in his already painfully hard erection, and he kissed down her stomach to the waistband of her pants. He unbuttoned, slid the zipper down, and groaned when he saw the black lace panties she was wearing.

In a breathy voice, Paige asked, "Do you like them?" as he pulled her pants down her legs. She gasped and put her head back as he placed an open-mouthed kiss on the crotch of her underwear, dragging his teeth over the silky fabric, his breath hot on her even through the material.

"I love them." His voice rumbled against her, making her squirm. "And they're going to look even better on the floor."

He positioned himself between Paige's legs, stroking his fingers along her slit through the panties, teasing her, pressing and sliding against the damp fabric. "You are so wet already." He moved his fingers to the side to reach under and stroke her skin.

Paige gasped at the increased sensation.

Grabbing her panties at the hips, he dragged them down her legs, dropped them on the floor, and started kissing his way up her inner thigh. "So gorgeous." When he finally dragged his tongue from her entrance to her clit, Paige bucked against his face, making a sound that was a combination of a scream and a groan, completely overwhelmed by the intense sensations.

Chris began kissing her with the same passion and thoroughness as when he kissed her mouth, reveling in her taste, her smell, the sounds that she was making. He moved his hands under her rear, lifted her up slightly, and made himself comfortable between her thighs.

"I love doing this," he said between breaths, pausing to place gentle bites on the tops of her thighs and up to her right hip, making a return path with wet kisses. He licked her with the flat of his tongue, saying, "You taste like heaven, Paige."

He nuzzled his nose against her clit as he pushed his tongue into her and was rewarded with another gasping cry. Dragging his tongue back up, he flicked it against her clit, and she grabbed the sheets.

"I fucking love this." This growled sentence was the last thing he said before beginning his final assault on her senses.

Sucking and licking her clit, Chris entered her with two fingers, stretching down gently in a way that made Paige moan, grab his hair, and thrust against his face. Shifting and twisting within her, he curled his fingers, searching for her G-spot.

Flicking. Licking. Sucking.

Chris was getting lost in his own desire, grinding his hips against the bed in search of friction as Paige moved against his mouth. She was panting and moaning, climbing toward release; her passion was driving him on, increasing his arousal. Chris clamped his lips around her clit and moaned against her, feeling her fingers tighten in his hair as he moved his fingers inside her one more time.

And then she came, muscles spasming around his fingers, thighs clamping against his head, wailing out a sound of passion and release that was music to his ears.

Chris tried to be gentle, stroking her slowly with his tongue, not wanting to stop kissing her in this way, but it didn't take long until she pushed him away, saying, "Too much." One final lick of her clit caused another full-body shudder, and he chuckled in satisfaction at her response.

He kissed his way back up her body, and Paige could smell and taste her own desire on his lips and face as she kissed him, holding his face in her hands. "I want you," she said between kisses. "I need you, Chris."

With a groan, he backed away enough to take his pants off, his erection throbbing. Paige raised her eyebrows and her eyes grew wide; he was a large man, in every way. She smiled and wrapped her hand around his shaft, causing a sharp intake of breath from Chris and a strangled kind of groan.

"I think you need to lie down," she said, slowly moving her hand along the silken steel of his length, causing him to close his eyes and shudder. "I'm going to need to be on top to handle this for the first time." His hands gripped the sheets.

"Oh God. Paige."

He shuddered again as she reached his tip and began sliding her thumb through the lubrication there. He put a hand on the back of her neck and said, "Oh shit, Paige, stop, I'm serious. I won't last."

Smiling, she pushed gently against his shoulder with her other hand until he was lying on the bed and then climbed over to straddle him.

"Do I need to get a condom?" He was vaguely proud of himself for remembering to ask.

"I've been on the pill for years," she replied, positioning herself to begin sliding down his shaft.

The feeling was so intense they both groaned as she pushed down over his tip. She slowly moved further down his shaft in short shallow thrusts, reveling in the feel of being stretched and filled by him, as he groaned louder.

Chris gripped her hips, willing himself not to pull her down onto him in one thrust, trying to make this last, knowing it was futile. He had been on the edge of climax going down on her.

Paige felt herself building to another orgasm from the combination of feeling his length inside her, his girth stretching her, and watching and listening to him struggle for control. His desire for her was so intense it was intoxicating, and when Chris started shifting his hips to meet her movements, she felt that familiar chain of sensations begin.

She pressed down harder, sliding against him, taking him all the way into her, and put her head back with a moan at the feeling.

He couldn't stop himself. It was too much. The feeling of her wrapped around him, the sight of her, the sounds…he held her hips tighter and thrust against her, feeling his muscles tighten as the orgasm began to overwhelm him.

"Oh God, Paige. Yes…yes…oh fuck, I'm coming." He groaned low as he climaxed. She rode him bucking into her and joined him in release, saying his name over and over.

***

"Fuuuck. That was amazing." The words were dragged out, almost a groan as Chris finally recovered his breath. Rolling over slightly, he brushed Paige's hair away from her eyes. "Although I swear I will be able to last longer from now on, baby." He thought he saw a little look of pleasure as he used the diminutive, calling her the pet name without even thinking about it. "That first time with you, though…there was an awful lot of want built up."

"That," Paige responded, "was spectacular sex." Leaning across to kiss him quickly, she said roughly, "The want was on both sides, Chris. Trust me."

She got up and walked across the room for her phone, completely nude. Chris leaned on one elbow and stared, watching her, letting his eyes devour her curves and valleys, vaguely surprised to feel himself beginning to harden again as she walked slowly back to the bed, looking up something on her phone.

Apparently she had asked him a question, and Chris finally dragged his eyes up to her face. She was smiling.

He said, "Um, what? I missed that."

"What kind of Chinese food do you want?" Paige's eyes sparkled, and she blushed a little. "Your distraction is very flattering, though."

"God, Paige, distraction doesn't half cover it…"

He trailed off, letting his eyes roam again, until she cleared her throat loudly.

"Chinese food, remember?"

"What? Oh, right."

They ordered, finally, and got dressed enough to lounge in the living room again. Liz had not returned from wherever she had gone, so they were still alone.

Chapter Eight

"So, there are probably some things that we should talk about. You know, sex-wise." Paige settled on the couch with a glass of wine as they waited for the food to be delivered.

Chris looked at Paige, surprised by this turn of conversation. Nervously, he replied, "Okay…" Trying to keep things light, he added, "I would like to say let's have more of it…?" He joined her on the couch with his own glass of wine.

Paige laughed lightly and reached over to touch his leg. "Me too, big guy."

He felt a quick squeeze in his chest at the playful nickname. And the idea of more sex.

She continued, "I mean about, you know, other aspects." She looked serious for a moment. "You won't get any risqué pictures or texts from me. Or even emails. Nothing electronic. It's too easy for there to be a breach or a hack, or I could accidentally leave my phone somewhere."

She held her hand up to stop him from saying anything and continued, "It's not that I'm worried that would ever do anything to intentionally hurt me in that way. It's just too risky for me. I work with kids, and I can't risk my career like that. Not for a thrill, you know?" Paige stopped and took breath and added, "I hope that's okay with you."

Chris was surprised by this straightforward discussion. "Yes, of course. That's fine with me, Paige."

"Now," Paige went on, "inside the bedroom is a totally different story." Chris sat up straighter suddenly. "No pictures. No videos. But…I am at least open to discussion regarding other…fun things…" Her voice trailed off, and Chris just looked at her in shock. "You know, other possible variations of adult entertainment…"

Chris was staring at her. Paige felt a bit nervous.

"Chris? Are you okay?"

He paused for a moment before answering. "I'm trying to figure out if this is real or all just an elaborate dream created by my subconscious as a reward for good behavior. This whole evening already seems like a dream come true."

Paige laughed.

"It's real. I'm sorry, because this is an awkward conversation, and I just really wanted to get it out of the way, in case the lack of electronic stuff would be, I don't know, some kind of deal breaker for you."

"What?" Chris shook his head. "No. No way."

Paige breathed out in relief. "Oh, good. I was a little worried, because you spend so much time on the road, you know?"

Chris chuckled, looking at Paige, and rubbed the

63

back of his neck. "Um...so, this is a little embarrassing to admit, but, well..." He cleared his throat. "To this point, my sex life has been rather...vanilla."

Paige smiled and felt her heart squeeze a little at this admission.

"That's fine, Chris!"

"No! I mean, yes, it's all right. But there are things that I've wanted to...I mean, I've thought about, but..." *Shit, I sound like an idiot.* "I mean..." Chris rubbed the back of his neck again, feeling his heart thumping. "I suddenly feel rather inexperienced."

Paige blushed deeply and moved to take his hand.

"Oh God, I hope I'm not giving you the wrong idea. I haven't had a ton of partners, and I'm not particularly...worldly? Would that be the right word? I just mean that I don't have a whole lot of hang ups about sex, if that makes any sense."

She shifted, trying to find the words to express her thoughts. "There are things that I have no interest in doing, and of course I want those boundaries respected, but as long as you're okay with me saying no to something, I won't be offended if you ask. That's all I meant. I just think that people shouldn't be afraid of asking for what turns them on, I guess..." She paused to take a breath. "Geez, this is turning into a horribly complicated and awkward conversation. I'm sorry, was this a terrible idea on my part? I feel like this might not have been the best plan I've ever had."

At the sound of the doorbell, Paige said, "Saved

by the bell," and got up, intending to pay for the food.

"No, wait, I'll get this." He answered the door, and they settled themselves down on the couch again after getting everything prepped on the coffee table.

"Thank you for buying dinner, Chris. You didn't have to do that." She wolfed down some of her chicken with cashews and made a sound of food-induced pleasure. "Oh God, I'm so hungry." Flashing him a quick look, she said, "I can't imagine why."

Chris chuckled, his mouth full. Swallowing, he said, "Me too. So, about our earlier conversation…"

"We don't have to if you don't want to."

He smiled, looking at her. "Not at all. I actually think it's a great idea. I was just floored. I've never met a woman who would be so comfortable talking like this."

"Please believe me that I wouldn't have this conversation with just anyone. Truth is, I've never been this forward and open before." She cocked her head to the side and looked at him thoughtfully. "But you're different, Chris. I trust you, and I want to be up front about things. I really want open communication between us."

Chris just sat on the couch, smiling at her.

"What?"

His smile was getting bigger.

"What are you thinking about?"

Chris moved closer to Paige on the couch. "Oh, just a few things I'd like to do with you…"

Paige laughed lightly. "Really? Already?"

65

"Mmm hmm." He snuggled her in close and moved his lips to her neck.

"That didn't take long." She drew in her breath as he kissed under her ear and moved her hand to his thigh. "What are you thinking that has caused this development?" she asked, running her hand along the length of his growing erection.

He chuckled against her neck. "Just being near you causes that particular development, baby." He chuckled again. "Hell, just *thinking* about you causes *that*. But I was thinking about a few simple things like taking a shower with you." His voice was getting lower. "Taking you from behind." He cupped her breast and rolled her nipple in his fingertips, loving the sound of her gasp. "Maybe a little sexy librarian role play?" he whispered into her ear. "Is that on the table?"

"Oh, that is most definitely on the table, big guy." She gripped him through his pants, enjoying how his breathing hitched. "All of those things are on the table." She moved to whisper in his ear, "Actually, sex on the table is on the table."

Chris growled and captured her mouth in a kiss. She smiled, gave him a little shove, and said, "Dinner first."

Chapter Nine

The differences in their schedules enforced a certain amount of slowness in their relationship. Being in and out of town and home games that sometimes ran late enough that there wasn't even time for a telephone call meant they couldn't rush things. It also left both of them on a low simmer.

"You guys must have ample opportunity for, shall we say, 'female companionship,' when you're on the road," Paige said, sipping a margarita at a little hole-in-the-wall Mexican restaurant that she and Liz had discovered years earlier. It was a dive, but it had the best burritos and taco salad, not to mention the fresh guacamole, of anywhere around.

"Well, I guess." Chris was munching on a taco. "You were right. This place is great."

"You guess?" Paige gave him a skeptical look. "I find it hard to believe that there aren't women just dying to get their hands on a hot hockey player. I mean, look at you!" She gestured to him right as he took another large, messy bite of taco. "Okay, not right at this very moment," she teased, and he tried not to laugh as he managed to swallow his food. "But really, Chris, come on. You can't tell me that you don't have women throwing themselves at you after games." She lowered her voice. "You are incredibly handsome."

Chris felt a deep warmth at the compliment and a quick squeeze in his chest. "There are some women who are mostly trying to notch their bedposts with players. And I'm not gonna lie, my rookie season that attention from the puck bunnies was overwhelming and really, really flattering. I had never experienced anything like that before, so I had the occasional, um, 'encounter' shall we say, but I haven't dated much. And I've never been too into casual sex—I'm not against it, mind you, and as I just said, I've indulged on occasion—but it's not who I am, if that makes any sense. I've always been pretty shy, really, so randomly picking up a woman at a bar was never going to be in my wheelhouse."

Paige flagged down the waiter and asked for more guacamole and chips, as well as drink refills.

"I'm still amazed at the thought of you being shy. I know you do media interviews sometimes after games; I've seen you do them." She picked at the little shards of chips still left in the bowl. "You seem completely at ease in front of the camera."

Chris smiled, obviously pleased at the comment. "Thank you. I really appreciate that; it's part of the job, so it's important to me to do that well, and I've worked really hard at it." He paused a moment as the waiter brought the replenishments. "But that's just what it is—part of the job. It's part of hockey.

That makes it easier for me, somehow. It's the personal stuff that gets me all flustered and makes my palms sweat."

Paige returned his smile, feeling the now familiar warm glow in her chest. His quiet openness, his vulnerability when they were together, was precious to her. She reached across the table and took his hand, rubbing her thumb across his palm.

"Not sweaty now."

He held her hand and brought it up to kiss her knuckles. "Not anymore, baby. Not with you."

"Thank you."

The corner of his lips twitched in a little smile. "For what?"

"For trusting me."

He stared at her for long enough that she asked, "What is it?"

"We need to get the bill paid and get out of here. Soon." At her questioning look, his voice dropped into a low growl. "I need to get you alone. It's been way too long."

Flutters, butterflies, and a rush of tingling arousal hit her all at once, almost making her dizzy with want. It must have shown on her face, because Chris flagged the waiter, handed him enough cash that it probably covered the bill twice over, and pulled Paige toward the exit.

***

"Hey, Liz, the team is going to be on a three-game home stand, so I was thinking of having Chris and Zee over for dinner Friday night. Would that work for you?"

Liz grinned broadly and said, "Look at you, throwing around hockey lingo. 'Three-game home stand.' Ha!" Paige gave her a look of mock irritation. Liz added, "Of course. Do you want me to be here or to make myself scarce? Either is fine by me."

"Here! I'm sorry, I was trying to invite you, not ask you to leave."

Liz smiled, saying, "I guess if you're inviting Zee, you're going to need a buffer zone to keep your sanity."

With a small smile, Paige replied, "That thought might have occurred to me. But I really just think it will be fun." She paused for a moment. "I'm a little nervous too. That's kind of weird, right?"

"Nope, not weird."

Paige looked unconvinced, so Liz moved over to put her arm around Paige. "This guy is different. It's okay to be nervous. You're a great cook, and Zee is a perfect distraction. You're a genius."

***

Paige had decided on something simple. It was the first time she had invited new people over for dinner in forever, and it was the first time she was going to cook for Chris, so she went with a staple that made her feel confident—spaghetti and meatballs.

Her grandmother had taught her how to cook. Paige had lovely fond memories of hours spent in the kitchen with "Grammy," learning how to make pasta from scratch, how to form perfect ravioli, and how to make exceptional sauce. While she wasn't going to take the time to hand-make pasta on a weeknight for Chris and Zee, she was fully intending to make an amazing sauce.

Chris arrived first, with a bottle of wine and a small but beautiful bouquet of flowers. Liz answered the door with a surprised, "Oh, for me? You shouldn't have."

"And you know that I didn't." Chris had quickly become completely comfortable around Liz and took her teasing in stride. "But how about a hug and kiss on the cheek. Deal?"

Liz rolled her eyes, made a "tsk" sound, and said, "Whatever," while offering her cheek to Chris.

Zee arrived a short while later, with beer. Liz grinned broadly as Zee practically bounced in the door and scooped her up for a feet-off-the-floor hug. "I've missed you! How am I supposed to manage meeting chicks in bars without my wing-woman? You're going to have to start traveling with the team."

Chris grimaced while the women laughed.

"Sweetie, I'm quite certain you have no problem chasing down puck bunnies on the road." Liz pinched his cheek playfully.

***

As expected, dinner was cooked to perfection—al dente pasta, sauce that was just the tiniest bit spicy, meatballs tender and flavorful. Liz suspected that if she measured each meatball there would only be millimeters of variance in size between them. Paige had a gift.

Chris and Zee ate like…well, like pro athletes who would be burning up every calorie the next time they were on the ice. It was astounding how much food they could put away. Especially Zee. At only twenty-two, it was entirely possible that he was still growing, at least in the sense of bulk.

***

One magnificent meal, a bottle of wine, and a whole lot of beer later, Paige and Chris quietly vanished, leaving Zee and Liz chatting.

"I'm so glad you're here, Zee. It gives me someone to talk to now that the inevitable has happened…they've wandered off to Paige's room and have forgotten that the rest of the world exists."

"No way! Fascinating." Zee got an evil gleam in his eye. "How often does that happen? Are they loud? Are we going to be treated to a show this evening?"

Right on cue, they heard a low, distinctly masculine groan of pleasure.

"All the time, yes, and apparently so," Liz answered Zee's questions in order. She got up to turn the volume up on the music.

"Oh, man." Zee looked practically giddy. "I should record this."

"Don't!" Liz reached out to stop Zee from pulling his phone out of his pocket. "Don't. Paige wouldn't find any humor in that at all. She would be very upset."

"Fair enough." Zee relented and gave Liz a look of interest. "I get the feeling that if it was you, you'd probably laugh. Am I right?"

"Ha! Possibly." Liz's eyes sparkled a bit. "But it's *not* me, so don't get any ideas, buster."

Zee settled back on the couch and looked more intently at Liz, shifting the topic somewhat. "I've been meaning to ask you—why isn't it you?"

"What?"

"Where's the guy in your life, Liz? There must be one."

Liz smiled. "Nope."

Pressing the subject further, Zee asked, "Are you not into guys?" Thinking just briefly, he continued, "Are you into girls? Holy shit, you and Paige?" Eyes wide, gathering steam now, "And Becks? What the fuck kind of kinky joint are you running here, Williams?"

Liz was laughing hard, and she paused to wipe her eyes before responding. "No, I am so sorry to disappoint you, but I am one hundred percent into guys. There just doesn't happen to be one right now."

"I could set you up…"

Still chuckling, Liz said, "No. Thank you, though."

"Are you sure? There are some guys I know…"

"No, really. I'm just not currently interested."

"Bad breakup?" Zee was now just curious. He had become close enough with Liz that he felt comfortable asking for more information, although he suspected he might be overreaching.

"Oh, sweetie," Liz sighed. "I promise I will tell

you all about it in the morning."

Perking back up immediately, Zee asked, "Is that a proposition?"

Liz chuckled and replied, "No, but you're definitely not driving. I will take the couch; you can have my bed."

Zee stood up and stretched, giving Liz a pouting look. "No threesomes…no girl-on-girl action…and now no girl in my bed. You're lucky I like you so much or this would be a very disappointing evening."

"You are an idiot." She cuffed him and gave him a shove in the direction of her bedroom. "Go to bed."

Zee gave her a big hug and said, "Good night, Liz."

***

The next morning, Liz was up and had already made coffee by the time Paige and Chris emerged from the bedroom.

"Good morning. Cinnamon rolls are in the oven," Liz said, taking a seat at the table with her mug.

They both got cups and joined her, chatting quietly as they waited for the pastries to be done.

"Dinner last night was inspired, Paige." Liz sipped her coffee, adding to Chris, "Apparently, inviting hockey players over brings out the best in her cooking. You guys have to come over more often."

"Are you kidding? Any time." Turning to his

girlfriend, he added, "That was an amazing dinner, Paige."

Zee emerged from Liz's room, shirtless and rumpled, drawn by the delicious aromas. "Oh, thank God, I smell coffee."

Chris's mouth was hanging open slightly, and Paige turned to Liz with a look of silent shock.

"Good morning, sweetie," Liz greeted him. "Sugar and creamer are next to the coffee pot; cinnamon rolls will be done soon."

Chris and Paige were still staring in mute disbelief when Zee joined them at the table. Liz sipped her coffee to hide her smile. Zee seemed unaware of anything but the life-giving liquid in the mug he was holding.

Paige broke the silence.

"So, Zee, did you sleep well last night?"

Zee grunted an affirmative, adding, "Coffee before talking."

Chris was still looking slightly stunned. "Um…" He was searching for a way to address this. "So, you two…?" He left off in an obvious question, and Liz tried not to let her smirk show. Zee was oblivious.

Liz answered carefully, waiting, pausing, trying to time things just right.

"Yeah, definitely…" Chris took a drink, and Liz struck. "We were out here fucking like bunnies." Chris choked and spit out his coffee.

Paige said, "Oh my *God,* Liz!" and Zee, startled out of his stupor, started laughing deep belly laughs.

Liz continued, "I'm surprised you didn't hear us, Chris. We were loud."

Zee was having trouble breathing by this point, and Paige was shaking her head, trying not to laugh at Chris's expense. Chris was wearing his coffee, along with an expression of shock, which was slowly changing to realization and understanding.

"I'm trying to decide if I hate you," Chris said, shooting a look of exasperation toward Liz as he started toward the bedroom to change out of the coffee-soaked shirt.

"You love me," she responded. "I'm fun!"

He snorted in amused frustration, and Paige just shook her head at Liz.

***

After everything had calmed down, and after cleaning up the kitchen, Paige and Chris left to run a few errands, leaving Liz and Zee alone.

"So," he said, kicking back on the couch and making himself comfortable, "what's the story? You promised that you would tell me exactly why you're single and won't let me set you up with some strapping young hockey player."

Liz sat down. "Didn't forget about that, huh?" Zee shook his head.

"Nope. Not a chance."

Liz's smile was small and a bit sad. Zee sat up and reached out to her, realizing suddenly that there was more to this than simply a bad breakup.

"Shit. Do you not want to talk about this? Is there something I can do?"

Taking his hand, she said, "No. No, Zee, it's okay. If I didn't want to tell you, I would have said

76

so last night. It's just not a happy story."

He listened quietly as she told him about Jimmy, her fiancé who had died in a car crash more than a year earlier. Liz let the tears show, and Zee held her hands and then pulled her into his chest for a deep, squeezing, comforting hug, murmuring, "I'm so sorry, Liz," into her hair.

She hugged him back and then pushed back from his chest and wiped her eyes, smiling at him.

"Jesus, Liz, I'm an asshole. I'm so sorry I made you tell me."

"No! No, Zee, don't be ridiculous. I promise, if I didn't want to talk about it, I would have said so." She sniffled a little. "I actually need to be able to talk about him, and I'm really glad you're such a good friend already that I feel safe talking about him with you. Thank you, sweetie."

"Damn, Liz. I just made you cry and you're thanking me? Ya big weirdo." His mouth quirked into a grin, and Liz laughed.

"So, anyway, although I truly appreciate the offer of being set up, I have had a few dates recently, and they were singularly uninspiring. I realized that I'm just not ready. Not yet. But, truly, thank you."

She stood up, stretched, and then said, "Okay, you. Time for you to head out. I'm sure you have practice later, right?"

"Kicking me out, Williams?" Zee's eyes were sparkling with good humor again, and Liz grinned at him in return.

"Yup. Beat it, Zimmerman." Zee laughed, and they exchanged a hug as he left the apartment.

Chapter Ten

Chris had a weekly call-in segment on the local morning sports radio show. The hosts were a group of three guys who had grown up together in the suburbs of DC. They were irreverent and funny, knowledgeable about sports, and admittedly ignorant about most of the other things they talked about but talked about them anyway. They had been on the radio for well over a decade, and their interactions with each other were part of what made the show wildly popular. Most of the time the show just sounded like exactly what it was—a couple of old friends shooting the shit, giving each other a hard time, and arguing about whatever topic happened to come up.

For every local sports team the station had at least one player and one coach—or general manager or other front office person—call in weekly during the season. Chris was a natural for this sort of thing; he was generally comfortable handling press conferences and media interviews, kept his cool under pressure answering the hard questions when the team wasn't playing particularly well, and as a bonus, he was normally able to watch his language when he was off the ice. Not all the guys were quite as good at that, especially the younger players.

The hosts were easy enough to talk to, and Chris normally enjoyed interacting with them for the twenty or so minutes he was on the air during his call-in each week. One of the three hosts was a life-long Guardians fan, which made it even better.

Questions each week could be about serious team considerations—line changes, how they're handling the pressure of having players out with injuries—or they could be asking him which player listens to the most obnoxious music in the locker room or who is most likely to be looking for junk food. Or which player gets the most local female action on road trips. It took a bit of fine-line-treading to know how much information to share to be interesting and fun without compromising the privacy of his teammates, and Chris was adept at this type of interaction.

This particular week, after a few minutes of discussing their upcoming road trip, one of the hosts chimed in with, "So, I heard an interesting nugget about our friend, Chris."

The other guys jumped on this. "Really?"

"Tell us more."

On the show, one of the hosts, JD, was known for asking questions about two things: money and women. How much money do folks make, and how hot are the women in their lives?

"A little bird told me that Chris has a new woman in his life."

Chris was speechless. Even after having dodged all kinds of personal questions from these guys for most of the last season, this one caught him completely unprepared.

"Really?" was the best he came up with to keep the interview going.

"That's not a no! Is my source right?"

Momentarily flustered, Chris replied, "I'm wondering exactly what that bird told you."

The guys were practically giddy. "Ohhhhh, he's not saying no!"

"He's not denying it!"

"Do you have a woman?"

JD added, "My little bird mentioned that she is a serious hottie."

Chris paused to collect himself while the guys chortled and then finally said, "You appear to know a very well-informed bird."

The cheering and clapping was ridiculous, and Chris found himself grinning and shaking his head.

"Tell us more! Who is she? Where did you meet?"

"Is she really hot?"

"My man is gettin' some buns!"

When the noise died down a little, Chris laughed a bit and simply said, "When I want to share more, I will be sure to let you know."

After a bit more of the requisite poking and teasing, the hosts thankfully let him off the hook for the week, and he ended the call. Sitting back in his chair, he sighed, realizing that this would now be a recurring theme. They were nice guys, but they worked in radio, and this sort of thing was good for their show. This was going to be an interesting balancing act.

He wondered briefly who had said something to them—Zee, maybe? Maybe, but Chris didn't think that he would go out of his way to do that. Most likely someone who was a fan of the team saw him out on a date with Paige at some point. She was a gorgeous woman; some guy might just have been looking at her and then been surprised to realize he recognized Chris.

I hope that this goes over okay with Paige.

***

"Can I take you out to dinner Friday night?" Chris asked. He was calling from the road; they were on their way back from an east coast road trip to Montreal and New York, so there was no jet lag to worry about. "We'll be getting in around three o'clock, so I can pick you up. Or you could meet me at my apartment, if that would be easier."

Paige hesitated a moment before answering. "I'm so sorry, I have a work obligation that night. How long will you be in town? Are you free Saturday night?"

"We're playing a home game at seven Saturday night, so that won't work. But what's the work event? That's pretty unusual for you to have school commitments on a Friday night, right? Is it parent/teacher stuff? Or sports?"

Smiling at his interest in her life, she replied, "No, it's actually a fundraiser. The marching band is trying to raise enough money to purchase new uniforms, and the students have organized a silent auction. I'm going to attend to support it."

"Oh. That's cool." Thinking about it for a moment more, he asked, "Really? The kids organized it?"

"The whole thing. All of the donations, the flyers, everything."

"Wow, I'm impressed. That's so much more ambitious than I ever was in high school."

Paige laughed. "Right? Me too. These guys are really amazing."

There was a pause before Chris asked, almost shyly, "So, um, can you bring a date to this event?"

Her heart twisted in a way that had become achingly familiar when dealing with Chris.

"Really? You would want to go?"

Chris had to stop himself from staring at the phone. "Baby, of course I want to go. I would love to go with you." There was a pause on the other end of the line, long enough that he felt a little anxious as he asked, "Would it make you uncomfortable for me to be there? I don't want to upset your plans."

Paige started; she hadn't realized that she had been silent. There were all kinds of things running through her head.

"Are you sure you want to go to this, Chris? It's a high school fundraiser. This is not a big event, you know? It's just parents and some community people, and the bidding items are things like dry cleaning gift certificates. You don't need to do this, Chris. I mean, this isn't the kind of thing that you're…"

"Paige," Chris interrupted her. "Stop. Breathe. I

remember high school, baby. I'm not under any delusions as to the glamour factor here. This is a special event for your job, and if you're all right with people knowing that we're dating, then yes, I would really like to be there with you."

She choked out a little laugh and replied, "Yes, Chris, that would be great. I would love for you to meet some of my co-workers."

He let out a breath, relieved that she would allow him into this part of her life.

"Well, um, could I contribute something? For the auction?"

"Really?"

"Sure. Maybe a signed jersey? Would that be appropriate?"

Paige was floored. "Are you serious, Chris? That would be amazing. The kids would be thrilled."

Smiling, Chris said, "Well, I mean, it's not dry cleaning, but..." and was rewarded with an easy laugh from the other end of the phone line. The conversation had become strained at some point along the way and was finally starting to feel normal again.

"Well, dry cleaning is difficult to top." Taking a quick breath, she added, "I would never have asked you. You know that, right?"

"Why on earth not?"

"Because I don't ever want you to think that I'm trying to take advantage of your position, of your job. Of the fact that you're a famous pro-athlete. I don't ever want you to feel like I'm interested in what you do more than who you are."

She heard a deep sigh on the other end of the

line.

"Thank you, baby. I never would have thought that of you. Not ever. But thank you." He chuckled for a moment. "And it's very sweet of you to call me a 'famous pro-athlete.' Not remotely accurate, but very sweet. I'll be amazed if anyone recognizes me on Friday." Another sigh. "I know you have to go to bed. Thank you for staying up to talk with me. It's the best part of my day."

"Me too, Chris. Safe travels. I'll see you on Friday."

***

Chris arrived at the apartment Friday night dressed in a full suit and tie.

Liz let out a low whistle when she answered the door.

"Damn, Chris." She spun him around before she let him in the doorway, checking out the whole effect. "I like it. Very stylish. I mean, you always look nice, but I don't think I've seen you in a full suit before. Except on TV, arriving at the rink before games, of course. But they only show you guys for a second."

"Well, thank you." Chris came in the door and sat down at the kitchen table when Liz finally released him from her inspection.

Paige called, "I'll be right out, Chris!" from her bedroom.

"Have you always…I don't really know how to put this…'dressed up' when you were younger? Or is that a more recent thing?" Liz gestured to herself, adding, "As you can see, my fashion sense runs toward jeans and…well, jeans. That's about it."

"Well, you know that we're required to dress in a suit to travel with the team," Chris started, and Liz nodded in agreement. "So when I started playing with Columbus, I just, well, got a little over-zealous in my clothing purchases."

Paige emerged from her room, wearing a beautifully simple red wrap dress that accentuated her figure, and Chris made a low rumble of appreciation.

Standing to greet her properly, he took her hand and twirled her around slowly, whispering, "Wow, baby."

Paige blushed and said, "Thanks," giving him a kiss. "Please keep telling your story. It sounded like you weren't finished."

Chris looked confused for a moment, until Liz said, "Your suit-buying spree?"

"Oh, right! Sorry…"

Liz interrupted with, "Oh, please, you got distracted by my beautiful roommate. Like that's the first time *that's* ever happened around here."

Chris chuckled. "Anyway, for a little while my teammates called me 'Suits' rather than 'Becks.' Thank goodness that was short-lived. But I ended up just, you know, liking the way I looked dressed this way, I guess." He looked slightly embarrassed by this admission, and Paige felt that familiar heart twist.

"Nothing wrong with that," Liz said. "I agree—you always look great, Chris." She gave him a quick kiss on the cheek and hugged Paige. "Have

85

fun tonight!"

She walked back to her room, and Chris offered his arm to Paige. "Shall we?"

***

"Thank you again for coming with me, Chris." Paige called him Monday afternoon after school. "Not only was your jersey one of the highest-bidding items Friday night, but apparently I am now deemed the coolest teacher in the entire school."

"Really?"

"Really. Evidently the word got around fast, because I had students more attentive and engaged in class than ever before, and even past students were stopping me in the halls to say hi and, you know, *ask me.*" She said the last two words in way that made it sound like a great mystery.

"Ask you what?"

Paige laughed and said, "If it's true, of course! 'Are you really dating a hockey player, Ms. Smith?' And then the occasional Guardians fan that would ask with obvious awe, 'Are you really dating *Chris Beckman?*'"

She sounded joyful and at ease, and Chris found himself grinning and laughing along with her.

"I'm so glad, baby. I wasn't sure how you'd feel when people knew."

"Oh, um, speaking of knowing things..." Paige paused for a moment and then rushed on, "So, I accidentally mentioned that you like poetry in my senior class."

"Excuse me?"

"I'm so sorry, Chris! It slipped out. One of the guys was saying disparaging things about poetry being boring, and I just…well…it was a target of opportunity, and I didn't think before I spoke."

"Oh. Okay." Chris was feeling a little odd about this but couldn't put his finger on exactly why.

"Are you sure?" she asked, and when he responded affirmatively, she said, more quietly, "I didn't say anything about *'Cloths of Heaven,'* I promise. I wouldn't share anything that intimate."

Chris breathed out, relaxing. "Thank you, baby," he responded quietly.

"Of course." He heard a little catch in her voice. "I'm sorry I said anything without checking with you first. I'm not used to this kind of interest in my personal life, you know? I need to learn to navigate this."

"I understand. It can be weird suddenly having this kind of attention."

"Thank you."

There was a pause for a few moments. It seemed to happen periodically when they were talking, even on the phone. Just a quiet sharing of space together.

"Can I see you tomorrow night?" Chris finally asked, his voice carrying his desire.

"Yes," she said, sounding suddenly slightly breathless. "Yes, Chris. Tomorrow night."

***

At practice the next afternoon, his area of the locker room was covered in bright yellow Post-it notes, each with a truly horrible limerick. They weren't even all in the same handwriting, although he was certain Zee was behind it.

"Are you fucking kidding me?" he asked, pulling yet another Post-it out of the sleeve of his jersey as his teammates laughed, all adamantly denying any knowledge of how, or even why, there would be such an abundance of lewd verse floating around.

Chris was laughing as he called them all a bunch of assholes.

***

The next morning was his weekly call-in.

"So, we are joined again this morning by Chris Beckman of the Washington Guardians. Hey, Chris. How's things?"

"Hi, guys," he responded. "Thanks for having me on. Going well."

JD chimed in, "How's that little hottie of yours?"

Chris shook his head and said, "Really? Leading off with that today? You do remember that there's a whole lot of hockey we could talk about."

The guys laughed, and JD continued, "True, but I heard more from my little bird."

The other hosts were, once again, giddy.

"Really? What's going on?"

"What are you not telling us, Chris?"

"Well," said JD, "apparently our man, Chris, is very secure in his masculinity and enjoys poetry."

After the locker room prank, he wasn't really surprised by this. He said, "So, what you're saying is that you have forgotten that we play hockey here. Okay, I'll humor you. Yes, I enjoy poetry." He paused and then added, "And long walks on the beach and sunsets and rainbows."

The guys started laughing, so he threw in, "And puppies, piña coladas, and walking in the rain."

"All right, all right, we get the point, Chris. Just teasing. But it has now been confirmed that your hottie is an English teacher, right?"

"Come on, guys, can we please talk about hockey?"

They relented finally. "Yes, we'll talk about hockey. Just one more quick thing, though: Is it true that there were Post-it notes with limericks all over your gear in the locker room yesterday?"

Chris laughed out loud, finally, and said, "Yes. I can confirm that the Guardians players are borderline illiterate and that the only poems they know are about men from Nantucket."

***

He gave Paige a call after school to let her know what had happened, finishing with, "Sorry, baby. There were no names given, but I just wanted to let you know that the news is out that I'm dating an English teacher. And that I like poetry."

There was a pause before she replied.

"Oh." She sat down while processing this. "All right. I mean, do I need to worry about this?"

"No, not at all. There shouldn't be any problems. I doubt that anyone would contact you."

"Is this my fault? Because I blurted that out in class?" She was starting to sound a little panicky.

"No! No, Paige." Chris sighed. "It might have

made this happen a little faster, with a little more flash, but with me doing the weekly radio spot, and then we went to the silent auction together…a few more specifics about you were bound to come out sooner or later. Folks already knew that I was dating a stunningly beautiful woman. People would notice you no matter who you were with."

Paige was quiet for a little while before responding.

"I understand. I am really sorry, Chris."

"Baby, this is part of the deal for me. It's fine. They ask questions; if it's too personal, then I dodge giving answers. It's part of the job." Sensing her discomfort, he tried to reassure her further. "Paige, it's not a problem for me. Not at all. I love…" He caught himself. "I love being seen with you. You're amazing."

"Thanks."

Still not convinced that all was well, he asked quietly, "Is it a problem for you? Are you upset?"

Paige paused for another moment before answering. "No, I'm okay. This is just all really new for me."

"I know. I appreciate it. Truly."

They talked for a few more minutes, making plans to see one another, and then hung up.

Chapter Eleven

Chris was leaning against the kitchen counter, sipping coffee, watching as Paige finished grading the last of the papers stacked on the small dining table. She had begun spending more time at his apartment, sometimes coming over directly after work to wait for him to get home from practice. He had already given her a key and was almost surprised how quickly it felt completely normal to have her there and just how much he loved it. How much it made this place where he slept feel like home.

He had even started idly looking at houses, realizing that this was the first time in his adult life that he found himself wanting to set down roots somewhere. When they were traveling, he often found himself browsing real estate websites, imagining what he would want in a permanent residence.

"Seriously?" she said aloud, talking to the paper in front of her. "One, two, three…" she continued counting silently and then continued, "Ten. Ten!"

Turning to Chris, she clarified. "He used the word 'excited' *ten times* in a two-page paper. *Ten. Times.*" Turning back, she addressed the page again, "How about 'enthusiastic,' huh? 'Giddy?' 'Vibrating with anticipation?'" Tossing her red pen down in disgust, she muttered, "Make a small effort already."

Chris was trying not to smile. She was frustrated, but he was finding it adorable.

"So...not a fan of repetitive word usage, I take it?"

She rolled her eyes and walked over to him.

"Don't get me wrong. I understand, I really do. They're kids. I don't expect Shakespeare. But for God's sake, Chris, they all have the internet. An interactive thesaurus is *literally* at their fingertips." She pulled down a wine glass and poured herself a glass of merlot as she continued, "Hell, the word processing program has suggestions built right in. We're talking a minimal amount of effort to make an enormous difference in writing quality."

"You are so damn cute."

She rolled her eyes at him again, but there was a smile starting.

"Just cute?" she asked. "Not stunning? Spectacular? Groin-tighteningly beautiful?"

Chris laughed out loud at the last one and moved to pull her to him, one hand on her backside, pressing his groin against her, enjoying her small intake of breath as she felt the evidence of his attraction growing against her.

"You tell me, baby," he said, caressing her ass gently.

"What would you like me to tell you, big guy?" she asked, her earlier irritation giving way to a more playful mood. Moving her hand across the fly of his pants, she continued, "That there appears to be a tent forming in your slacks? That you seem to be sporting a stiffy? How about that I like the feel of your wood under my palm?"

He was unable to keep a straight face, torn between laughing at her increasingly absurd phrases and arousal from her continued stroking.

"I do like the feel of your Johnson, your twig-and-berries, your one-eyed trouser snake coming out to play…" She put her wine glass down so she could continue with both hands. "…the way your family jewels start to tighten as I fondle your nuts while stroking your salami."

He pushed her away, laughing. "Enough!" Looking at the sparkle in her eyes, he said, "I can't believe you know all of these euphemisms."

"Big guy," she said, pushing against his chest, maneuvering him toward the couch, "I'm a word junkie. I want to know *all* the words." Pausing to stroke his length again, she said, "I could do this all night, talking to you about the increasing angle of your dangle, the heat of your meat, the feel of your one-holed-friction-whistle."

The last one made him laugh out loud again, and he put up his hands in surrender. "I give. You win. Even I have never heard that last one."

She now had him standing in front of the couch.

"Words have power, Chris. They're practically magic, the way they can shape how we feel. They can uplift or devastate, amuse or arouse, comfort, captivate, tantalize…" She began to unbuckle his belt and undo his pants. "…frustrate, irritate, tease…" She pushed his pants and boxers to the floor and began to unbutton his shirt, running her hands up his chest. "…and I want to know them all. The proper names, as well as the slang."

"Really?" His voice was rough with desire as she pushed him to sit on the couch.

"Absolutely." She gently slipped off his shoes, socks, pants, and boxers and grabbed a pillow from the nearby chair, placing it under her knees.

He felt her hands run up the outsides of his thighs and murmured, "Oh, fuck." Her hands ran over the top of his thighs, tantalizingly near his balls as she moved them down to his inner thighs, and he groaned as she dragged her hands gently down his inner thighs to his knees, pushing his legs apart as she went.

"So, big guy, I was thinking about a vocabulary lesson."

"Vocabulary?"

"Yes." She settled herself comfortably between his knees and gently encouraged him to move his hips forward on the couch just a bit, so that everything was in easy reach.

Stroking his inner thighs gently, she started talking.

"I love knowing all of the words for things." She paused to drag her fingers gently on the underside of his scrotum, causing him to twitch.

"For instance," she continued, "this, as I'm sure you are aware, is your scrotum, containing your testes."

She cradled his balls, weighing them in her hand. They were large and heavy, and she rolled them gently in her fingers briefly.

His eyes were half-lidded, and he was breathing more heavily than normal already.

"In singular, one may be referred to as either a testis or a testicle. The plural is testes, although testicles is also generally accepted.

"But did you know that the midline of the scrotum is called the raphe? Right here." She bent her head down and drew her tongue along the center up toward the base of his shaft, and Chris gasped.

Paige took the loose skin of his scrotum in her lips and tugged gently and then took one testicle into her mouth, using her tongue to move it around within the pouch.

Chris groaned and instinctively moved his legs further apart so that she had room to repeat her actions on his other testicle, lightly sucking as she manipulated it with her tongue before releasing it.

He was already fully erect, and she wrapped her hand around him, saying, "This is the shaft of your penis." Dragging her hand slowly upward, she added, "And this is the head, also known as the glans."

Paige began using fingers and tongue to draw attention to the various parts as she described them to him.

"This area right here, the ridge where the glans meets the shaft? This is the corona," she said and then circled her tongue around him. "And the area just up under the corona is the sulcus." She circled her tongue around him again, catching that sensitive area underneath the head.

"Christ." It was a whispered groan, and Chris closed his eyes and put his head back against the couch cushions.

"The foreskin is also known as the prepuce." Pulling down slightly so that the skin was taut, she said, "And this, where the foreskin connects to the shaft, is known as the frenulum." She kissed and sucked at his frenulum, moving it with her tongue while he twitched and moaned.

One of her hands was holding the base of his shaft, and she shifted the other to cradle his balls again.

Paige met his eyes, which were heavy-lidded with lust, and smiled.

"As I said," she continued, "I like knowing all the words for things. I've already mentioned a few, but colloquially, these are your balls." She moved her hand to roll them in her fingers. "And this is your big, hard, cock," she said as she started stroking him, watching his reactions carefully. His eyes had widened at her last words.

"Oh, Chris," she said, pausing to swirl her tongue around him again and then speaking with her mouth teasingly close to his glans, "your reaction to the word 'cock' makes me think that it's possible you might like dirty talk."

His breathing got a little faster.

"Words are powerful, and context is everything." She licked the underside of his shaft and said, "So, if hearing me say that I want to suck your big, thick, hard cock turns you on, I want to know."

The responding involuntary thrust of his hips

was enough of an answer for her, but he also whispered, "Oh, fuck."

"Oh, yes. You like hearing just how much I want to suck you off, how badly I want to feel your fat cock in my mouth, don't you?"

Chris stared, almost unable to believe what he was hearing from her, unable to connect the words with the woman.

"Don't you?" she repeated, hovering over the head so that he felt her warm breath. "Does it make you even harder, Chris? Does it turn you on hearing me talk about wrapping my lips around your thick, hard cock?"

"Yes." The word rasped out of his throat, the admission almost painful.

Smiling at him, maintaining eye contact, she took him into her mouth until her lips met her hand.

"Oh, fuck, fuck, fuck." It was almost a mantra he was repeating as she began moving on him.

She started with moving her mouth slowly up and down on his shaft. Bringing her left hand back down again, she reached under to cup him, rolling her fingers in time with the sliding of her mouth. She added a bit more suction pressure and allowed him to pop out of her mouth, only to swirl her tongue around his crown again.

Chris was groaning and cursing softly under his breath.

"Do you want to come in my mouth, Chris?"

"Oh, fuck, Paige."

"Do you?"

"Goddamn, baby," he growled. *"Yes."*

Releasing both of her hands, she took him back

into her mouth, taking him in as far as she could while she moved her hands back along his thighs to his lower back. He felt her run her short nails across his back and down to his thighs again as she held him deep in her mouth for a moment before resuming her hold on his shaft and her shallower strokes into her mouth.

Increasing speed slightly caused an audible intake of breath from him; when she opened her mouth around him and rapidly breathed in, causing a rush of cold air around his shaft, he jumped, gasping, "Holy shit!"

She moved back a bit, chuckling, her eyes wickedly playful when they met his.

"I'm going to suck this big, throbbing cock of yours until you come, Chris," she whispered and then licked the underside of the head again, still stroking him. "Until you come in my hot, wet mouth. Is that what you want?"

"Oh fuck, yes."

And then, her gaze shifting to pure heat, she took him into her mouth again and began to move her hand on his shaft with a firm, sure grip, stroking him slowly at first. While she increased the speed of her strokes incrementally, she started treating the top half of his cock as she would a lollipop—sucking, moving her tongue to press and slide, swallowing while using her tongue to press him against the roof of her mouth. Allowing his cock to pop out of her mouth with hard suction and then sucking him back in again. All the while increasing the speed of her stroking. Holding his balls with her left hand, touching, rolling, tugging.

He was panting, groaning, moaning.

"Fuck. Oh, fuck. *Yes.*"

He started moving his hips as she increased the speed and pressure of her stroking yet again.

Suction. Pressure. Stroking. Tonguing.

She was now jacking in the short, fast strokes that she knew would finish him off. Hips shifting, cursing, thrusting…and then she pushed her lips down to her hand and moaned loudly, the vibrations finally sending him over the edge into a pulsing, shooting, shouting orgasm.

Chris grabbed her head, pushing his hips up toward her mouth, thrusting frantically as his climax crashed over him. He twitched repeatedly as she kept up suction and pressure, continuing to stroke him as she swallowed.

And finally, finally, he began to relax as she released him from her mouth and hands, running her hands up to his chest while she kissed the inside of his thighs before getting up to sit next to him on the couch.

"Holy shit." Chris looked at Paige, feeling almost as if he had never met this version of her. "I…holy shit."

She laughed softly, deeply pleased by his reaction, and he smiled at her, looking a little confused, unfocused. After a few moments of just breathing and returning to his own body, he said, "I had no idea."

"About what, in particular?"

Chris thought for a moment, still having trouble putting thoughts together.

"That you would say…stuff. And that I would

like it."

Paige laughed out loud. "As I said, all words are powerful in their own way, and there's a time and place for them when they will be at their most powerful."

He looked at her and said, "But you..." The pause lasted so long he just gave up trying to put his thoughts into words and just laughed, relaxed and satiated.

"So, big guy," she said, nipping at his earlobe, "now I know another thing that turns you on. It's fun."

"I didn't even know. I'm not so sure if it's the words themselves or hearing them come out of you."

"Either way." Paige shrugged and then snuggled up close to his ear and whispered, "By the way, you can go down on me any time you want. I love feeling your soft tongue on my clit."

Chris murmured, "Sweet Jesus."

Chapter Twelve

Paige did not get a chance to watch many of Chris's games from beginning to end. Between grading papers, lesson plans, parent-teacher conferences, and needing to get to bed at a decent hour, watching a full game that didn't start until at least seven p.m.—later if the team was traveling west—was simply not an option. So it was a while before she got a chance to sit and watch another game with Liz.

"That game we watched together was *not* rough, Paige." Liz was munching on popcorn as they were watching pre-game coverage on TV. "*This* game, however, is a different story altogether. In the other game, they were playing against Ottawa. Not huge rivals, and both teams are a bit more geared toward speed and skill rather than heavy hitting."

"There were hits in that game," Paige protested. "It looked rough to me."

Liz smiled and said, "Just wait. Tonight you'll see some fireworks, if I'm not mistaken. They're playing Pittsburgh *in* Pittsburgh. This is one of our *huge* rivalries. Pitt knocked them out of the playoffs last season, and there were a few, shall we say, 'questionable' calls by the refs. This is the first time they're meeting this season, and I have a feeling that things are gonna get chippy."

Paige shook her head at the gleam in Liz's eyes as she talked about the game. Liz always said she loved the physicality of hockey.

The game did not disappoint. Big, heavy hits slamming guys into the boards, lots of pushing and shoving, lots of after-whistle action, and quite a few penalties. And several things that probably should have been penalties that weren't called, which just amped everything up even more.

"Oh, this is gonna get ugly," Liz said, watching two players head off for matching roughing minors. She turned to Paige and added, "Just watch. There will be a fight between those two when they get out or soon after."

"Not an actual fight, right?" Paige asked. "Just more pushing and shoving."

Liz turned to her, looking surprised, and said, "No, Paige, an actual fight. How do you not know that there are fights in hockey?" Shaking her head, she added, "How long have you known me? Have you ever listened to anything I've said?"

"I sometimes listen, but hockey talk sounds a lot like 'blah, blah, blah, Ginger' to me."

Liz sighed. "They fight. For real. Not all the time, but you're gonna see it tonight, probably pretty soon. When it happens, both players involved will be called on a penalty—five minutes, haven't you ever heard the phrase 'five for fighting?'—but the refs will let them go on a while before they break it up."

Sure enough, it was only about three minutes after the roughing penalty when the first punch was thrown. It happened behind Pittsburgh's net and became quite a scrum. When the refs started pulling players apart, it was clear that there were two main altercations happening at the same time, and one of them included Chris.

"Holy shit! That's Chris!" Liz exclaimed. "I'm not sure I've ever seen him fight. He must be really pissed about that cheap shot from Malek."

His fight was quick, but he got in two good left hooks before it broke up. Liz cheered.

Paige was silent, and when Liz looked at her, she was rather pale. Liz moved over to sit next to her and put her arm around Paige.

"Paige, what's wrong?"

Paige turned to her, eyes wide, and said, "I can't believe he does that." She was breathing rather shallowly and said, "I feel a little sick."

"Oh, shit." Liz got up and brought her a glass of ice water. "Paige, look at me." When she had her friend's focus, she said, "He does *not* do this all the time. Almost never. And it's part of the game. Part of his *job*."

Liz turned off the television so she could focus solely on Paige, who was clearly having a hard time processing seeing this aspect of Chris's game.

"I don't know if I can do this."

"Do what?"

Paige turned to her friend and said, "Date him. Date someone violent."

"Oh God, no. Paige, he's *not* violent."

"How do you know?"

Liz stared at her. "How could you *not* know? Has he seemed the least bit violent to you? Ever?"

"No, but…"

"None of the Guardians' players—and I mean *none* of them—have any history of violence outside of the rink. There's no domestic assault charges, no bar fights, nothing. Chris is the same person now that he was to you two hours ago. Please don't make a decision this important based on one two-minute hockey fight."

Paige was calming down but still looked pale and shaken.

"Okay. That makes sense, but God, Liz. That's crazy. They do that all the time?"

Liz smiled. "It's part of the game. I think it's part of what makes the game amazing, that there's this built-in pressure relief valve. The players are passionate about the game." Tilting her head to one side, she asked, "Are you going to be all right? I'm sorry, I had no idea that you really didn't know about hockey fights. It feels impossible that you haven't seen one before."

"Yeah, I'll be fine. Still a little freaked out, though. He seems so…gentle." She was smiling. "And sweet. It doesn't seem like he could be the same person that just did…that." She gestured at the television.

"Everything I have ever seen or read about Chris says that he's exactly what you have seen from him…soft-spoken, quiet, kind. I promise I would never have pushed you toward someone who is

104

violent or mean, Paige."

Paige stood up and stretched. "I know. It was just surprising. Go ahead and turn the game back on. I'm going to go read for a while."

"Nope, I can live without watching this game. Come on, let's go get ice cream or something."

***

The team traveled back to DC the same night after the game in Pittsburgh, so Chris came over to see Paige after school got out the next day. She answered her apartment door with a smile, but when he reached his hand to her cheek to hold her face for a kiss, she flinched.

Chris drew back immediately, his face a picture of concern, bordering on fear.

"What's wrong?" he asked. "Paige, what happened? Are you hurt?"

She shook her head. "No, I'm fine, Chris. I'm sorry about that." She smiled at him, irritated with herself for her reaction, and said, "Let's try this again," as she moved toward him.

But he took a half step back from her, saying, "No, please. You flinched away from me like you were afraid. Paige, tell me what happened. This is scaring the hell out of me, because I don't know what's wrong."

Paige sighed and stepped out of the doorway to invite him in. "Come in, have a seat, and we can talk. I am sorry, Chris."

"Are you breaking up with me?"

"What? No!" Paige shook her head in irritation.

105

"Shit! This is not going well." She saw Chris raise his eyebrows in surprise at the language, and she laughed out loud. "Oh, for fuck's sake, come inside, Chris. I'm making a mess of this conversation nine ways to Sunday, and I'm sorry about that. And yes, I can cuss too."

Chris relaxed a bit at the abrupt change in tone and walked into the apartment to take a seat on the couch.

"I watched the game last night with Liz. Or, at least, I watched most of it." She took a breath. "I stopped watching after the fight."

He stared for a moment and then said, "I still don't think I understand what's going on."

"Your fight," she said. "It…" She felt her eyes tear up a little, which she hadn't expected. "It kinda scared me," she finished in a whisper.

"Oh God, Paige…shit." He covered his face with one hand, the anxiety that began in her doorway beginning to make him feel ill.

"Liz talked to me about it. Explained things. I mean, I get it now, I think. I think I understand the way this works, but I haven't ever seen you…" She trailed off with a vague gesture.

Chris took her hands very gently and said, "Paige, I'm sorry. I should have realized that you wouldn't have known…that you don't watch…" He looked up for a minute, trying to get his thoughts together. Looking back into her eyes, he said, "I feel like an ass for not having talked with you about this. That's part of the game, but it's not *me.* Not off the ice. I hardly ever get into fights even *on* the ice."

Paige interrupted. "That's what Liz said."

He continued, "It's not my role, really. There are guys that tend to take the lead on that sort of thing—they're known as 'enforcers'—and I'm not one of them. But it's part of the game to stick up for your teammates, and sometimes that means that even I will take a swing at someone. Last night was one of those times. Pittsburgh was throwing some really cheap shots at our guys."

He brought her hands to his mouth and kissed the knuckles on each of them. "That is not me off the ice, Paige."

"I know. I'm sorry, Chris."

He looked somewhat better but still not quite right, and he pulled away from her to sit back.

"There's more, right?" she asked, probing gently.

He shook his head slightly and said, "No." And then said, "Yes. Kind of." He breathed out slowly. "I'm not sure I can explain."

Paige waited as he gathered his thoughts.

"On the one hand, I'm really pissed off at myself for not talking with you about this, not anticipating this issue. And I'm so sorry that this happened…" He trailed off.

Paige prompted, "And on the other hand?"

Chris looked at her with a rather pained expression and said nothing.

Quietly, Paige answered her own question. "And on the other hand, you're terribly hurt that I could think that of you."

He exhaled, rubbing his hand on the back of his neck. "Yeah."

"I get it, Chris. I do. And I'm sorry. It was completely unfair of me to jump to that conclusion." Moving closer to him, she asked, "Can we try to move past this?"

Chris gathered her in close and held her. "Definitely." He gave her a little squeeze and said, "Thank you for understanding."

"You too."

They spent the rest of the evening quietly reconnecting with each other—talking, enjoying each other's company, gentle touches soothing the discord between them. Paige fell asleep curled in his arms on the couch, and Chris smiled as he stroked her hair, realizing the embodiment of his vision during their first date.

Chapter Thirteen

"So, Paige, I would really like to bring you to a game in person." Chris handed her a gift bag, and she looked at him curiously.

Opening the bag, Paige pulled out two matching Guardians jerseys with his name and number—fourteen—on the back.

"One for you and one for Liz," he said, smiling.

She giggled and said, "Cool! I get to wear your jersey?" as she pulled the smaller of the two over her head. "How do I look?"

His eyes got surprisingly lusty looking at her, and she felt her heart beat faster in response.

"You absolutely get to wear my jersey, Paige," he said, and then his voice got a little rougher, and he added, "It looks perfect on you. And makes me want to take it off you."

Flashing him a flirty little smile, she pulled up the hem just a bit as if she were going to take it back off again, and he gave a little growl of approval.

"And you can *only* wear *my* jersey, Paige. I think

109

that Zee knows I will kill him if he tries to convince you otherwise, but he's got weird ideas about pranks, so if he gives you one of his and tells you that I won't mind, he's lying to you. I will mind very much."

"Interesting," she responded. "That seems surprising coming from you."

Chris sighed. "Yeah, it's a holdover from teenage days. I can't stand the idea of seeing my girl wearing another guy's jersey." He turned her around to look at the back. "There's something unbelievably sexy about seeing you wearing my name. It makes me feel all caveman possessive." He kissed the top of her head gently as she laughed.

"Thank you for *not* being an actual caveman, big guy." Turning around, she added, "I find your wonderful brain as sexy as you find my tiny panties."

Chris groaned, "Paige, you're killing me. I can't even remember what I was asking you about in the first place." Trying not to fondle her breast was a challenge that was eluding him at the moment.

"Something about a game."

"Oh, right." He tried to focus on her face again. "We are playing in Tennessee this weekend. How would you like to come to Nashville to watch the game? You and Liz, both?"

"Nashville? This weekend? That's a big trip on short notice, Chris."

"I know, but it would be a lot of fun, and you mentioned wanting to go there sometime. You and Liz could fly in Friday night—it's a short flight—go to the game Saturday, and then fly back Sunday.

Would you like that?"

Paige was stunned. Sure, it sounded great, but this wasn't the kind of thing that she did, living on a teacher's salary. Liz made more money at her job, but even she would need time to plan and budget for this kind of trip.

"I don't think I can do that, Chris. Flights, and hotel, and food...I would need more time to be ready for a trip this big."

He looked at her curiously for a moment and then understood. "Oh! No, baby. I would take care of all of that. All you would need to do would be to show up at the airport. I will arrange the tickets and the room and a rental car—or a driver if you would prefer that. I'll take care of everything."

Now she was stunned and felt a press of anxiety in her chest.

"I can't accept that, Chris. That's too much. I could never pay you back for all of that."

"Pay me back?" he asked, getting more confused. "Why would I expect you pay me back, Paige? This is a gift—for me as much as for you. I would love to have you there."

"But paying for all of that? For me *and* for Liz?" The pressure in her chest was getting worse. "I can't ask you to do that."

He was now looking at her as if he truly didn't understand.

"You're not asking me to do this. I'm asking you. All you need to do is say yes."

"I can't."

Chris sat down heavily at the kitchen table, leaning on his forearm. "Why not? Do you not want to go to a game? I thought if Liz came along too, it would make you feel more comfortable."

"That's not it."

"Please, Paige. Sit down and explain this to me. You're acting so skittish all of a sudden, and I don't understand why."

She sat down across from him and took a deep breath, trying to push past the anxiety, wanting to have him understand.

"It's just too much, Chris. I don't feel right accepting something so big from you, as sweet as it is for you to offer." Trying to put the pieces together in her head, she continued, "I mean, I'm a public school teacher. Odds are that anyone I date is going to make more money than me. But I don't ever want to take advantage of that; it's just not right. And this?" She gestured vaguely around toward him. "It's so far beyond that. I know you have the right to make your own decisions about how you spend money, but that's a lot, Chris. It's too much."

Chris sat back in the chair and looked at her, head cocked slightly to one side, a small smile on his face.

"You have no idea how much money I make, do you?"

"Of course not." Paige sounded incredulous. "How would I? This isn't something we've talked about before."

He shook his head, amused and amazed.

"Paige, my contract and salary are public record. The team releases that information whenever a new contract is signed." He sat back up, reached across the table, took her hand gently, and said, "I'm in my second year of an eight year, two-and-a-half million-dollar contract with the Guardians."

She stared at him and then whispered, "Holy crap."

Chris chuckled.

She did some quick math. "That's, what, more than three hundred thousand a year? Holy crap, Chris," she repeated.

"Oh, baby," he said, shaking his head and smiling. "You don't understand sports deals at all, do you?"

She shook her head.

Taking both her hands gently, he said, "Paige, my contract is two-and-a-half million *per year.*"

She paled and then very quietly said, "Oh."

"Baby?" he asked, getting concerned. "Paige, honey, are you okay?"

She nodded.

Chris moved to the chair next to her, put his hand behind her neck, and kissed her forehead. "So, can I take you to Nashville this weekend? Please?"

With a little squeak, she said, "Yeah. Okay, I guess." Looking up at him, she added in a smaller voice, "I kind of feel like an idiot."

He cupped her face in both hands and said, "No. Never." He brushed her hair away from her face gently. "You don't know what it means to me that you cared about me without having any idea. I have friends who have to worry that any woman they date is only interested in the money or attention that goes along with being in the pros. I have never felt that way with you. Not for one minute." Another kiss to her forehead and he added, "I really did think you knew, though. It just never felt like it mattered."

"It doesn't."

"I know. It's one of the things that makes you amazing." Looking in her eyes again, he said, "So, now, I'm going to make arrangements for my girlfriend and her best friend to have an amazing trip to our game against the Chords. Thank you, baby."

Paige started laughing out loud and shook her head.

"You're thanking *me?*"

***

True to his word, Chris handled all the preparations for the trip to Nashville. Liz and Paige were met at Nashville International by a man holding a sign with Paige's name—Chris had decided that he wanted Paige to have a driver, so they wouldn't have to worry about finding their way around a new city.

"Oooh," Liz whispered to Paige. "It's like you're a celebrity!"

Paige swatted her.

Their driver, Sam, took them directly to their hotel, unloaded their bags, and made sure everything went smoothly with check-in. Chris had set them up in the penthouse, which was a luxury two-bedroom suite.

"Mr. Beckman has asked me to be back here at nine-thirty tomorrow morning to take you ladies anywhere you would like to go around Nashville. If you don't have any specifics in mind, he has given me a list of suggestions." Sam smiled warmly. "He has been very clear that you are both to have an exceptional time. He won't be able to see you until after the game tomorrow night, so you are to consider me at your beck and call from nine-thirty tomorrow morning until I deliver you safely back to the hotel after the game."

He gave them a bow and said, "Have a lovely evening, ladies. Sleep well."

As he walked out the door, Liz and Paige looked at each other and started giggling like kids.

"This is ridiculous!" Paige whispered. "Do people really live like this?"

Liz grabbed her elbow and steered her to the elevators. "I have no idea, but it's fun!"

Even Liz was struck speechless when they entered the suite.

"This is bigger than our apartment." Paige felt that knot of anxiety in her stomach again, and her voice started rising in volume. "Liz, this is *bigger than our apartment*. I can't do this. What is he doing? I don't belong here!"

"Paige, breathe."

"I'm breathing!" she almost shouted and then shook her head. Glaring at Liz, she took an exaggerated calming breath.

"Think for a moment. You've been to his apartment. Does he live like this?"

"No."

"Is it possible that he's doing this because he wants to do something incredibly special for you?"

Paige sighed. "Do I have to answer?"

"Yes," Liz said, smirking. "Because as you well know, the brain learns better when the information is processed in multiple ways, including speaking said information aloud."

Paige threw up her hands. *"Now* you decide to prove that you've listened to me when I talk about teaching."

Liz just looked at her, still smirking.

"Fine. Chris is doing all of this because he wants to make this weekend very special."

Liz raised her eyebrows.

"For me. He wants this weekend to be special *for me.* Satisfied?"

"Yup!" Liz chirped. "So, there's a full bar here. What do you want, Paige?"

Chapter Fourteen

The next morning they took advantage of the in-room dining and ordered a breakfast that was only moderately extravagant.

Sam was waiting for them in the lobby at nine-thirty, and they spent the entire day out and about, visiting The Country Music Hall of Fame, Ryman Auditorium, Bicentennial Mall State Park, and The Parthenon, stopping in between for lunch at an upscale local restaurant. All as suggested by Chris.

He had also, somehow, contrived to arrange for all their food to be paid for. They assumed that Sam was taking care of all of this somehow.

By four-thirty in the afternoon, they were back at the hotel to change into jeans and jerseys to be ready for the game. For dinner, Chris had made reservations at a nice sports bar very close to the arena.

"Mr. Beckman suggested that this would be a fun place for you to get into a hockey mood," Sam told them. "Apparently, lunch was geared toward Ms. Smith, but dinner is especially for you, Ms.

Williams."

Liz laughed and clapped her hands like a kid.

"It's like magic, Paige. This is crazy, and so much fun, and how the heck am I supposed to go back to being a regular person after this weekend?"

"Just order a beer and look at the menu, Liz."

***

By the time they reached the arena, Paige was not remotely surprised to find that Chris had them seated in a suite along with the players who hadn't dressed for the game and just two other women— both wives of players—that had made the trip. Everyone was friendly and kind, and Liz got a kick out of talking to the players.

The wives both approached Paige and introduced themselves.

"You must be Paige," said a lovely, elegant woman with long brown hair and a Russian accent. "I am Natalia. Dmitry is my husband." Sensing Paige's discomfort, she smiled and pointed to the ice where the team was warming up. "He is number six. The team captain."

"Oh," she replied. "Thank you. Very nice to meet you."

"Chris has said so many nice things about you, Paige. Dmitry and I would very much like to have you and Chris over for dinner sometime soon."

"That would be lovely, thank you."

As Liz walked up to join them, Natalia said conspiratorially, "Chris looks so happy lately. I am very happy to be able to meet you tonight. And please, let me know if you have any questions. It can be…overwhelming…to come into a new situation. Or a new country." Her smile to Paige was warm and comforting.

The game was very exciting, with lots of heavy forechecking and backchecking, although much less than the Pittsburgh game. And no fights. Chris scored one of Washington's three goals, and Paige found herself on her feet cheering with everyone else in the suite. The atmosphere in the arena was loud and exciting, and it was a completely different experience to see the game in person.

During the second intermission, Liz turned to Paige and said, "So? What do you think? Are you having fun?"

"Actually, yes, I really am!" Paige replied. "I'm not sure it's something I would want to do all the time, but it is fun to be here in person. Hearing the sounds from the ice is amazing. I can't believe how fast that puck is moving and that you can hear it ring off the metal when it hits the crossbar! And I truly had no appreciation for just how fast those guys skate. It's impressive."

Liz hugged her friend, pleased and relieved that she was having a good time.

"Natalia and the other woman, whose name I have already forgotten, darn it, have been so nice too. I didn't expect that, you know? That they would reach out to me and welcome me? I don't know why, but it's been such a pleasant surprise. I guess I never thought about Chris being friends with the other players off the ice and knowing their families."

119

"I think a lot of the players are friends off the ice," Liz responded. "With how closely they play together, it makes sense to me that they would form some pretty tight relationships. And then, some of them pretty much grow up together on their teams, get married, have kids…they probably have team barbecues in the summer with all of the families."

The third period started, and Liz and Paige watched and cheered as the Guardians went on to beat the Chords four-three in regulation.

Chris had arranged for special access passes for them, and Natalia walked with them to reach the part of the arena where the players would be emerging after their media interviews.

Natalia introduced them to Dmitry. His English was far more heavily accented, but he was exuberant in greeting Paige, picking her up in a hug.

"You are the beautiful Paige!" he said as he put her back down. "You make Becks happy man."

Natalia swatted him and said something quickly in Russian; Liz assumed it was an admonishment not to embarrass Paige, but Dmitry just grinned and kissed his wife.

Chris could not have looked happier as he left the locker room. He scooped Paige off her feet, just as Dmitry had, and kissed her and then put her down and kissed her again, all the time saying, "I'm so happy to see you! I'm so glad you're here!"

He finally gave Liz a hug too, just as Zee emerged.

Zee said, "Hey! Share! You've got your own personal hugging…person…to hug. Leave some for the rest of us," and then he grabbed Liz in his signature bear hug.

"My wing-woman!"

"Hey, sweetie! So, are we going out dancing?"

Zee thought for a moment. "Sure, why the hell not? I can be your wingman this time." He playfully shoved her shoulder. "I can try to get you laid."

Liz stared at him and said, slowly and with a certain edge to her voice, "Do you think that I need assistance in that area? Do you think that it would be so difficult for me to find a willing partner without your help?"

Zee stopped and stammered out, "Liz, no. I mean…" He flailed his arms a bit and continued, "I'm sorry…I just…shit!"

She was biting her lips by this time to keep from laughing, and both Paige and Chris were looking on with glee.

Liz kept her voice icy. "I assure you that, should I want to, I can find my own fuck-buddy, thankyouverymuch." And then she burst out laughing, unable to keep up the facade any longer.

Zee shook his head, looking at the ceiling. "Son of a bitch."

Chris came over, kissed Liz on the forehead, and said, "Thank you. That was priceless."

Zee punched him in the shoulder.

Chris and Paige went back to the hotel with Sam, and Zee and Liz called for an Uber to head out for drinks and dancing.

***

Chris gave a low whistle when he saw the suite.

121

"Damn, this is nice."

Paige gave him a light smack on the arm. "Like you didn't know."

"I didn't! Well, I mean, I saw pictures, but…" He looked around for a moment. "Yeah, this is nice. I could get used to this." He winked at her, but she had stiffened.

"Paige," he said, pulling her into his arms. "I'm just teasing. This isn't my lifestyle, you know that. Right, baby?"

"Yes," she mumbled into his shirt.

"Then what's wrong?" he asked. "I just wanted to make this a really special weekend for you. And for Liz too, but especially for you."

"I know."

Chris pushed back to look in her eyes. "Did you have fun? Where did you guys go today? Did you enjoy the game?" He realized he was asking too many questions in a row, but he found that he was really excited and couldn't help himself. "You met Natalia, right? Was she nice to you? Did you like her?"

Paige laughed at his enthusiasm and couldn't help but smile at the joy on his face. She pulled him to the big, comfortable couch and sat down with him.

"Yes, I had fun. Lots of fun. It was a wonderful day, and Sam was amazing…"

"Sam?" he interrupted.

"Our driver," she clarified. "Sam the Driver," she said, the capitalization of his full title clear in her voice.

"Oh, right! Please, continue."

Paige went on to tell him all about their day and their evening and the game.

"It was really fun, Chris. Man, that arena is *loud*. Is it always like that?"

Chris chuckled and said, "Wait until the playoffs. On our home ice, it always seems to me like the sound of the crowd is going to peel the paint off the walls. Nashville has a good home crowd," he leaned in a bit, "but DC is the best. Don't tell my Columbus teammates I said that," he added with a wink.

Paige just looked at him for a few moments. He was so happy, so in his element. She smiled as he pushed a lock of hair behind her ear with a soft caress, stroking his thumb along her jaw, and then drawing gently it across her lower lip.

"I had an amazing time, Chris. It couldn't have been better." He was still smiling, but his eyes were looking softer and were focused on his thumb as he drew it back across her lower lip. Paige closed her eyes briefly and sighed.

"I'm really glad, baby." He kissed her very softly, his thumb moving down to her chin. "I just wanted everything to be perfect for you today."

"It was," she whispered and tucked her head a little to slide his thumb into her mouth. She sucked gently on his thumb, watching his face and eyes run through about fifteen different thoughts and emotions in the few moments before she allowed his thumb to pop back out of her mouth.

In a ragged voice, he said, "Do that again." He struggled not to close his eyes as she complied, wanting to simultaneously lose himself in the sensation and watch how incredibly sexy her lips looked wrapped around him. Around any part of him, apparently.

She swirled her tongue around his thumb for a moment more and then, with a little sparkle in her eye, changed over to his middle finger. His breath caught, and as she descended toward his hand, he just stared, breathing harder, until she sucked at the base of his finger and flicked her tongue along the connecting skin.

"Jesus." The sensations were plowing straight through his body, his brain trying to make him accept the simultaneous yet contrary information that he was watching her suck his finger but practically feeling her suck...other things.

Seeing how much he responded to this, she kept going for a minute, licking and sucking, enjoying the complicated look on his face and the lust in his eyes.

When she slid his finger back out of her mouth and kissed the palm of his hand, she said, "So, I take it you like that?"

"Fuck, yes."

"First time anyone has done that to you?"

He nodded.

Leaning in, she asked quietly, with a gleam in her eye, "Did it feel kinda like I was sucking your dick?" And then she squeaked in surprise as he grabbed her, put her over his shoulder in a fireman's carry, and headed toward the bedroom.

"What happened to scooping me up romantically?"

"If you're talking dirty to me, all bets are off."

Chapter Fifteen

"Do you have plans for Thanksgiving?" Paige asked Chris as they were washing dishes after dinner at his apartment one evening. "I know you don't have a game that day, but it seems like it wouldn't be enough time to go home to see your mom. Or does she come to see you?"

"I don't have plans. It is too short a turnaround to go home from here; I wouldn't really get any time at home. It would be an eat-and-run," Chris responded. He was on drying duty. "Last year I had my mom fly in and we went to Thanksgiving dinner at a nice restaurant, but this year I'm on my own. How about you? Do you go to Philly to see your family?"

Paige made a face that was almost a sneer, saying, "Oh, no. My sister and my niece are awesome, but my mom is a completely different story. And not a pretty one, at that."

"Oh, geez, I'm sorry."

"No, no. It's fine, really," Paige reassured him. "*Not* seeing my mom on holidays is a gift I finally started giving to myself several years ago. Long overdue. It's very unfortunate, but it's just…" She paused for a moment and then decided that she didn't want to hide any of this from Chris. "She's an alcoholic. It's really bad and has been since my sister and I were kids. I think 'toxic' is not too strong a word to describe our family situation."

Chris had paled and looked somewhat uncomfortable. "I'm so sorry. Baby, you don't need to tell me this if you don't want to."

Paige finished up and shut the water off, shaking the last drops from her hands and wiping them on the dishtowel that Chris was holding. "I'll stop if you don't want to hear about it. That's okay."

"No." Chris shook his head. "That's not what I meant. I just don't want you to feel like you owe me any explanation."

Paige gave him a wry smile and said, "I don't mind unloading my family baggage. I carried it around by myself for most of my life. It's been nice these past few years to give some of that up."

Chris put away the last of the clean dishes, grabbed two wine glasses and a bottle of wine, and they sat on the couch together.

"I'm all yours, Paige," he said, handing her a glass of merlot and settling in with his own. "I want to hear everything about your life."

"Everything?" she asked, with a raised eyebrow and a small smile.

"Everything," he responded seriously, although he knew that she was teasing. "The good, the bad, and the ugly."

"All right, you asked for it." Paige clinked her

glass together with his gently. "I have one older sister, Becca, who is four years older than me. Our dad left when we were little—I barely remember him at all—so we were raised by a single mom our whole lives.

"Mom is an alcoholic. I'm not sure when it crossed over from drinking some every day to not being able to stop drinking, you know? Not only was I just a kid, but I think that line is really blurry for everyone. That's one of the reasons denial is so easy. 'I can stop anytime' is actually true for some people. Just not for everyone."

She paused for a moment, trying to think of the best way to tell the story.

"Well, at some point when Becca and I were still young, it became clear that things were just not right, you know? It was bad even when my Grammy—her mother—was alive, but after Grammy passed, things got worse…I don't want to drown you in sad details, so I'm trying to pick out the synopsis of the story, if you will."

Chris smiled at this comment. "Always the English teacher."

"Definitely." She took a sip of her wine. "Becca and I dealt with things differently. I think that's both a function of siblings—the second one almost always goes in the opposite direction from the first one—and because of our ages when things started to really fall apart at home. Becca was in the beginning of rebellious teenage years; I was still in the 'make people happy' stage. So we kinda both got stuck there, you know?

"That's what seems to happen…both for the

127

addict and for people in their lives…they get developmentally stuck at the point where the problem starts. Anyway, rebellious Becca got pregnant at seventeen, while dutiful, co-dependent Paige was trying to do everything right, get straight A's, make everyone happy, and keep shit together at home."

"Damn." Chris was slowly shaking his head.

"It's weird to tell this story, because it's simultaneously worse than it sounds and yet not as bad as it sounds." She looked over at Chris. "I realize that makes no sense, but it's true. On the one hand I had a good middle-class suburban life, with friends and activities and an awesome sister, and while Grammy was alive I had a wonderful relationship with her. She was the one who taught me to cook. On the other hand, shit was a mess, everywhere, and I was constantly trying to make things look right and clean up the problems caused by my mom. Because I felt like that was my responsibility."

"Why?"

Paige shrugged. "Because that's what co-dependency is. Anyway…" She poured them both a second glass of wine. "Becca had my niece, Margot, who is beautiful and amazing. Long story short, Becca managed to pull her life together in a stunning way and became a wonderful mother. She's a single mom but for the last year has been dating a super nice guy who loves them both. She's got a great job, and Margot at fourteen years old is self-confident and talented and just a joy to be around.

"I went off to college and found myself. I met fantastic friends—Liz and I met our first day of freshman year—and started getting help understanding the problems with how I grew up and how they affected me. I read a lot..." Chris chuckled, and she said, "Shocking, right? And I found people and organizations to help steer me where I needed to go to accomplish what I want in my life."

She spread her hands and said, "And here I am."

"God, Paige." Chris's eyes were filled with admiration. "You are amazing." He put his wine glass down and leaned forward to take hers from her so that he could hold her hands. "Truly, you amaze me." He kissed the knuckles on each hand gently.

"Thank you. Thanks for listening, Chris."

"Of course, baby." He moved over to tuck her under his arm so that her head rested on his shoulder. "I meant it—I really do want to know everything about you." Moving his hand up, he stroked her cheek with his thumb and turned to kiss her hair.

The words were sitting there on the tip of his tongue. God, he wanted to say them.

"Oh, so, I almost lost track of my original question." Paige sat up and turned back to him. "If you have no plans for Thanksgiving, would you like to come over to our apartment? It's nothing huge, but I cook a real turkey dinner for Thanksgiving every year. And Liz and I always try to invite strays."

"Strays?" Chris asked with amusement.

"You know, people who, for whatever reason, have nowhere to go on Thanksgiving. Strays."

"So, I'm a stray?"

She smiled. "Apparently. Would you like to join us for Thanksgiving dinner?"

"I would love to."

***

Thanksgiving morning Paige was up early, getting the turkey ready to be put in the oven. She had done most of the prep work, and good bit of the cooking, the night before, so the only big thing left to manage was the turkey. Dinner would be around two o'clock; Chris would be coming over earlier than that.

Once the bird was started, Paige sat down for a moment, steeling herself for the one obligation that she dreaded every year.

She had to call her mother.

Becca would be at their mother's house soon, if she wasn't already, so that would make some of this more palatable. Paige had realized over the course of the years that it was far better for her to call in the morning, when there hadn't been as much time for drinking. Things got worse, and deteriorated faster, the longer she waited to call. She would get the unpleasantness over with as soon as possible, and then she could enjoy the rest of her day.

"Paige! I was waiting for you to call!"

There was no slurring yet, so that was a good sign.

"Hi, Mom. Happy Thanksgiving."

"Your sister and niece have just gotten here. I still don't understand why you can't come to our house. It's selfish of you not to join us for Thanksgiving."

Paige ignored the opening dig. "Please tell Becca and Margot I said hello. Is Jose with them?"

She heard a huff on the other end of the line. "He's here. I don't know what she sees in him."

"He's a very nice man, and he makes them happy. He's great with Margot, Mom."

Paige had responded without thinking it through first—always a mistake when dealing with her mother.

"You always take her side. You're not here. You don't know. I do."

Realizing her error, Paige tried to change the subject before this line of discussion spiraled.

"So, how are things in the neighborhood? Did Mrs. Miller finally cut down that dead tree?"

Success. Her mother ranted on for a few minutes about how the neighborhood was going downhill, that people didn't care about property values anymore, and the danger that the offending tree posed to her and her property.

Paige half-listened, inserting agreeing sounds here and there where appropriate. But then, disaster.

"When were you going to tell me that you're dating someone?"

She froze. *Shit. Becca must have said something.*

"Oh. Well, eventually. We haven't been dating for very long."

"That's not what I heard."

Paige's phone chimed with a text.

131

Becca: I'm sorry!! She overheard me talking to Jose!

"I heard that he's some rich hotshot hockey star."

She heard the clink of ice hitting a glass...not good news. That meant the hard liquor was coming into play.

"Well, he does play hockey."

"I knew it!" And then more distantly, as if her mother were talking to other people in the room, "I told you!" Back to talking into the phone now, "I knew you would finally find a man to take care of you. Why else would you have gone to college for a degree in *education* of all things? No one makes money in *teaching*. You can't make any kind of life for yourself that way."

Paige's heart sank. This was it. This was the recurring horrible conversation with her mother that she could never escape, even if she managed to avoid it occasionally. She braced herself, feeling sick in the pit of her stomach, holding the phone away from her mouth, while her mother ramped up.

"I knew that you would finally end up using that hot little body of yours to get a man. You acted all noble, but I knew it." The glee in her mother's voice was poisonous. "Better get him tied down soon, before you get any older and your looks fade." The slurring was starting; her mother must have started drinking earlier than she had originally thought.

"Mom..."

Her mother continued without pause. "A prenup! That's what you need. I've always told you that. Make sure that you're set for life when he moves on to someone younger. It's how I managed to raise you two girls after your no-good father left us…"

"Mom, it's not like that…" Paige knew before she said it that it was useless; the only way to get out of this was to hang up the phone, but the nagging sense of obligation kept her from doing that. Kept her hanging on the line because this was one of the few phone calls that she made each year.

"Of course it's like that! I know you better than you know yourself. You always flaunted your figure, trying to get attention from men. Don't bother trying to deny it. Just make sure you don't get screwed in the prenup. Get a good lawyer. You don't want to be left high and dry when he moves on to greener pastures. You're not going to look like that forever, you know."

Panic was starting to press against her chest. She needed to get off this call soon, before things got even worse.

"Mom, I need to go. The timer on the oven is going off."

She tried to ignore the comments that started about her cooking, about how was she going to keep this man if she couldn't even cook well.

"Bye, Mom. Happy Thanksgiving."

She disconnected and sat, shaking, heart pounding, until Liz walked out of her room.

"Hey, I thought I heard you talking with someone…" Looking more closely at Paige, she finished, "…oh, *fuck,* it was your mother. Goddamnit."

Liz hurried to get Paige a glass of water, cursing under her breath the whole time.

"I'll be okay. I just need a minute."

Liz sat down at the table with her. "What was it this time? Same shit? Or do you not want to talk about it?"

"Some of the same but worse. She overheard Becca say that I was dating someone. A hockey player."

"Motherfucker."

"Yeah. Becca texted to apologize as soon as she heard Mom start in on it."

Liz sighed. "I'm so sorry, Paige. You *know* the shit your mom says isn't true. You *know* that."

It was Paige's turn to sigh. "I know. But God, Liz, it *still* gets under my skin right away. Every time."

"Well, Chris will be over in a few hours, and I know that will help you feel better. Please feel free to take some 'alone time' with him if you need to. You can either leave me to watch the food or tell me to go out to run an errand or something."

Paige laughed and said, "Thank you for the offer. But you know I would never trust you to watch the food." She stood and stretched. "I'm feeling a bit better already."

"She makes me so fucking angry, and I don't even have to deal with her."

"I know. There's nothing to be done for it, really. She'll never change unless she stops drinking, and she has no desire to stop drinking. I know that Becca only allows her to see Margot very sparingly and then never without supervision. And *then* she and Margot have a debriefing session afterward."

Liz shook her head. "Well, that's good to know.

But Paige, Becca was always kind of better about handling the criticism than you were. I think that's why your mom focuses so much of her negative energy on you, because it works."

"I know. I'm still working on it."

"You are." She gave Paige a hug. "And you're doing amazingly well, and I'm so proud of you."

***

Paige was feeling much better by the time Chris arrived, and Liz was pleasantly surprised that Zee was with him; Paige had forgotten to mention he was tagging along as another stray.

"My whole family is in Alberta," he said, "but we Canadians celebrate Thanksgiving on the correct day. Second Monday of October, as God intended."

"You complaining?" Liz asked. "Because it sounds like you already had Thanksgiving this year, so you could just head on home." She started pushing him back toward the door.

"No! Not complaining!" Zee laughed. "Don't send me away without food! This smells *amazing,* Paige."

Dinner was wonderful, and the four of them lingered, enjoying too much food and wonderful company, until it was time for Chris and Zee to head out. The team was traveling in the morning, the start of another road trip.

Chapter Sixteen

When the team was back in town again, Chris drove straight to his apartment. They had spoken the night before, so he knew Paige would be there. She was waiting for him, perched on the edge of his desk, legs crossed, reading a book.

"Hey, baby, I missed you," he said as he closed the door behind him.

She looked up from the book she was reading and peered at him over her glasses.

Glasses?

She put a finger to her shiny red lips, said, "Shhhhh," and turned back to her book.

Chris's mouth quirked into a grin as he took a moment to really look at her. Paige had her hair up in a slightly disarrayed bun, and in addition to the glasses she was wearing a tight pencil skirt, hose, and sexy pumps...and a tight cardigan sweater unbuttoned too far with what appeared to be a black lace bra peeking out from underneath.

Chris made a sound that could only be described as a soft growl, and Paige struggled to keep her stern demeanor while continuing to study her book.

"You look so hot."

"Shhhh!" She repeated her admonishment and added, "This is a library!" in a whisper with what was supposed to be a harsh glare. It almost succeeded, but Chris was now standing next to her, and his presence was more distracting than she had anticipated. He was warm—she could feel the heat flowing from his body—and his breathing had already picked up.

"Oh," he whispered quietly, his mouth close enough to her neck that she could feel his breath. "I'm sorry," he breathed into her ear. "Can you help me find something, miss?"

Paige sat up straight, closed her book, and uncrossed her legs.

"Of course, sir," she replied, standing up in a way that accentuated the shortness of her skirt.

Chris thought he caught a glimpse of the top of a stocking but wasn't sure. Just the idea added to the already rapid blood flow to his groin. As did looking down the open front of Paige's sweater as she stood in front of him.

"What are you looking for today?" she asked, pushing her glasses up on her nose.

Chris glanced around his apartment quickly and replied, "Poetry. British poetry." His voice was rough as he tried to keep to a whisper. "Do you have anything like that?"

"We do," she replied, briefly taking hold of his tie near the knot and then running her fingers down it. "Please follow me."

Paige was standing close enough to him that she

137

brushed the front of his suit pants as she turned, and she smiled to herself when she felt the hard bulge underneath and heard his quick intake of breath.

Walking slowly, with a sway that emphasized every curve, Paige made her way over to the big bookshelf near the window. She took her time, first reaching up over her head standing on her toes, which pulled the cardigan up and exposed her midriff. Chris was standing close behind her and ran his hands softly across the exposed skin.

Paige turned her head and said quietly, "Sir, please, keep your hands to yourself while I find your book," and grinned to herself again at the resulting sound of aroused frustration.

She continued perusing the bookshelf, bending over at the waist to look closely at the book bindings, which allowed the back of the tight skirt to lift over the tops of the stockings, showing the garters that held them up.

The groan from Chris was loud enough to allow her to shush him again, turning from her bent position, causing more exposure.

As she reached the lowest shelf, she got down on her knees, spreading her legs slightly, hitching the skirt higher on her thighs to make room. Tilting the compilation of English poetry from the shelf, she asked over her shoulder, "Is this what you were looking for?"

Chris knelt down behind her, one knee between her legs, and said, "Yes, that's exactly what I'm looking for," as he ran his hands up the outsides of her thighs, moving her skirt even higher.

"Are you sure, sir?" Paige's voice was a breathy

whisper, and she gasped as his hands now came over her skirt and up over her sweater to cup her breasts.

"Are there other books that might be better than that one?" he asked into her ear as he tweaked her nipples through her clothing.

Paige could feel his swollen arousal pressed against her, and the insistent throbbing between her own thighs was making it more difficult to keep up the conversation.

"Possibly."

"Then please keep looking." Paige felt him smile against her neck as she shuddered from the nipple play.

She made a point of "looking," whispering the titles and authors of each book across the shelf. Chris had now backed up a bit and had pulled her skirt even higher.

"Isn't it customary for librarians to wear panties?" he asked, his hands having reached her hips.

"Yes, sir," she replied.

"Then it seems you might be somewhat of an unconventional librarian, as it appears that you are wearing none."

"Yes, sir."

She lost track of what he was doing for a moment, and was going to turn, when she felt his hands wrap around her thighs as he moved his head under her, between her legs, lying face up on the floor. Paige gasped at the sudden feel of his hair brushing her inner thighs and panted as he gently blew on her swollen lips.

"You are absolutely not wearing panties, miss."

She whimpered loudly as he placed one kiss on her labia.

"Shhhhh." He had his face near her skin so that she would feel the sound. "This is a library. You need to stay quiet."

And then he pulled her down onto his mouth.

Paige gripped the bookshelf as she moved against his hot, teasing, oh-so-talented mouth, unable to keep still, and unable to keep entirely quiet, as he drove her to distraction.

But he wasn't trying to take her over the edge. He was trying to bring her to the edge and keep her there.

And he was succeeding.

Paige moved against him more desperately and had given up trying to be quiet. She reached down with one hand and gripped his hair.

"Chris, *please,*" she panted and then made a sound of desperate frustration as he pushed away from her, slid back out between her legs, and moved into position behind her.

"Put your hands back on the bookcase and don't move." He rasped the instructions into her ear as he unzipped and pushed his pants and boxers down.

Heart pounding, hips shifting in desperate need, Paige complied. Her moan mixed with his low groan as he slid into her from behind, all the way in on the first thrust, and then held there.

"Now," he said, reaching around to stroke her clit with his fingers, "don't make a sound. This is a library, miss."

Paige disappeared, transformed into hot, wet

bliss as Chris thrust deeply into her again and again, circling his fingers in a rhythm with his hips. She tried to comply with his request for silence. She pressed back against him, trying to take him even deeper, feeling the pressure building, spreading underneath her skin, ready to envelop her entire being.

He lost himself in her, his breath hot against the back of her neck as he bent to be closer to her, even in this moment of complete intimacy. The pulsing rhythm of their joining increased, and he felt the rush of impending climax.

"Oh God, baby." He couldn't stay quiet any longer. "Oh God, I can't wait. I can't wait any more, Paige." With one rough final thrust, he emptied himself into her, hearing her cry out her own release, and said, "Oh God, I love you, Paige."

Chris held her close to his body, holding her up, his arms wrapped around her from behind.

"I love you, baby," he murmured into her hair. "I love you so much."

"Chris…"

It sounded almost like a sob, and he quickly turned her, moving to see her face. Her eyes were bright, and her bottom lip was trembling.

"Baby, what's wrong?"

"Nothing, I'm okay." She smiled and moved to put a hand against his cheek. "I promise, Chris," she said to reassure him as he looked so worried. "Sometimes, I get a little teary, after…well," she shook her head, suddenly feeling a little shy, "after a *really* intense orgasm."

Chris let out his breath. "Oh."

He relaxed some, and she smiled at him, even though there were a few tears leaking from her eyes and her bottom lip still trembled a bit.

"So this is a good thing?" He still looked a little confused and concerned.

Paige gave a small laugh and said, "Yes, it's a good thing." Gathering her courage, she took a breath and added, "It's more likely to happen when there's a really deep emotional connection."

Chris felt the muscles in his chest contract, waiting for her next words.

Paige reached up to pull him to her for a kiss and whispered, "I love you too, Chris."

He felt a rush of adrenaline, his heart racing from hearing her say those words, and their kiss was tender as they lingered in the afterglow.

Chris finally brushed her hair away from her face; the bun had come undone sometime during their activities; he didn't remember when. Holding her face in his hands, he kissed the tears away from her eyes and then stood, ready to pick her up to take her to bed, only to realize that his pants were around his ankles. Paige laughed, trying to get up off the floor, unsteady on the high heels, and ended up on her rear on the floor again.

He grinned at her and said, "This is the part the romantic movies don't show...the aftermath." Bending down to retrieve his pants before giving her a hand up off the floor, he said, "There's just no way to be manful and sexy when trying to pull up your pants."

"Also no way to gracefully stand up off the floor in a tight skirt and heels." Once standing she pulled the skirt down over her hips, smoothing it down. "At least, I've never figured out how to do it."

Chris pulled her to him, saying, "Thank you, Paige. That was…unbelievable. Incredible." He pushed back from her to look at her face. "Mind-blowing sex." Pausing to cup one hand on her cheek, he added quietly, "And I meant every word. I love you."

"I meant it too, Chris. I love you."

They kissed for a moment more before Paige pushed back, stroking his chest, and teased, "And damn, big guy. I'll be your sexy librarian any time you want."

***

When Chris came out of the bedroom the next morning, the sight that greeted him was Paige, wearing his dress shirt from the night before, hair down and slightly sleep-ruffled, in his kitchen cooking breakfast. The feelings almost overwhelmed him as he stood in the doorway. She looked over her shoulder, smiled, and said, "Good morning," and it was as if every dream of domestic bliss he ever had was materializing in front of his eyes.

The feeling was so powerful he took a moment before responding, almost unwilling to risk breaking the spell.

"Good morning, baby." He moved behind her and put his arms around her. "You are so incredibly beautiful."

She smiled a bit shyly and said, "I hope you

don't mind that I grabbed your shirt. It smells like you, and it made me feel good this morning."

"Are you kidding?" He slid his hands up to cup her breasts from behind. "I love seeing you in my shirt. It's that caveman possessive thing again." He tweaked her nipples gently and started to run his hands down to her thighs.

"Hang on, big guy, or you'll have burned pancakes." Paige shimmied out of his grasp. She looked back over her shoulder at him and added, "Besides, there's plenty of time after breakfast."

Chris made a *grumph* sound and retreated to the table.

For a few minutes he just watched her and then said, "Paige, baby, will you please come to Minnesota with me at Christmas? I want you to meet my mom."

She turned around and stared at him.

"I'm sorry, I should have asked sooner. I know that. I think I was nervous that you might say no. And now I've waited long enough that I know you might already have other plans. It would only be for a quick up-and-back trip; we only have those few days right at Christmas where we don't play any games."

She stared at him a moment longer then hurriedly turned to flip a pancake that was starting to get overdone.

"I don't know, Chris." She said it quietly, focused on the stove.

The tone of her voice made him get up to come closer. He leaned against the counter and watched her, trying to see her face.

"Do you have other plans?"

Pause. "No."

He touched her under her chin to look at him. Her eyes were a little too bright.

He asked quietly, "Is this about your mother?"

Another pause and then, "Maybe. Probably."

He brushed the hair from her face and kissed her forehead before sitting back down at the table.

"My mom is amazing, Paige. She's been my biggest supporter my whole life. She's dying to meet you, because she knows how much you mean to me."

Paige flipped the last pancake onto the platter and walked the food over to the table. When she sat down, Chris took her hand, encouraging her to look at him. Her face showed her anxiety.

"Baby," he said, "I don't know what your mom says to you, but I can guarantee you, one hundred percent, not one doubt in my mind, that *my* mom will love you."

Her mouth curved a little in the right direction.

"How can you possibly know that?"

Chris shook his head and chuckled. "Really? Paige, I love you. And, if I remember our conversation last night," she smiled at the memory, "then you love me too. Being with you makes me incredibly happy." He took her other hand and said, "And that's what my mom wants for me."

Paige blinked.

"Really?"

Chris leaned over and kissed her gently. "Really. So please come with me at Christmas."

"Okay," she said and then smiled gently. "Thank

you. I would love to meet your mom."

"Perfect. I'll make all the arrangements. Now, I'm gonna eat these pancakes before they get cold, because the smell is making my stomach growl." He wolfed down a huge forkful of pancake and then said, "Oh, and I'm going to take you to visit my best friend too. I'm pretty sure he still might think I'm making you up. Or at least exaggerating."

Chapter Seventeen

"I bought a house."

"What? Are you kidding me?" Micky's voice conveyed to Chris every bit of the surprise that he was feeling. "When?"

"I closed on it two days ago."

Chris was finding it a little hard to believe too. The opportunity had presented itself, and he had jumped on it. The right price, great neighborhood, and everything he was looking for. The agent he was working with came highly recommended by his teammates, and everything had just fallen into place like it was meant to be.

He told Micky, "It's pretty cool. Four bedrooms, three and a half baths, and a pool."

"A pool? Really?"

"Yeah, man. It actually gets hot here in the summer. People go swimming. It's a thing."

Micky was having a hard time imagining Chris being a homeowner. "This is crazy. When did you start house hunting? And, no offense, but why?" Before Chris could answer, Micky added, "Oh, shit,

147

is this because of Paige? Are you going to tell me you bought a house for her?" Chris was quiet for a moment, and Micky said, "Holy shit, you did. I can't fucking believe it. Becks, did you have her pick it out? Or is this something else she doesn't know about? Like the fact that you're planning on marrying her?"

"Hey, a house is an excellent investment. Maybe I'm just starting to act like a grown-up, you asshole." There wasn't any real heat behind his words.

"Damn." Chris could hear Micky laughing under his breath. "I'm going to have to meet this woman who's turning you into a responsible adult without even realizing it. Are you still planning on bringing her for Christmas?"

"Yes, definitely. I can't wait for you to meet her. She's smart and kind. And gorgeous. Did I mention gorgeous?"

Micky chuckled, saying, "You might have mentioned that detail. Once or twice. So, when are you going to tell her about this house?"

"I'm going to call her after I talk with you. There's no furniture, and the stuff from my apartment would fill like a room and a half, so I'm not entirely sure how I'm going to handle any of this."

Micky thought for a moment and said, "You could hire someone to furnish it. Like an interior designer or something like that. However that works. Although I wouldn't have the first idea how to go about finding one." He laughed out loud. "It's not like I have any interest in become a responsible adult any time soon. You're on your own with that shit."

Chris grinned. "That's a good idea. I'll ask around and see what I can come up with. And how irresponsible are you being, anyway? Still just sowing your wild oats amongst the puck bunnies, or are you seeing someone?"

"Shit, Becks, just because you're settling down with one woman doesn't mean anyone else needs to." Micky was grinning too. "Wild oats exist to be sown. That is the way of nature. But, to answer your question, there isn't anyone in particular. That doesn't mean I'm lonely, though, if you know what I mean."

Chris could practically hear Micky's eyebrows moving up and down with that last comment. "God, Mick, leaving a trail of broken hearts." This earned another laugh from Micky. "I'll send you pictures of the house. And I'll see you at Christmas."

"I told Mom you would be there. She's thrilled. And Colleen can't wait to see you, either. Although I suspect that she's going to be a little disappointed to hear you've got a serious girlfriend." Micky's youngest sister was ten years younger than they were and had always had at least a bit of a crush on Chris.

"Is she a senior this year?"

"Yup. It's looking like she's going to UConn. They're offering her a full ride academic scholarship."

Chris gave a low whistle. "Damn. That's no joke. I'm impressed."

"Yeah, she's too smart for you, anyway. It's

probably a good thing you're taken."

Chris laughed again. "Yeah, whatever. Like you're a prize. Talk to you later, asshole."

"Fuck off, Becks. Later."

Chris hung up the phone and sat back, wondering what Paige was going to say when she found out he had bought a house. Even though he had been looking for a little while, the actual purchase was fast and seemed almost impulsive, and he was not normally an impulsive guy. But everything about her made him not want to wait, not want to slow down, but to start a life with her immediately.

He didn't have any time during the season to worry about moving and buying furniture, anyway, so Micky's idea of hiring someone to take care of things was a good one. There was no rush for him to move in; he had bought the house outright. With a few exceptions, he hadn't spent any appreciable amount of money since joining the NHL, preferring to live in apartments or sometimes with roommates. He had purchased the occasional expensive car, taken a few nice trips, and supported his mom, but mostly he had just saved. A career-ending injury could happen at any time, and Chris wanted to make sure he was able to take care of himself without worrying about finances.

And he had always intended to settle down at some point. Chris was a bit of a homebody at heart. Micky was too, when it came right down to it, although his broken engagement had damaged his ability to trust on multiple levels. Possibly permanently. Chris hoped fervently that his best friend would find someone, but in the meantime, Chris would settle for Micky just having some fun in his life.

He broke out of his reverie and called Paige. He was smiling before she even picked up the phone.

"Hey, baby! So, I've got some news."

"Hi, Chris! Really? What's up?"

"I bought a house."

There was a pause while Paige tried to process this information.

"Wow. I didn't even realize you were looking." She wasn't sure why this information made her slightly uncomfortable, but it did. "Have you been looking for a long time?"

"No, not terribly long," Chris replied, with a measure of caution. Paige was definitely not sounding as excited about this as he had hoped. "It's a good market right now, and it's a good investment, and the perfect opportunity kind of fell into my lap."

"Oh! Sure, that makes sense." Paige tried to adjust her reaction. It wasn't fair to Chris to put a damper on something this big. "So, where is it? What's it like? Are you moving soon?"

Chris smiled, glad that she was starting to sound more enthusiastic. "It's in McLean, and no, I'm not moving any time soon. And it's four bedrooms, three-and-a-half baths…and a pool!"

"Wow!" Now she did sound excited. "That's really cool! I've always thought that would be fun, to be able to go swimming whenever you want."

Now Chris was grinning. She liked the pool! He silently fist-pumped.

"I closed on it two days ago," he said. "You wanna see it? I can pick you up and take you there. No game today, so after practice I'm completely free."

"Okay, that sounds great. I'm really happy for you, Chris." Paige smiled at his excitement. He sounded thrilled and a little giddy.

***

"This place is *amazing,* Chris!" Paige was truly impressed. While the house wasn't enormous, it was beautifully appointed, with updated appliances throughout. The bathrooms and kitchen looked brand new, and there was an abundance of natural light throughout the whole house. And the pool…well, the pool was fabulous, with a large concrete deck area complete with a full array of patio furniture, which had conveyed with the house.

"I'm so glad you like it, Paige." He had watched her face for her reactions as they walked around, absurdly pleased that she liked it so much.

"So, what are you going to do about furniture?" she asked. "This is *way* bigger than your apartment."

"I'm not sure yet." Chris looked around. "I'm not really good at that part."

"Your apartment is really nice!"

Chris looked sheepish. "Yeah, well…I went into a furniture store and just bought the rooms they had on display that I liked." Paige laughed out loud. "I figured if they were good enough to display, they must be okay, you know?" Paige laughed harder.

152

"Oh, Chris. Well, you do have good taste, because you picked nice rooms for your apartment, and this house is spectacular." She smiled at him, eyes shining, and his heart melted.

"So, I was thinking…" He paused and then threw caution to the wind. "I was thinking if you like doing interior decorating, maybe you would want to furnish the house for me."

Paige was startled and said, "What?"

"Um, I mean…I would pay for everything, obviously. I could just give you a credit card and you could buy whatever you think will look nice."

Paige stared at him. She felt a tightness in her chest that had anxiety written all over it.

"You're really good at this! Liz said that you picked out almost everything in your apartment and that you love doing this kind of thing…" He was starting to worry this was a misstep on his part.

"I can't do that, Chris." She tried to play it off, but there was an obvious tightness in her voice that made it clear there was more going on under the surface.

"Sure you can! I would love it…" *Oh, crap.* "Unless you don't want to, Paige. That's okay too." Chris took her hand. "I can hire someone."

"That might be better." Paige's face had gone rather blank, and Chris gently pulled her to him.

"Paige." He tucked her in his arms. "Baby, it's okay. You don't have to do this. I thought you would enjoy it, that's all. I thought you would have fun."

She pushed back from him and looked him in the eyes. "Chris, I just don't think it's a good idea. If things don't work out between us, you would have an entire house of furniture picked out by your ex. That sounds like a horrible plan. Especially for your next girlfriend." She tried to smile gently at him, but there was a strain in her eyes.

Chris felt his chest constrict the moment he heard, "If things don't work out between us…" He pulled her back in for another gentle hug.

"All right, Paige. I see your point."

He did, really. On the other hand, he had the feeling that if things didn't work out between them he would simply sell the house, fully furnished. But he definitely wasn't going to tell her that. Things had already gone downhill in a way he hadn't expected.

Paige gave him a squeeze and took a step backward. "I'm sorry, Chris. I feel like I just disappointed you."

"No," Chris responded. "No, it's all right. I'll hire someone." His mouth hitched into a small smile. "But I really do like your style, and I think you have a great eye. Would it be okay to ask your opinion on a few things when the time comes?"

She smiled, and this time it was a more relaxed smile that reached her eyes. "Yes. Of course." She looked around briefly and added, "It really is a great house, Chris. I'm happy for you!"

Chris tucked his arm around her as they walked to the front door to leave. "I'm happy for me too. And I'm very glad you like it."

Chapter Eighteen

With Chris and Paige spending so much time together, Liz had taken to doing more travel on the weekends, visiting friends within easy driving distance. This particular weekend in December, Liz was on her way to western North Carolina to visit her friend, Kaitlyn. She was just driving past Richmond when her phone rang.

"Hey, Lizzie. I'm so sorry to do this to you, but I've got to bail on this weekend." She sounded upset.

Liz responded, "Oh, no! What happened?"

Kaitlyn's voice choked as she said, "We lost one today. Harvey died."

"Oh, shit."

Kaitlyn worked as a keeper at a zoo. It was more than just a job to her, and the animals she worked with were incredibly important to her. Harvey was one of her chimps—one of the alpha males, if Liz remembered correctly.

"I'm so, so sorry, Kates. Are you sure you don't want me to come and keep you company? We could just hang out."

"No, I really just want to be alone and deal with this. Let's reschedule for another weekend."

"If you're sure, then of course." She paused, her heart breaking for her friend. "Call or text me if you need to talk, any time, okay?"

"I promise."

Liz pulled off the highway into the city and made a few phone calls, figuring that she might as well make the best of things and see if she could hook up with some college friends for dinner.

Once her plans were set, she tried to call Paige to let her know, but there was no answer, so she sent her a quick text message:

Liz: Hey, K had to cancel. Having dinner in Richmond with James and Brenda, then heading home. Maybe we can catch a movie this weekend?

***

It was around eleven o'clock that night by the time Liz opened the door of the apartment and walked in with her bags, stopping short as she took in the scene in front of her.

Looking like a deer caught in headlights, Paige was standing by the kitchen table in a cheerleader outfit, complete with pom poms. Chris was slightly behind her with his hands on her hips. He was wearing his hockey jersey.

And, apparently, nothing else.

He looked up, saw Liz, said, *"Oh, shit,"* and did

his best to hide behind his much smaller girlfriend.

Paige shrilled, "What are you doing here? You're not supposed to be here!" Her eyes were wide with shock.

"I texted…" Liz trailed off, genuinely at a loss for words, but as Chris hid his very red face in his hand, she had to bite her lip to keep from laughing.

She turned on her heel and said, "I'll see you guys tomorrow." She added, "I'll call first," over her shoulder as she went back out the front door.

Just before the latch caught, they heard her burst into laughter.

After a few moments of complete silence between them, Paige cleared her throat and said, in a slightly squeaky voice, "Okay, then. All role-playing at your place only from now on." She peeked over her shoulder at the still-silent Chris and said in a small voice, "I am so sorry!"

"I…" He paused, not even sure what he was even trying to say. Starting again, he said, "I have no idea how to handle this."

Paige giggled. And then snorted.

"Are you sure this is funny?" he asked.

Paige took a few steps away from him, looked down at herself, looked over at him, shook her head, and started laughing.

Chris was starting to grin but said, "I don't know if I can ever look her in the eye again."

"Oh, Chris, she's never going to look at you anywhere *except* your eyes after this."

He started laughing and just said, "Fuck."

Chapter Nineteen

School got out for Christmas break, and Paige was able to go to another home game with Liz before she and Chris were going to leave on their trip.

"Are you nervous at all?" Liz asked while Paige was packing.

Paige stopped and thought for a moment.

"Maybe a little. But I trust Chris, and we're only going to be there a few days. And honestly? This has *got* to be easier than a trip to my mom's house, right?"

Liz blanched at that thought. "Oh God. I had not thought of it in those terms. Never mind, pack faster!" She started pushing clothes into the suitcase, making Paige laugh. "Hurry up!"

***

Their first stop in Minnesota was the house of Chris's best friend.

They were greeted at the front door by a big guy,

well over six feet tall, with sandy brown hair and deep blue eyes. Chris and the behemoth greeted each other like brothers, with handshakes and hugs.

Chris started to introduce Paige, saying, "Micky, this is…"

Micky interrupted him. "This is the lovely Paige." His eyes flashed as he took her hand and bowed, gently kissing her fingers while keeping eye contact, flirting shamelessly. "I have been dying to meet you, Paige. You seem to have turned Becks here quite upside down."

Chris shook his head and rolled his eyes. "All right, that's enough of that." He removed Paige's hand from Micky's and held it in his own. "Behave yourself, you idiot."

Micky held his hand to his chest in mock surprise.

"Moi? Je suis sur mon meilleur comportement." He turned smoothly to Paige and said, "My apologies, I work in Montreal and sometimes forget to speak English when I return to the US."

Chris guffawed, "Oh my God, you are so full of shit! Paige, I swear, he has always been an idiot, but this is the first time I've seen him put on a 'pompous ass' display."

Micky's façade finally broke, and he laughed along with Chris. Pulling Paige into a hug, he said, "It is really nice to meet you. Please come in."

"What did you even say?" Chris asked.

Paige spoke for the first time, answering with a smile, "I'm pretty sure he said that he is on his best behavior."

This prompted an impressed look from Micky, as

159

well as another burst of laughter from Chris. "Oh, please. You memorized that line specifically for this moment. I know it."

The returning grin confirmed Chris's suspicions.

They reached the kitchen, where Micky's mom and some of his siblings were having coffee and chatting.

"Christopher!" Micky's mother, who was much closer to Paige's height, greeted Chris with an enormous hug and a kiss on the cheek. "I have missed you, my extra son."

Chris picked the smaller woman up to hug her, saying, "It's so good to see you!"

Swatting him with a dish towel when he set her down, she said, "You don't write, you don't call..." And then catching sight of Paige, she stopped and held out her hands in welcome. "Paige. It is so good to meet you. Come in, sit down, and please call me Kathleen. What can I get you to drink? Water? Coffee? Tea?"

One of Micky's sisters stood up to greet her, saying, "She just met Tommy, Mom. She probably could use a big glass of the mulled wine." Holding out her hand, she introduced herself. "Hi, Paige, I'm Colleen."

"Nice to meet you," Paige responded, taking a seat at the table. "Mulled wine sounds wonderful, thank you. But who is Tommy?"

Colleen laughed, pointing at her older brother. "That's Tommy. The one Chris calls 'Micky.' Hockey players don't seem to be able to use first names." She rolled her eyes. "They are big, overgrown kids."

Chris grinned at Colleen, and said, "Hey, Squiddo!" while giving her a big hug. "Heard you're heading to UConn next year. Congrats!"

Colleen returned the hug and punched him in the shoulder. "I can't believe you're still calling me that! See what I mean about the nicknames, Paige?"

Chris explained, "She was really little when I met her, so she was 'Squirt' or sometimes 'Kiddo.' Naturally, they merged one day…" Colleen rolled her eyes at him. "…and 'Squiddo' was born. And so shall she forever be. You're doomed, Squid." He ruffled her hair, and she poked him in the side, hitting a ticklish spot.

After a few more minutes of greeting Micky's family, Chris put his hand on Paige's shoulder and said softly, "Baby, we're going to go into the living room, you okay here?"

"Yes, of course, I'll be fine." She squeezed his hand briefly. "Thank you."

As the two men walked away, Colleen raised her eyebrows at her mother and said in an exaggerated whisper, *"'Baby?'"*

Kathleen shushed her, saying to Paige, "Don't mind her."

Another sister, a few years older than Colleen, chimed in. "Hi, Paige, I'm Erin. Col is just jealous. She's always had her eye on Chris."

"Oh my *God,* Erin!" Colleen shot a glare at her older sister. "Paige, ignore all of these people. I do *not* have a thing for Chris." Betrayed by a blush, she added, "I might have had a bit of a crush on him when I was younger, but *oh my God,* Erin! I can't believe you said that."

161

Turning to her mother, Colleen added, "And please, when have you *ever* heard him call anyone 'Baby?'" Addressing Paige again, she said, "He hasn't brought a girlfriend over here since college, I think, and I have *never* heard him call one by a pet name."

***

Micky grabbed a few beers from the fridge on their way to the living room.

"Holy shit, Becks. You were not kidding. She's beautiful."

Chris had a grin a mile wide. "And smart. Brilliant, really. And funny. And sweet and kind."

Micky just shook his head slowly, smiling, listening as Chris extolled Paige's virtues to him.

"I'm really happy for you, Becks. You know that, right?"

"I know. Thanks, man." He clapped Micky on the shoulder and asked, "Hey, where's your flavor of the month?"

"Ha! More like flavor of the week lately. And I unloaded the latest flavor two weeks ago. I enjoy flying solo during the holidays. Makes the odds ever in my favor, if you know what I mean."

Chris shook his head. "Damn, Micky. I do hope you wear party hats."

"You're kidding, right? I *always* wrap it. I do not need any complications in my life. Shit, the last thing I need is some puck bunny trying to tell me she's pregnant." Micky shuddered dramatically, and Chris rolled his eyes again.

Micky got a sly grin on his face and asked, "So, are you gonna tell me or what? What's she like behind closed doors?"

"Jesus, Mick. Remind me why the hell we're friends again. I am *not* going to tell you anything." But his smile said everything, and Micky threw back his head and laughed.

"I knew it. Grace in public; tiger in the sack. You've found the perfect woman." He wrapped his arm around Chris's shoulder. "Okay, Becks, now tell me about the rest of your life."

"You've just seen it. Hockey and Paige. That's about it for me. And I'm a happy man." Taking a drink from his beer, he said, "What's going on with you, besides your never-ending parade of willing women? Still a spiky bastard or have you finally warmed up to your teammates?"

Micky's eye darkened slightly. He scowled at Chris momentarily and said nothing.

"So," Chris responded, trying to lighten the mood again, "clearly still a spiky bastard. Got it."

Micky relaxed, not even realizing that his whole body had tensed in those few moments. "Sorry, Becks. Some things don't change, I guess." He stood up, put his arm around Chris's shoulders, and said, "Come on, let's go rescue Paige from my mom and sisters."

***

They spent several hours with the McCullins, laughing and reminiscing, with Colleen embarrassing Chris as often as possible with stories from when Chris and Micky were younger. Paige had a wonderful time.

As they were preparing to leave, Kathleen pulled Chris aside for a moment and gave him another hug and a kiss on the cheek. "She's lovely, Christopher. Treat her well."

"You know I will." Chris beamed at her.

Kathleen patted him on the cheek, saying, "I do, sweetheart. I do. You take care of yourself, now too. And for heaven's sake, come visit more often! Your mother might not tell you, but she misses you terribly."

"I will do my best." Chris picked her up in a hug one last time before they went back to the car to head to his mom's house.

***

The drive to Chris's mother's house was just about an hour and a half, and Paige spent most of that time asking more questions, now that she had met the McCullin family.

"So, tell me again how you met them. And did I hear Kathleen call you her 'extra son?'"

Chris chuckled and said, "Yes, I'm the extra son. You didn't meet Joe, Micky's younger brother—he's a really nice guy too—but there are the two boys and then three girls. I'm the extra.

"When I started really playing competitive hockey, it was tough on my mom. It was just the two of us—my dad had left when I was really little—so my mom had to try to work full time and get me where I needed to be *and* somehow make ends meet. Which was amazing of her. She did so much to ensure that I had a chance to do what I dreamed of doing. But anyway, lots of things were not close by where we lived.

"I went to a development camp when I was right around thirteen or so that was not too far from where we are now. My mom dropped me off for the week, and I didn't know anyone else. That first day, there were a bunch of guys who obviously knew each other and had been playing in the same clubs for a while, and one of the guys started giving me a hard time. You know, the usual, bragging about his goal scoring, where he's been playing, naming impressive coaches, making comments about how my teams and coaches weren't as good, that kind of thing. Scooter was acting like kind of a jerk…"

"Scooter?" Paige interrupted. "Seriously?"

Laughing, Chris said, "Yeah. Colleen really wasn't kidding about the nickname thing. I don't even remember the guy's real name anymore.

"Anyway, we were starting camp off with a scrimmage, and Scooter and I were on opposing teams. Right after he walked off with his little fan club, this big guy on my team came up, nudged me in the shoulder, and just said, 'No worries, I got this.'"

"That was Micky, I assume?"

"That was Micky. He was big and intimidating even then. I was feeling like crap—I didn't know anyone and was really shy and not feeling particularly confident by that point—and didn't know what to expect."

Chris started laughing at the memory. "We had

165

our scrimmage game, and Micky put Scooter into the boards every single time he was out there." Looking over at Paige briefly, he said, "Seriously, Paige. Every single shift—*wham*—into the boards. He even got called on a few penalties for doing it when he shouldn't have based on what was going on in the game. It was nuts."

Turning back to the road, he continued, "After the game, Micky came over, gave me a big grin, stuck out his hand, and said, 'Hi, I'm Micky.' I knew right then that we were gonna be friends for life. I just knew it."

"What happened with Scooter?"

"Scooter came over to me and mumbled a quick, 'Nice game,' and that was it. He ended up being an okay guy, and we got along. He played through college but didn't end up trying to make a career out of it."

They were quiet for a few minutes, and then Paige said, "Wait, that doesn't explain your 'extra son' status with the McCullin family."

"Oh, right! Well, at the end of camp, when my mom came to pick me up, Micky brought his parents over to meet my mom and explained to everyone that it would make a lot of sense for me to stay at their house sometimes for tournaments and travel." Chris chuckled again. "I'm sure he had worked it out with his parents already, but he sounded like he was presenting the entire idea as his own. Once my mom realized that this would really work, she was thrilled. And so was I."

He had a wistful look on his face and a small smile. "I spent so much time with them, Paige. I stayed at their house as much as I stayed at my own—maybe more—and they took me to tournaments and practices and games. They really are my second family. They were so unbelievably generous with their time and space, and just themselves. Micky's parents are a huge part of how I ended up being a pro hockey player. I owe them so much."

Paige reached over to hold his hand and said, "They clearly love you and consider you part of the family."

"Yeah, it's amazing. Micky is my brother in everything but blood. I'm telling you, I knew it when I met him." Stealing a small look at Paige, he said, "There are a few things in my life like that…things that I have just *known*. It's hard to explain, but it's true. I just *knew* that I was going to play hockey or die trying," he joked, "pretty much from the first time I put on skates. And I just *knew* that Micky was going to be my friend for life."

For a brief moment, he considered telling her that she was the third thing in his life that he was absolutely certain of but decided it was not quite the right time.

Chapter Twenty

They pulled up to a moderately sized, beautifully kept house, decorated with Christmas evergreens and accented with white lights. It was dusk, and the house looked like it could be on the front of a Christmas card, elegant and inviting.

"It's beautiful, Chris. Did you grow up here?"

Chris turned into the driveway as he answered, "No, but close to here. We lived in a double-wide trailer in a trailer park about five miles away." He shut the car off and turned to Paige briefly. "The first thing I did as a pro was to buy this house for my mom. She didn't want anything big, and she had always liked this neighborhood, so I thought it would be perfect."

Paige watched him get out of the car and walk around to open her door. A gentleman, without a doubt.

She took his hand and stopped him for a moment as they walked toward the house.

"What?" he asked her with a smile.

Paige stood on her toes and put her hand on his

cheek, encouraging him to bend down for a kiss.

"You're wonderful," she whispered.

Chris tilted his head a bit, and his smile conveyed his pleasure at her comment.

"Come on," he tugged on her hand, "let's have you meet my mom. She's going to love you."

***

Emily Beckman opened the door before they reached it, beaming at her son. She hugged him, stood back to look at him, as if he had grown since she last saw him, and then hugged him again. And then turned to Paige.

"Mom, *this* is Paige." Turning to address Paige, he said, "Paige Smith, Emily Beckman. My mom." He gave his mom another squeeze, adding, "And my biggest fan."

Paige put her hand out, but Emily ignored it and pulled her in for a hug.

"Welcome, Paige! I'm so glad to finally meet you. I don't hear from Chris as often as I should," she threw a playful, chiding look to her son, "but every time I do, I hear about you." She bustled a little, saying, "But come in, come in. Paige, what can I get for you to drink? Are you hungry?" Paige demurred as Emily turned to say, "Chris, why don't you get the luggage out of the car so you can get settled? The guest bedroom is all set up for you two."

Chris was grinning and kissed Paige on the top of her head before going back out to the car.

Emily chuckled, watching him walk away.

"He's crazy about you. You know that, right?"

Paige smiled and replied, "I'm pretty crazy about him too. Your son is a lovely person, through and through."

"He is at that," she agreed, preparing cups of tea. "So, tell me about you. You teach English, right? What's that like? How big are your classes? Do you enjoy the work?"

Paige told her about her work, finding Emily to be very friendly and easy to talk to. Chris made a few trips to the car and back, peeking at the two of them chatting each time he passed, a grin permanently on his face.

After the luggage was all set in the guest room, he returned to the kitchen just in time to hear his mom say, "Oh my goodness, I agree! Grammar is so important. It just isn't stressed as much now, at least not in the media. It makes me crazy to hear a news reporter make basic grammar errors."

"Yes! Or commercials! It's like nails on a chalkboard to hear them. Did no one notice? No copy writers? No producers?"

Chris sat down at the table, saying, "So, I guess I need to thank my mom for correcting me all of those times."

"Absolutely," Paige answered immediately.

"I could never get away with saying, 'Me and Joe are going to the movies.' There was always, *always* the immediate correction: 'Joe and I.'" He chuckled. "I had to repeat it back properly, or no one was going anywhere with anyone."

They shared a laugh, but Paige said, "Good grammar is very sexy, Chris."

He immediately turned to his mother and exaggeratedly bowed over her hand, saying, "Thank you, thank you," over and over until she laughed and swatted him away.

***

They spent the evening talking and laughing, until Chris's mom went off to bed.

"I will see you two in the morning." Kissing Chris on the cheek, she added, "Christopher, you being here and bringing Paige is the best present I could ever hope for."

Paige was amazed at the relationship Chris and his mother shared. Her own upbringing had been so…different. This seemed almost idyllic. And yet she had grown up living a comfortable middle-class life in a big, single-family home, while Chris had grown up in a life of financial struggle, living in a trailer park.

"Your mom is wonderful, Chris."

"Isn't she?" He held her hand as they sat on the couch together. "She worked two jobs so I could play hockey. She was a secretary by day and then had a moonlighting job doing transcription from home so she didn't have to leave me alone and could tuck me into bed each night." She could see the emotion on his face talking about it. "She sacrificed so much so I could have the life of my dreams, and every year she says that the best Christmas present in the world is me coming to visit.

"Between my mom and the McCullins…" his

171

voice rasped, "they gave me everything, Paige. Absolutely everything. I can never repay them."

Paige gently pulled him down so he was lying on the couch with his head in her lap and then ran her fingers through his hair and stroked his face.

"I'm the luckiest man in the entire world," he said quietly.

***

Christmas morning Paige awoke early, climbing out of bed quietly so as not to wake Chris. Emily was awake already, in the kitchen, making breakfast for the three of them.

"Merry Christmas!" Paige said quietly, and Emily greeted her with a hug.

"Merry Christmas, Paige! I take it Christopher is still sleeping?"

Paige accepted the cup of coffee Emily offered to her, replying, "Yes, I didn't want to wake him up. My schedule is skewed early, so it's rare for me to sleep in very late, at least not during the school year. During the summer is a totally different story."

She offered to help Emily with breakfast, but as expected, Emily insisted that Paige sit and drink coffee while she prepared the food.

After they had been chatting for a bit, Paige said, "Chris mentioned last night that you sacrificed a great deal to help him succeed in hockey. Being a single mom, working two jobs...it's amazing, really."

Emily sat down at the table with her, everything

172

now either baking or staying warm until Chris woke up.

"It was all worth it. Every minute. Look at how successful he has become. And now, how happy he is. Truly, Paige, I'm not sure I've ever seen him this happy without skates on his feet and a hockey stick in his hand.

"It's what every parent wants for their children—for their kids to be happy and more successful than they were."

Paige responded without thinking, "Not every parent." At Emily's surprised look, she added, "Only the good ones," with a smile.

Feeling that more of an explanation was called for, Paige opened up, saying, "My relationship with my mother is not…good. Not healthy. I would go so far as to say unhealthy, except I'm much better about controlling the situation than I used to be. Mostly that means very limited contact."

"I'm so sorry, Paige."

Paige smiled and said, "Thank you. Me too."

They sipped quietly for a few more minutes, until rustling sounds and footfalls indicated that Chris had awoken and was out of bed.

"Ah, finally," Emily said with a smile. "I knew he wouldn't sleep too late. It is Christmas, after all. He's never been able to sleep late on Christmas."

***

They opened gifts after breakfast; Chris gave his mom several small things that he knew she would love, along with the complete itinerary for a trip to

St. Paul for the Grizzlies home game against the Guardians in February.

"One of these days I will get you to come visit DC again," he said.

Emily responded with a smile. "And one of these days I will take you up on that offer again. But I always look forward to seeing you play in Minnesota."

Paige gave Chris three pairs of cufflinks.

"I noticed that you have several shirts with French cuffs," she said, "but I've only seen you wearing one set of cufflinks."

He looked closely at them. "Guardians logo— very nice, the guys will love that, thank you. And the seal of the University of Minnesota!" He looked up at her, touched that she remembered where he went to college. "And…"

"The last ones are tiny hockey rinks," she said. "Because you taught me about the game."

Chris tilted his head slightly as he looked at her.

"What?" she asked. "Do you like them? I was afraid that the ones you have might have a great deal of sentimental value or something…"

"I love them," he interrupted. "I love them, Paige. Thank you."

She smiled. "You're welcome. Merry Christmas."

"I have something for you too," he said, moving to pick up a box and interrupting her protest, continuing, "I know you said the trip was your gift, but this is just something small I really wanted to get for you."

She tore the paper and opened a box to find a

pair of white figure skates.

"Oh, Chris…thank you. I've never owned a pair of skates before!"

At the shocked looks from both Emily and Chris, Paige laughed and said, "You forget that in Pennsylvania and Virginia, people almost always have to go to *rinks* to skate! I didn't grow up being able to just head out to a pond. I've always just rented skates from the rink. But I haven't been for years." She thought for a minute. "A lot of years. I'm not sure I remember the last time I went skating!"

"Well," Chris said with a smile, "I have a solution for that. Later tonight, I'm going to take you to the pond where I skated all the time as a kid."

"As long as you're ready to hold me up!" she replied. "I make no promises about my ability to stay on my feet on skates."

***

Later that afternoon, Emily approached Paige out of earshot of Chris and sat down with her at the kitchen table.

"Paige, this is presumptuous of me, but…if you ever need to talk to a 'mom' figure, well…" She paused for a moment. "I mean, I don't have a daughter. I love my son more than life itself, but I always wondered what it would be like to have a daughter. So, well, you can call me, if you'd like. I guess that's what I'm trying to say."

Paige was touched and felt tears prick her eyes.

She had just received more motherly affection from a virtual stranger than she could recall receiving from her own mother. Ever.

"Thank you," she said, blinking back the tears as she gave Emily a hug.

Chapter Twenty-One

Chris drove them down a gravel road into the woods, stopping when the headlights were shining on a frozen pond. He left the car running and the headlights on and got out to open Paige's door.

"Are you sure about this?" she asked, feeling slightly wary of the rustic nature of this adventure.

"Absolutely. It hasn't gotten above twenty degrees in weeks. It's perfectly safe." When she still looked suspicious, he added, "This is where I used to skate all the time. Really, Paige, it's safe."

He helped her with her skates and then put his own on, helping her to the surface of the ice.

"It won't be completely smooth like an ice rink, but just relax your knees."

She stumbled a little, saying, "Oh God, it's been a long time since I've been on ice skates."

"Hang on a second, I'll be right back."

"Wait! Where are you going?"

Chris sped off in a quick arc, calling back over his shoulder, "Just looking out for tripping hazards. Hang on."

Paige took a moment to admire his athleticism, the inherent grace in the way he moved across the ice, and then smiled as he looped back around and came up behind her, putting his arm around her.

"Okay, baby, just relax. Bend your knees a little."

"I'll try."

She did her best to relax, and Chris started to skate the two of them around the ice. He moved slowly at first, until she was feeling more comfortable, and then sped up a little.

"Don't worry, baby. I won't let you fall. Just relax and trust me."

It was beautiful and romantic and magical, and Chris finally slowed them down near the edge of the reach of the headlights, toward the middle of the ice, and turned her to him.

Paige looked at him, her face glowing, eyes shining, and they kissed for a moment as Chris held her close.

Brushing his glove across her cheek, Chris said, "There are actually three things in my life that I have just...*known*. That I wanted to play in the NHL, that Micky and I would be lifelong friends," he paused and looked at her, "and that I want to spend the rest of my life with you, Paige."

In a heartbeat, her eyes went from softly focused to almost panicked, and Chris held her face in his hands, his heart suddenly racing. "Please don't freak out. You already know that I love you, Paige. Now you know how much. I won't pressure you, but I knew after our first date. Every moment since then has made me more certain. You're it for me,

Paige. You're the one."

Paige's hands were gripping his jacket, and she felt a bit like she wanted to run; the panic was compounded by the fact that she suddenly felt trapped on the ice, felt like she was too far from the car to make it back on her own, even though she knew that wasn't really true.

"Please, baby," he said quietly, "don't panic. The only thing between us that just changed is that you now know how I feel. I want you to know, Paige."

"This is a lot, Chris. It might not feel sudden to you, but it feels really sudden to me. I need some time to process this."

"It's okay. Take your time. I'm not going anywhere."

He maneuvered them back to the shore and helped her with her skates. When they were back in the car, Paige turned to him and said, "I do love you, Chris. You know that, right?"

Smiling at her, he kissed her forehead and said, "I know, baby. Thank you."

He held her hand as they drove back to his mother's house, and he said a silent prayer of thanks that he started talking to her *before* getting down on one knee to give her the ring that was sitting in the pocket of his jacket.

Chapter Twenty-Two

"He told me he wants to marry me." Paige had only just gotten back to the apartment and blurted this out to Liz without even a greeting.

"What? Oh my God, Paige! You're engaged?" Liz jumped up in excitement.

"No!" Paige's sharp response stopped Liz short. "No, I'm not. He just told me that he wanted to spend the rest of his life with me." She sat down heavily on the couch. "That he knew after our *first date* that I was 'The One.'"

"Whoa." Liz sat down next to her to absorb this information.

Paige got up and started pacing.

"Yeah. I mean, who says that? Who even *thinks* that?"

Liz smiled and said gently, "He does, apparently." Paige was clearly agitated. "You seem upset, Paige. What's wrong?"

"What's wrong?" Paige replied, now moving her luggage to a different part of the living room. "Really, Liz?"

"Yes, really. Take a breath. Have a seat." She waited until Paige sat down on the couch. "Now, what's wrong, Paige? What's going on in your head? The man you love just told you that he loves you enough to spend the rest of his life with you, and you seem to be taking it strangely."

Paige stood up again and resumed her pacing. "I just don't understand why he would say that. I don't need to change my life. I don't need to get married. My life is fine!" She opened the fridge for no reason and then closed it again. "It's great, actually! Job, friends…"

"…Amazing boyfriend," Liz interrupted, and Paige gave her a frustrated look.

"This isn't how I work." Paige sounded adamant. "This isn't how I do things. You know that!" She was winding up again, pacing, opening cabinets without even looking in them. "I plan! I prepare! I know what my life is going to bring! *I'm not you!*"

Liz paused for a moment before responding, quietly, "No, you're not me."

The soft response snapped Paige out of her random movements, and she turned to Liz and said, "I'm sorry. I didn't mean that. Not that way."

"I know."

Sitting back down on the couch, Paige continued, "I just meant that you are comfortable going off script, you know? Your motto is practically, 'Let's just wing that mother.'"

Liz laughed and repeated, "I know, Paige. I knew what you meant." She paused for a moment and then said, "This wasn't any kind of ultimatum, right? It sounds like he was just telling you how he feels."

Paige sighed. "No, it wasn't an ultimatum. He said that nothing has changed between us except that now I know."

"Okay, then. Nothing has changed. He still feels the same way as before, it's just…" she searched for a word, *"out* now."

Paige sat back against the cushions. "It feels like something changed, though."

"What?"

Another sigh. "I'm not sure. I think…maybe…" She struggled to find words to express the anxiety pressing against her. "This ups the stakes. For him. For me. For what happens if or when this ends." She must be getting close to the truth, because she felt tears starting. "He's such a good person, Liz. I don't want to hurt him. I don't want him to have wasted his time with me because he decided on the spur of the moment that I'm the one for him."

Liz had a look of concern bordering on confusion on her face. "He doesn't strike me as a 'spur of the moment' kind of guy, especially not with something important."

Paige shrugged. "Liz, he bought a *house.* He says it's a good investment, but he bought a house and then asked me if I wanted to decorate it. Like 'here's my credit card, go buy furniture.'"

Liz pushed, "I get it, Paige. But 'wasted his time' with you? Really?" She shook her head. "You know what I'm going to say."

Reluctantly, Paige answered, "I know. Love is never wasted."

"Love is never wasted," Liz repeated. "No matter

what. That time, those moments spent in love with someone—really in love, not lust or obsession—those moments change people. Real, honest love is transformative. It makes you somehow…larger. More connected with the world, the universe. And at the very same time it reduces your world down to that bright line connecting you to the other person. It's a beautiful, paradoxical, incomprehensible, intangible, yet very real thing. Almost like fire, now that I'm thinking about it. It transforms what it touches. Hardens steel, changes the color of minerals, reduces wood to ashes while providing light and heat.

"That part of love—the part that makes you want to be a better person—that is never, ever wasted. No matter how the relationship ends, be it infidelity or indifference or incompatibility or ''til death do you part.' The love you shared will have shaped you. And him."

Paige looked at her friend, taking the time to really "see" her for the first time in a long while. "Sometimes I forget you have the heart of a poet," she said with a weak smile. "You bury it under quite a bit of profanity."

Liz chuckled. "'Fuck' is the most versatile word in the English language. But you know I mean it. Trust this. Trust yourself, even if the feelings are racing faster than you feel safe. People flock to roller coasters for a reason. Enjoy the ride, Paige. Enjoy the ride."

Paige stood up and walked over to her very best friend for a long, comforting hug.

"I know you miss him," she whispered to Liz.

She heard a sniffle and then a short laugh.

"Damn it, Paige." Liz released her friend from the hug and wiped the stray tears away. "I was doing fine until that. You're a pain in the ass."

"Takes one to know one."

"Okay, enough of this. Tell me about his mom."

Paige couldn't help but smile at the thought of Emily. "She's *wonderful,* Liz. Compassionate. Understanding. Loving. Chris is her whole world, and he treats her so well. Their relationship is incredibly special."

Liz smiled, pointing out, "He treats you like that too. He shows old-fashioned manners that I thought didn't exist anymore."

Paige smiled in return. "I know, isn't it amazing?"

Liz got a wicked gleam in her eye and said, "I might be concerned that everything was all stodgy and old-fashioned between you two, but a certain scene involving a cheerleader outfit that is permanently burned into my retinas assures me otherwise."

Paige's eyes got wide and she started throwing pillows.

***

Chris hadn't mentioned marriage again, and after a few days Paige was more relaxed, and their relationship had returned to normal, which included her spending more and more time at his apartment.

Paige was sitting on the couch with a stack of papers in front of her on the coffee table, muttering to herself while marking up the top one. Her brows were knit together in a look of frustration, and Chris heard her say, "Damn it, Jeremy," under her breath. She got to the end of the paper, threw down her red pen, stood up, and huffed off toward the kitchen to get a glass of water.

"What's up, baby?" Chris asked. "What's wrong?"

Paige's voice reflected the frustration already evident on her face.

"It's this kid. He's a junior this year. Basketball player, and he's really good. He could be offered scholarships, I just know it." She was pacing. "And he's smart too. But now, there are girls and cars, and he's letting his grades slip. I'm watching it happen, Chris!" Paige turned to face him. "I'm watching this smart, talented kid let an opportunity of a lifetime slip away. He's not going to get scholarship offers without the grades to go with the talent. He's good, but he's going to *need* those grades to set him apart."

Chris was looking at her with a kind of wonder. He took her in his arms, smoothed back her hair, and kissed her forehead, holding her close to him until he felt her tension ease.

"You are amazing, baby. You care so much. Smart, kind, beautiful," he tilted her chin up to look at him and continued, "and sexy. I'm the luckiest man in the world, Paige."

She sighed and leaned against his strong frame again.

"Thank you, Chris," she murmured. "I always feel better when you hold me. It's like you're some

185

kind of trouble sponge." She snaked her arms around to hold him tighter. "You hold me and soak up all of the trouble, leaving me feeling better." She sighed. "It's like I can shut off the worrying part of my brain for a while and just…feel."

"I feel that way with you too. It's like your arms are home, Paige."

She tilted her head up to look at him, a small smile on her face, almost wistful.

Feeling a tad self-conscious, he asked, "Is that corny?"

She shook her head and then nuzzled her face against his chest again. "No. It's sweet. And wonderful." She peeked up at him again. "And okay, maybe it's a little corny, but that's one of the things I love about you."

He sighed and held her just a little tighter.

"Hey, baby, I've been wanting to ask you something."

She hummed a contented noise against his chest and asked, "What's up?"

Chris looked down and cupped her face in his hand before saying, "So, I'm expecting the house to be ready sometime soon, and I'm thinking about moving in at the end of the season." He moved his other hand to fully frame her face. He had thought carefully about how to ask this, not wanting to spook her. "Whenever you're ready, I would love for you to move in with me, Paige."

He felt her stiffen a bit, and he repeated, "Whenever you're ready, baby," and leaned down to kiss her forehead.

"It's just…" Paige was fighting the panicky

feeling that was trying to force its way in. "I mean…I don't think it's a good time yet."

Chris smiled and kissed her on the nose. "That's why I said 'whenever you're ready.'"

"I don't think I should leave Liz on her own. Not yet." At Chris's confused look, she said, "After Jimmy died, she was a wreck. I got us an apartment together so she wouldn't be living alone."

Chris cuddled her against his chest. "Of course you did. You took care of her."

"She's my best friend. We have been through some really hard things together. She would have done the same for me."

Chris pushed back again to look at her. "I don't doubt that for one minute. She seems to be doing really well now. She is, right? Or is that all a front?"

Paige smiled and said, "No, it's not a front. She's doing well. Trust me, she's not that good an actress. And 'subtle' is not a word I would use to describe her."

Chris laughed out loud and said, "True, but without her lack of subtlety, I probably would never have had the nerve to ask you out. So she's a hero in my book."

"Mine too. But I don't feel it's the right time to move out." There was more to it than that, but she didn't want to talk about it. She wasn't even sure that she understood her feelings about it.

"I understand." Chris kissed her again, slowly and gently. "Whenever you're ready, baby."

Chapter Twenty-Three

A few days later, they were at Paige's apartment.

"This road trip is the longest one of the season," Chris said, holding Paige close to him. "It's eleven days, including travel. I won't be back until Thursday after next, but I will be home by the afternoon. Are you free that night?"

Paige thought for a moment and then looked up at him. "No. Shoot, that's the start of the senior trip I'm chaperoning that I told you about."

Chris muttered, "Damn," under his breath.

"I've done it the past three years. It's been easy for me, because I don't have kids of my own to worry about, and I committed to it a long time ago."

"I know," he replied, "I'm not upset about that." He tilted her chin up gently to look in her eyes. "It's just that we're only at home two days until we leave for another five day roadie."

"Oh." Her shoulders sank. "Damn."

"Exactly. I'm not going to see you for a long time, baby. I'm going to miss you."

They kissed, lingering, and Paige let her

fingertips play in the soft, short hair at the back of his neck. He gave a little shiver and chuckled.

"I love when you do that."

"I love the way that hair feels. Like a soft little baby duck," she replied, continuing to stroke his neck gently.

Tightening his arms around her waist for a moment, Chris said, "Hey, can I ask a favor?"

"Of course. What's up?"

Chris gently cupped her cheek with his hand, stroking her face with his thumb and looking at her in a way that made her heart beat faster.

"Would you stay at my apartment a night or two while I'm gone?"

The request seemed oddly inconsistent with the way he was looking at her.

"Sure, honey. Are you worried about something?"

"No," he said, dipping his head down for a kiss. "I just want my bed to smell like you when I'm home for those two days." He rubbed his cheek along her face, burying his nose into her hair and breathing in the scent of her. "Would you mind?"

"Not at all," she said, taking the opportunity to rub her face along his strong chest. "I love the way you smell too. It reminds me of summer, even though you play on the ice all the time."

He chuckled and sighed. "Anything that smells the least bit like vanilla makes me think of you now. It can be very distracting to walk around in a bakery." With a rough whisper, he added, "Everything about you feels like home, Paige." He pushed away with a quick glance at the clock. "I have to go, baby. I love you. See you as soon as we can manage."

"I love you too, Chris. Safe travels."

They kissed one more time, and then he was off.

***

"Hey, baby. You leave tomorrow, right?"

"Hi, big guy. Yes, I do. But guess where I am right now." She rustled around to give him a hint.

His voice got quiet and rough. "Are you in my bed?" he growled softly.

"I am."

He held the phone a bit away from his mouth so that she only caught brief snippets of the string of low curses.

"God, baby, the things I want to say to you."

She smiled and stretched and then grabbed the second pillow and hugged it to her.

"It smells like you, Chris. This was a really good idea."

They were silent for a few moments, each just feeling the presence of the other across the miles.

When he spoke again, his voice was still a low rasp. "I'm not sure how to say this without breaking our electronic communications agreement, but…if you feel the need to…you know…take care of things, take care of yourself, while you're there, well, that would be amazing."

"Oh." Paige's breath came more quickly, the desire in his voice sparking tingles low in her body. "I hadn't thought about…" Her breath caught and then, with her voice mirroring his, said very quietly,

"I could do that."

His groan was involuntary, and the sound made her thighs press together as arousal started taking over.

"I have never been so tempted to break my phone policy." Her voice was breathy, and he could hear a little gasp at the end.

He closed his eyes. Without realizing it, his free hand trailed down to rest on his thigh, seeking the heat building in his groin.

"Oh, baby, I can't believe I'm going to say this, but don't."

"Don't?" The panting quality of her voice had him starting to throb.

"Fuck," he muttered. Trying to force himself to break the spell, he moved his hand to rub the back of his neck. "No, baby. Don't." His voice was still rough with desire. "I don't want you to ever feel bad about anything we do, and you might regret it later."

Paige laid her head back on the pillow and sighed.

She was quiet long enough that Chris asked, "Baby, are you there?"

"I'm here." She smiled, feeling tears pricking at her eyes. "I can't believe how much I love you, Chris. I didn't know it was possible to feel this way."

"God, me, either. I love you too, Paige."

"I can't wait to see you again."

"Me too. Good night, safe trip, baby."

***

Chris threw his bag to the side as he entered the apartment, loosening his tie as he walked toward the bedroom. It was still the afternoon, but he desperately wanted to put his face in his pillow and breathe her in. The sheet of loose-leaf paper sitting on the bed brought a smile to his face—it simply said, "Enjoy," and was signed with a lipstick print. He picked up the page, and beneath it, neatly folded, was a pair of black lace panties.

"Oh, fuck," he groaned, bringing the satin and lace up to his face and breathing in...her. The smell of her arousal caused such a sudden and intense visceral reaction that he leaned his hand against the wall before sinking down to sit on the bed, one hand still holding the panties, the other fumbling to release his belt buckle and pants. Dropping back to lie on the bed, he reached down with both hands, frantically attempting to free his throbbing erection, and when he had shifted his clothing out of the way, he brought the hand holding the scrap of material back up to his face.

"Oh, fuck. Paige."

Eyes closed, his mind brought him between her thighs, and he was moaning with each stroke of his hand along his hard shaft.

"Yes."

He was never this vocal when going solo. Then again, the scent of her was stripping away any remnant of control he might have normally had. His mind added in what she sounded like, what she tasted like, and he was already thrusting his hips up to meet his hand.

"Goddamn."

He dropped her panties on his face and reached down to cradle his aching balls with his other hand.

"Oh, God."

The pressure was rising, and he stroked his balls in time with his cock, feeling the contractions start deep at the base.

"Fuck. Oh, fuck, fuck, fuck, gonna come, baby—*Paige!*"

Her name was a shout followed by a deep groan as the orgasm overtook his body. Pulsing waves erupted, landing on his shirt, his abs contracting with every gasping one of them, his mind momentarily a white hot blank.

Breathing hard, coming down, he opened his eyes and reached up to his face to pull away the little bit of fabric that had triggered such an intense reaction.

His hands dropped off to the sides, he murmured, "Sweet Jesus," and then started laughing, emotional release following the physical.

***

When Paige checked her phone that evening, she saw a text message that simply read:

Chris: Thank you baby.
XOXOXO

She smiled.

Paige: You're welcome. Hope you enjoyed your present.

Chris: *You have no idea.*

Chapter Twenty-Four

The team got back in town in the early afternoon after the second road trip, and Chris had coordinated with Paige for her to come over right after she got out of work.

He knew she would be there soon, but she had a key, and he really needed to take a shower to get rid of that "I've been on a plane for a long time" feeling.

He had only been in the shower for a few minutes when Paige quietly slid open the shower door and slipped in behind him.

"No, don't turn around," she said to stop Chris from turning to embrace her. "I just want to look at you." She ran her hand down his back, reaching up to gently follow the shape of the toned muscles from his broad shoulders, stroking along his spine, moving down and over to end at his hip.

Chris exhaled, enjoying the hot water on his front and her caress on his back.

Placing her thumbs in the small of his back, near his spine, she pressed and rubbed, massaging away at least some of the tension from the tight muscles. He made a sound of contentment as she continued, pressing deeply.

A few moments later, she picked up a scrub, lathered it, and began the process of washing his back.

"Thank you, baby," he said with a sigh. Chris leaned his hands against the front wall of the shower, dropping his head down to allow the water to cascade over his head and down his back.

"Hey," Paige chided gently, "let me wash before you rinse." She shifted her scrubbing down to his firm glutes as Chris chuckled. His quiet laughter stopped abruptly with a sharp intake of breath. She had reach under to caress his balls with one soapy hand.

"Oh," he said with a soft groan. She continued soaping his scrotum far longer than was necessary for cleanliness. "That feels amazing."

Paige dropped the scrub and snaked her other hand around his hip, now using both hands to slide his soapy testes around, back and forth, exploring, listening to his breathing deepen. She shifted her front hand to slide up his expanding erection.

He groaned again, more deeply, as she stroked him slowly, soap making his cock slide easily through her fist.

"Just making sure you're really, really clean, big guy." Paige smiled against his back, placing kisses along his spine as she continued stroking, fondling. She tasted the skin on his back with her tongue and bit him gently. All the while continuing to slide his hard shaft through her fist and move his balls with her fingers.

In a slightly strained voice, he said, "I think I'm clean now." He tried to turn around, adding, "I should wash you."

Pressing closer to him to prevent the turn, Paige tightened her grip slightly and said, "No, I don't think so. I'm not convinced you're clean enough yet." She shifted to moving her hand more rapidly along his length, twisting her hand just a bit at the head each time.

It was making him crazy. She increased her speed until she heard his breathing hitch in the familiar way that told her he was close. They both knew there wasn't enough pressure or friction to get him off; it was just enough to keep him on edge, orgasm close but unreachable.

Finally relenting, she said, "Okay, you're probably clean enough…" She had barely finished the sentence before he turned to her, pressing her back against the wall of the shower. The cold against her back made Paige squeak in surprise as he pressed his mouth to hers. His hands found her breasts, his tongue found hers, and it was her turn to gasp as he shifted one hand from her breast to slide a finger through her slit and slip inside her.

"You're wet," he growled. He added a second finger and kissed her harder, pushing his tongue into her mouth in a rhythm that he matched with his fingers pushing into her, rubbing his hand along her clit.

Paige made a needy sound and rocked against his hand, seeking more pressure from his palm.

"Oh, no," he said, removing his hands from her

body and wrapping them around her wrists. "Not after all of that teasing. You have to wait for me." Chris held her hands together in one of his, over her head against the shower wall. He kissed her, hard, as he tweaked her nipple with his other hand as she squirmed and moaned.

Paige felt his hard cock trapped against her midsection, and she moved against him, trying to continue her teasing while he held her arms pinned to the wall. Chris shifted hands so he could pay attention to her other breast, tweaking, teasing, tugging at the nipple until she was making breathy sounds against his mouth.

Briefly releasing her hands, Chris turned Paige around, pressed her hands against the shower wall, and positioned her slightly bent over, pulling her hips back toward himself. He slid two fingers through her folds and into her, pulsing them in and out in a quick rhythm while Paige writhed, moaning, pressing back against him.

Crouching down slightly, Chris gripped his cock and slid it between her thighs, making sure the shaft was tucked between her lips, the tip bumping against her clit as he pushed forward. He moved his hands to the outside of her thighs to hold them together, with his shaft trapped between them.

Paige gasped out a cry of pleasure as Chris started moving, thrusting between her legs, allowing his cock to drag back and forth against her, pushing against her clit with every movement. She was pressing back against him, and Chris saw her muscles shudder with the sensations.

Chris released her thighs and stood up, turning

Paige around. Her face was flushed and her eyes were full of lust as she reached up to wrap one arm around his neck and kiss him, using her other hand to wrap around his hardened length.

Bending his knees again, Chris grabbed her ass and lifted, and Paige wrapped her legs around him. He positioned them both so that his tip pressed against her opening.

He pressed her back against the shower wall and entered her in one hard thrust, swallowing her shout of pleasure with another deep kiss.

Chris held himself buried deep inside her and looked into her eyes. "Now," he said. "Now I'm going to make you come, you sexy tease."

Her return gaze was full of heat, and Paige squeezed her legs around him and ground herself against him. "Yes," she replied and, grinding against him again, added, "Please."

"Please what, Paige?" He slid out just a little and then shoved in again, hard, filling her. "Tell me what you want, baby."

She looked at him, her eyes filled with passion, and said, clearly and distinctly, "I want you to fuck me, handsome man."

He grinned and started moving slowly in and out of her.

Paige closed her eyes, breathing harder. "Fuck me, Chris." He moved a little faster, a little harder.

She opened her eyes and smiled at Chris, knowing just what he needed to hear. She kissed and bit his lower lip and then slid her lips up to his ear and whispered, "Please shove your big, fat cock in me, and fuck me *hard.*"

Paige felt him shudder, and his arms tightened around her as he finally gave in to what they both wanted. He thrust into her hard and fast. She clung to him, feeling her orgasm build as he rocked his hips, pushing her against the shower wall, the pressure from the base of his shaft against her clit making her writhe.

They bucked against each other, building toward release until his long, drawn-out groan of orgasm finally pushed her over the edge into a shared climax. He felt her fingers digging into his skin as she held him tightly, muscles contracting around him in waves, drawing out his own orgasm as he continued to capture her moans with his kisses.

It was a few moments before they realized the water was starting to cool.

"Looks like it's time to get out, baby. Almost out of hot water." He put her down gently and chuckled, saying, "I'm not sure how much of me actually got washed. Not that I care anymore. God, I missed you, Paige."

She smiled at him in a slightly sleepy way as he turned to shut off the water, and she opened the shower door just enough to grab the two towels waiting on the rack, handing one to him.

"I'm pretty sure none of me got washed," she said with a smile as she stepped out of the shower to dry off. "Welcome home, Chris." She pressed one more kiss against his chest as he got out of the shower. "I missed you too."

Chapter Twenty-Five

"So, baby, there's this work thing that I have to do, and I was hoping you'd come with me." They were having dinner at Paige's apartment; she had felt inspired and cooked lasagna.

"Oh!" The request caught Paige by surprise; she had met some of the other players, and they had even had dinner with Dmitry and Natalia and gone bowling with some of the others, but he had never asked her to attend anything for the team.

"When?" she asked. "And what is it? If I'm free, I would be happy to go with you."

"It's a formal charity event—dinner and dancing, that sort of thing—and it's happening the third week of February. Are you free?" Chris sat back in his chair, wiping his face with his napkin. "And I know I've said this already, but my God that's the best lasagna I have ever had."

Paige smiled at the compliment, getting out her phone to look at her calendar once Chris told her the exact date.

"I'm free that weekend," she said, "but how

formal are we talking?"

"Black tie," Chris responded, getting up to start helping with the dishes.

Paige froze. "Like, tuxedos and ball gowns? That kind of black tie?"

"Yup." He turned back to the table to pick up more dishes and saw Paige standing, plate in hand, unmoving. "What?"

"I can't do that." Her voice was not quite steady, and Chris took the plate from her hand and brought her to the couch to sit down.

"Why? What's wrong?"

"I don't..." She paused, reaching for some reason to give him. She was feeling the beginnings of panic. "I don't have a dress. I can't. I don't have anything that I can wear for that. I'm sorry, Chris."

He looked at her curiously.

"I would love to get a dress for you, baby. Just go pick one out. You could go shopping with Liz."

"Liz wouldn't want to do that."

"Liz wouldn't want to do what?" Paige turned abruptly; Liz had just opened the door to the apartment. "And what smells so good? Holy crap, is that lasagna?"

Chris responded, "Yes, and it's fantastic. But Paige thinks you wouldn't want to go shopping for a formal dress with her."

Liz looked at Paige questioningly. "Well, that's just wrong. Since when wouldn't I want to go shopping with you? You look good in everything. That makes it fun and easy."

"You don't care about dresses." Paige knew that she was sounding strange, but she felt panicky.

Now Liz was staring at her. "I care about *you*. And I would love to go with you." Tilting her head slightly, she said, "What's really going on, Paige? What's wrong?"

Paige's eyes darted between Chris and Liz, suddenly feeling trapped, and she deflated.

"I just don't think that I'm the right person to go to a formal event like that."

Chris's whole demeanor shifted, and he chuckled. "Oh, baby. I'm a big, dumb hockey player. You are actually far more suited to this than I am. Or than any of the guys are. I need you to make me look good."

Liz smiled, gave him a little punch on the shoulder, and went to explore the leftover lasagna situation.

Paige looked skeptical.

"Seriously!" Chris was trying to convince her. "Paige, think about it. Think about Dmitry. And Natalia. Which one of *them* is more suited to formal wear?" Paige's mouth twitched. "And *Zee?* Please. Like that idiot is proper formal-event material."

She started to relax.

"Are you sure, Chris?"

He took her hands and looked her in her eyes. "*Yes*. One hundred percent. Trust me, baby, you will fit in so much better than I will."

"So, you're going, right?" Liz was talking with her mouth full, and Paige just shook her head and rolled her eyes.

"Yes, I will go."

"Excellent. Let's start looking at dress styles for you!"

Liz scurried off to grab her laptop, and Chris put his hand on Paige's cheek.

"Thank you, baby." He leaned in and kissed her gently. "I really appreciate it. You're going to be amazing. You're always amazing."

"So you won't leave me alone there, right?"

Chris smiled, pulling her toward him so she could rest her head on his shoulder. "Only when I have to do something like take pictures. But then I'll make sure you're with someone you know. Deal?"

"Deal."

***

Paige ended up having a lovely time. Chris knew his way around these kinds of events, and he talked with people effortlessly.

"I still find it amazing that you consider yourself shy, Chris," she said as they were sipping cocktails. "You seem to be a complete natural at this sort of thing." She took a moment to appreciate just how handsome he was. "And you look incredible in a tux."

His smile was genuine, and she felt that little flutter in her chest.

"Thank you. I have worked really hard at handling the social part of being in the pros. It didn't come naturally at first, so that's a huge compliment, baby. I really appreciate it."

He paused for a moment, suddenly looking slightly shy, and took her hand, looking down at her fingers. "I've always kinda hoped that maybe, when

204

I'm done playing, I might be able to get into the broadcasting side of things."

He glanced up at her. She looked thoughtful for a moment and then said, with all sincerity, "Chris, I think you'd be great at that."

"Really?" He sounded hopeful.

"Really. I mean it. I think you would be amazing."

Picking up her hand and kissing her knuckles, he said, "Thank you. That means a lot to me." He smiled at her for a moment before adding, "By the way, you are, by far, the most beautiful woman in the room. But I knew that before we even got here."

She had already met a few of the other wives and girlfriends who were there, so she had people to stand with while Chris and the other players took care of their team-related duties. Paige was impressed again at how easily they accepted her and how kind and welcoming they were.

Chris held her hand in the car on their way back to his apartment, gently stroking the back of her hand with his thumb.

"Thank you for coming with me."

"You're very welcome, Chris. I had fun."

A few minutes later, he added quietly, "You know, you do belong."

She looked at him questioningly.

"I just sometimes get the feeling that you think, maybe, that you don't." He grimaced a bit. "I'm not saying this very well."

She squeezed his hand and said, "I think I understand. And thank you."

He looked over at her briefly. "I can't tell if you

believe me or not."

She didn't answer, and he let it go. He twined his fingers through hers and just held her hand.

Chapter Twenty-Six

They stayed at Paige's apartment the weekend that Liz went to North Carolina for her rescheduled visit with her friend. Before leaving, she had solemnly vowed to them that she wouldn't return until Sunday night, no matter what.

She ended with, "So, Paige, cheer your heart out!" before racing out the door ahead of the incoming pillow thrown by Paige. They could hear her laughing from the hallway.

***

"What do you mean 'trade deadline'? I thought all of the players had contracts," Paige asked while sipping on a glass of wine. They had just finished cleaning up after dinner at her apartment and now were just sitting together, talking about their lives.

Chris had mentioned the upcoming trade deadline in passing, but Paige had stopped to question him about it.

"We do all have contracts. But the teams can

decide to trade to get players they feel they need to make a run at the playoffs. Or, on the other hand, if teams are definitely not in the running this season, they can trade players to get more draft picks or minor league prospects that look promising for the future."

"But you have a *contract,* right? With the Guardians." She pressed him harder on this point. "That's what you told me, that you're in the second year of an eight-year contract."

"Yes," he replied. "And I want to be here the whole eight years. I love this team." He paused and looked at her. "And you. I love being here with you. But my contract isn't a one hundred percent guarantee that I won't get traded."

"That doesn't make any sense," she said, shaking her head. "What's the point of having a contract if you can still just be traded away? I mean, that makes it sound like players are baseball cards or lunch snacks." She was starting to get upset.

"If there's a trade, the new team takes on the player's contract, so that there's no financial loss for the player," he tried to explain. "The contract is to make sure that players don't suddenly get cut, or traded, without being paid."

"No *financial* loss to the player, maybe. But picking up and moving? With no notice?" This was clearly affecting her more than Chris thought it would. "Players have families too. What about their kids? This sounds completely crazy. Does this really happen?"

"Well, yeah, it does. There aren't tons of trades each year, but players do get traded, and they move to their new city to finish off the season." Chris was trying to be matter-of-fact about this.

"Just like that?"

"Kind of, yeah. Just like that. It's the way that all pro sports work."

"Really?" She was agitated now. "Tennis? How about golf? I don't see golf players traded to wherever the hell someone else wants them to be."

"Those are both individual sports, Paige. Football, basketball, baseball, hockey, soccer…they all have trade deadlines, and players can be moved from team to team." He was trying to be soothing, trying to calm her down. Chris reached out for her hand, but she pulled away from him, and he started to feel concerned.

"Oh my God, you just don't get it, do you?"

"I can see that you're upset, baby. This is the way that hockey works. In the minors, players can be switched back and forth too, sometimes even between minor league teams in the same feeder structure. And there are guys who sign two-way contracts with the AHL and NHL every year—they play in Hershey just *hoping* they'll be called to DC on a moment's notice, because it's an amazing opportunity to be in an NHL game." He reached out again to hold her hand. "Even if it's just to sub in for an injured player. Even if they get sent right back down to the minors again because the player is back. Any minor league player would gladly hop a flight right this minute if they thought they were going to get a chance at the NHL level."

She stared at him as if he had lost his mind.

"So you'd be fine with this?" she asked,

incredulous. "You'd be fine if you were traded in the next few weeks?"

He didn't know how to answer.

"No, of course not. I wouldn't be *fine*. I don't want to leave DC. I love it here. This team has fantastic chemistry, and God knows I wouldn't want to leave you in the middle of the school year when you couldn't come with me right away. But I don't think they're looking to trade me, Paige."

"Oh my God, Chris. You really just don't understand."

"No, I'm not sure that I do." He took a breath, thinking, trying to explain. "My window for playing professionally is limited, Paige. It's finite. There's an end date...there is for all players, as much as none of us want to think about it. Aside from a career-ending injury..." Paige blanched, "...there's simply a limit as to how old you can be and still play in a way that is of value to your team. Sometimes that's when the trades happen." She was getting paler. "When a player is getting closer to the end of his career, sometimes he'll be traded a few times, to teams that need his specific skill set for a year or two or for a playoff run.

"Every player wants to play as long as possible. I've worked my whole life for this; I don't want to give it up. So, if that means I get traded to another team, well, I'll go. So I can keep playing. But baby, I would want you to come with me."

"So, there comes a time when players are moving every year?" Paige had stood up to put her empty wineglass on the counter and hadn't sat back down.

"Sometimes, but baby, that's years down the road. We can work this out. And there's a need for good teachers everywhere."

"This is insane." She had started pacing.

"It's sports. It's the way the game is played. Literally." He was still feeling slightly ill about this whole conversation.

"I can't do this." Her anxiety was clear in her voice, and she was gesturing with her hands while continuing to pace.

Chris felt sudden pressure in his chest.

"Can't do what?" He didn't want to ask the question, but he had to.

"This. This lifestyle. This craziness. I can't function not knowing where I would be living from year to year. Why did you even bother to buy a house?"

"Baby…" Chis stood up and walked toward her, trying to calm her, but she interrupted, continuing to pace.

"You don't understand!" Paige was beginning to raise her voice. "I have a great life here. I love it *here*. I make a difference *here*. I love my school. I love the teachers and the rest of the staff. I love my students! I love…"

"Me?"

He asked it very softly, but it stopped her in her tracks, and she spun to face him and choked on a sob.

She whispered, "Yes…" Tears were forming in her eyes.

"But." There was no questioning in his voice. He felt the qualification that was coming and steeled

211

himself as if he were watching a punch heading for his gut.

"Chris, please…" Paige took a step toward him, realizing suddenly where this conversation was heading.

"But it's not enough." His voice was harsh and gravelly. It was the best he could do; he could feel tears threatening, and he didn't want to go down that road.

"Chris…"

He closed his eyes for a moment, bracing himself for the next step. Opening his eyes again, he took her hands in his and looked her in the eye.

"Paige, stop. Don't say anything more. I get it."

"But…"

"Stop. Please." Paige was quiet. "I love you, Paige. I love you, and I want a life with you. That's simply not going to change; I know you don't understand that, but it's true. You are in my heart, and that's not going to go away, not ever." He paused a moment. "You just told me that you love me. Is that true?"

She nodded, tears in her eyes.

"You're sure?" His voice was rough again as he pressed her to answer. "I *need* to know, Paige. It's important."

On a broken sob, and sounding a little frustrated, Paige said, "Yes, it's true. I love you, Chris. But…"

He put his fingertips on her lips to stop her from saying more and then continued quietly.

"Then here's what's going to happen. I'm going to give you your space. I'm going to walk away right now and give you the space you need, for as long as you need it." He saw her start to cry, and he felt his own heart breaking but continued, pushing through the lump in his throat. "But I'm not giving up. Unless and until you tell me you don't love me, I'm not giving up on this, on us.

"I *know* we are meant to be together, Paige. I *know* it." He wasn't sure anymore that he was going to make it through this without breaking down. "So I'm going to do what I do, and I'm going to chase my dreams. And that's you. A life together with you is my dream. I will give you your space, but I'm not going away."

Paige was crying and looked a bit confused.

Chris summoned every last bit of courage he had, put his hands on either side of her face, drew her to him gently, and kissed her softly, lingering, trying to savor the feeling of electricity between them, not knowing when he would feel it again.

And then turned and walked away before she could see the tears that were starting.

Paige stood, stunned, as the door closed behind him, not fully understanding what had just happened. They had just broken up? Maybe? They were at least taking a break in their relationship.

But he doesn't understand. I can't do this.

Then again, she wasn't sure she understood. Sadness and confusion gave way to a kind of grief, and she sat on the couch and let herself cry.

***

Chris sat in his car, trying to breathe past the feeling of panic gripping him, trying to swallow around the lump in his throat.

Fuck. Fuck. Fuck.

He wasn't sure he had done the right thing, except he *knew* that letting her break up with him was absolutely the *wrong* thing, and it was clear that was where the conversation had been headed.

He had no idea how to navigate this. He had sounded very sure of himself when he walked away from Paige, but the truth was it had been a kind of Hail Mary pass to keep her from shutting the door on their relationship. As long as it hadn't ended for certain, and as long as he knew that she loved him, there was hope.

Chris put his head back on the headrest and closed his eyes, steadying his breathing. When he had calmed down a bit, he started the car to drive home.

Instinct had him dialing the phone before he even realized what he was doing.

"Hey, Becks, what's up?"

"Fuck." Chris shook his head. "Fuck, Micky, I didn't even realize I was calling you. I don't know what I'm doing."

Five hundred miles away in Montreal, Micky sat up straight, worry creasing his face. "Becks, where are you? What's wrong? What's going on?"

"She wants to end it." The brutality of what he was saying finally hit him. He choked on the words and pulled the car over into a parking lot, realizing he wasn't able to keep driving.

"Oh, shit. Becks?" Micky heard a sob on the other end of the line. "Becks, are you there?" One more choking sob. "Talk to me, Becks. Please."

A few deep breaths and Chris said, "Yeah, I'm here. Fuck me. I'm sorry. I shouldn't have called."

"Bullshit. That's bullshit. I'm exactly who you should have called."

The vehemence in his voice brought a small smile to Chris's face.

"Talk to me, Becks. Tell me what happened."

So he did, and they talked about it—well, Chris talked, and Micky mostly cursed.

"And after all of that, you still want this, Becks? Really?"

Chris sighed and responded, "More than anything, Micky. Fuck, almost more than playing."

Another curse from Micky, followed by a gruff, "Don't you dare quit for a woman. Don't you fucking dare."

"Shit, Mick, I'm not gonna quit. I'm just fucking wrecked right now."

"Okay." There was a longish pause before Micky continued, "I mean it, though. You call me if you are ever thinking of that shit again, right? You have worked your whole fucking life for this career, Becks."

"I know. I'm not gonna quit." With a rough edge to his voice, he added, "But goddamn it, Micky, I've waited my whole fucking life for her."

Micky sighed and simply said, "I'm here for you, brother. You know that."

"Yeah. Thanks, Mick. I'll be okay."

***

When Liz got back to the apartment, Paige was

curled up on the couch, asleep. She awoke as Liz finished getting her stuff in from her weekend in North Carolina.

"Hey."

"Hi, Paige. Sorry, I didn't mean to wake you." Liz sat down on the couch and looked at her friend curiously. Paige almost never napped, and it was a rare thing to find her asleep on the couch. "Are you feeling okay?"

Paige sat up, stretched, and rubbed her eyes. "Yes." She thought a moment and then said, "No. No, I'm not okay."

Liz was startled by the sight of tears in her eyes. "Paige, what's wrong?" she asked worriedly.

Paige said, "We broke up."

Liz stared at her. "What?" She shook her head. "No…what?"

"We broke up. I think."

"You think? I don't understand, Paige." Liz moved in to give her a hug, and Paige started crying.

"He wants a commitment, Liz. He wants more than I can give him. He could be traded, and that would mean moving God-knows-where, and I *can't.* I have a life here. Everything I've been working and planning for in my life is *here.*" Paige paused for a moment and then got up and went to get headache medicine and a glass of water. "God, my head is pounding."

"He broke up with you because you wouldn't commit?"

Paige sat back down again. "No."

"He broke up with you because of something

else? What happened?"

"No…"

Liz looked confused and then said, "Wait, Paige…did you break up with him?" Paige sniffled, and Liz whispered, "Oh, shit."

"It's too fast, Liz. And it's too much, and I can't give him what he wants, and I don't want that lifestyle. I don't belong."

"What lifestyle?" Liz asked carefully. She didn't want to upset Paige more than she already was but wanted to understand what her friend was thinking.

Paige waved her hand, saying, "The whole thing. The pro-athlete, in-the-news, life-is-not-your-own thing. The uncertainty. The scrutiny."

Liz sighed, feeling the press of Paige's sadness. "So, what happened? Do you want to talk about it?"

Paige sniffled a little. "We were talking about how contracts worked and how it was possible for him to be traded even though he has a contract, and I just…I couldn't take it, Liz." She shrugged. "I told him that I need to be *here* and that everything I love is *here*…" She gave a short sob. "And then he asked if I loved him…and I said yes…and then he said, 'But.'" Paige looked at Liz, eyes starting to well up again.

Once again, Liz whispered, "Oh, shit…"

"Yeah."

"Paige…" Her heart was breaking for her friend but also for Chris.

"So he said he's going to give me space but that he won't give up unless I tell him that I don't love him. But that doesn't even make sense, because he could be gone by the trade deadline." She choked

217

out a sob. "Or next year, or whenever the team decides they don't want him anymore, and I can't live my life like that." Another choking sob and then she just sat and cried.

Liz hugged her again. "Oh, Paige. I'm so sorry."

A few minutes later, she sniffled and then sighed. "Thank you. I'm sorry too." She sat back again and then stood up. "I'm going to take a shower and go to bed. I don't even understand how we left things. I'm confused and tired, and my head hurts."

One more hug and she headed off to her room.

Chapter Twenty-Seven

There was a cloud of unhappiness hanging over the apartment the next few days. Liz didn't want to push Paige to talk if she didn't want to, but there was a subject that needed to be addressed, so she sat Paige down on the couch.

"You know I'm not great about subtlety and dancing around tough subjects, so I'm just going to come out and ask and hope that you give me a pass on tactlessness because, you know, it's me." Taking a deep breath, she asked, "I need to know if you will be upset if I stay in contact with Chris."

Paige had some tears starting, but she didn't look angry.

"I will be staying in touch with Zee—we've become really good friends already—and that means, by extension, I will sometimes see Chris." Another deep breath. "But Chris feels like a really good friend to me too, and I don't know what to do about that."

She continued kind of in a rush, trying to just let her thoughts flow out and see where they led; she had known Paige long enough to have a solid hope that she would understand this manner of processing.

"He's not a jerk, and he didn't treat you badly—you know I wouldn't stay friends with an asshole—but on the other hand, you're my best friend in the entire world, and I don't want you to be more upset by this, so if you need me to not see him, I will, Paige. But I'm also kind of worried about him, because I know this has got to be wrecking him too…" She winced a little at Paige's reaction to this statement. "…and I know he's not my responsibility and he has other friends, but shit, I feel like I need to talk with him, but I don't want to do anything that will make you more unhappy, and I don't want to lose his friendship, or Zee's, but you've been with me through pretty much every hard time in my life, so I *can't* lose you, so I don't really know what to do."

Paige stared at her for a moment before saying, "There was so little sentence structure to what you just said that I want to get out a red pen."

Liz gave a brief laugh and got a smile from Paige in return.

"It's okay, Liz. He's your friend too."

Liz squeezed her hands. "Are you sure?"

Paige sighed and said, "Yeah, I'm sure."

Liz gave her a tight hug. "Thank you."

***

Liz: Do you want to get coffee sometime?

Chris blinked in grateful surprise to see the text from Liz.

Chris: Yes when and where?

Liz sighed in relief, and they made plans to meet at a local Starbucks. She was waiting on the sidewalk when Chris walked up, and she hugged him fiercely enough that his emotional walls crumbled a little. When he squeezed her back in return, he said, "Shit, we should have met at my apartment. I don't want to be unmanly right here on the sidewalk."

She chuckled but said, "I'm so sorry, Chris."

One more squeeze and he said, "Me too. Let's go get coffee."

Once they were seated with their drinks—regular coffee for Chris and a sweet, frothy concoction for Liz with extra shots of espresso—he asked the obvious question. "Does Paige know you're here?"

"Here, specifically? No. But she knows that I want to stay in contact with you and that I will be seeing you." She looked at him sideways and said, "That is, if it's okay with you. Fuck, these things feel so complicated. I consider you a good friend, Chris, and would like to still get together sometimes, you know, with Zee or whatever."

"Of course, you idiot." He smiled at her. "I was really glad you texted."

Liz exhaled in relief and then asked, quietly, "Do you want to talk about it?"

Chris rubbed the back of his neck and looked at the ceiling. "I guess? I don't know. Honestly, I don't understand what happened. Everything seemed fine, and then, suddenly, it wasn't."

"You're an athlete," she said. "You live in that world and you always have. It feels completely normal to you. The risks, the public attention, the uncertainty. To Paige it's scary as hell. I think the idea that it's possible for you to be traded was the final catalyst for all of this. That's not something she had considered; she thought having a contract meant you were here for sure, at least for the next six years. I think that started a cascade of fear and doubt about, well, everything."

"Shit." Chris fiddled with his coffee cup. "Yeah, that fits with the timing of this."

"If the two of you were together, and you were traded, it would mean moving to God-knows-where, at essentially a moment's notice, with almost no input from her.

"There are places that you will never live, no matter if she would want to. Like, say, Omaha." At a strange look from Chris, she clarified, "I'm not saying she would ever want to move to Omaha, or Santa Fe, but the minute she commits to being with an NHL player, those options are gone."

Chris was looking thoughtful and a bit sad.

"Paige plans her life, Chris." Liz so wanted him to understand. "It's one of the reasons she's so good at her job. It's not that she has no flexibility—she does—but she is prepared and organized. Plan and contingency plan. Always."

He sat back and asked, "Are you saying this is doomed? Because I can't accept that. Three things, Liz. There are three things in my life that have been crystal clear to me. And she's one of them."

"No, sweetie, I'm not saying anything like that." Liz put her hand on his arm. "She loves you, Chris. In a way and with a depth that I have never seen in her before. But I think something about that is scaring her to death."

Chris's face became almost unreadable; there was a mix of emotions that seemed to war across his features. Hope, joy, sadness, love, desperation.

"I won't just walk away from this," he said in a voice that had gone rough with emotion. "I can't. I won't push her, but I won't leave, either. Not unless she tells me she doesn't love me, Liz. As long as she loves me, then I'm in this for the long term."

Liz smiled at the conviction in his voice and said, "So, low-speed chase?"

He smiled too but said, "You're goddamn right I'm going to be chasing Paige."

"You know I love you, right, Chris?" She stood up and walked toward him as he rose from his chair. "You're already family to me. Paige just isn't quite ready to believe it yet."

Chris hugged her tight for a moment and said, "So you believe in this?"

Liz pushed back from him and looked him in the eye. "I wouldn't be here if I didn't, sweetie."

Chapter Twenty-Eight

When Paige got to her desk at school Monday morning, there was a vase with one perfect red rose and a card that simply said:

> *Had I the heavens' embroidered cloths,*
> *Enwrought with golden and silver light,*

She smiled a bit sadly and tucked the card into her wallet.

***

Chris wasn't particularly looking forward to the next weekly radio call-in. There were some real hockey-related things to talk about—the trades that had just happened, for one—but it was inevitable that they would poke at his relationship to try to get details about Paige, and this week, that was not going to be fun.

"Hey, Chris! Thanks for calling in. Things have been on a little hot streak lately for you guys. Nice score the other night, by the way."

"Thanks! Happy to talk with you guys. Yeah, we've had some puck luck, and a bit of it rubbed off on me the other day. I got a great pass from Navee—he put it right on my tape. It would have sucked to miss after such a nice setup."

"Yeah, that guy seems to be really kicking up his game this season. Seems to be winning a good number of face-offs too."

"Definitely. He puts in a lot of work on that. He's an important part of our penalty kill in that way too. If you can keep the other guys from getting the puck and maybe send it down the ice so they have to chase it, it knocks a few seconds off the clock until you get your guy back." *So far, so good. Keep talking hockey, please.*

They discussed the trades—Washington had picked up a veteran forward as well as a defenseman—and the upcoming schedule.

"So, are you guys looking at the playoffs already? Or do you not talk about that yet?"

"No, we're looking at tomorrow night's game, always. Gotta get after what's right in front of you if you even want to make it to the playoffs, right?"

Keep talking hockey.

"Yeah, but you gotta have it in the back of your mind that you guys are only one point down from New Jersey in the division."

Chris laughed and said, "I truly try not to think about it. One game at a time."

And then JD chimed in, "So, Chris, how's that hot girlfriend of yours?"

Shit.

"She's…" *What? What is she? Not really my girlfriend, that's what she is.* "I'm sure she's doing well. It's a busy time of year for her too."

As soon as the sentence was out of his mouth, Chris was kicking himself.

"You're 'sure she's doing well?'" another host asked. "That sounds like you don't really know."

"What's going on with you two? Trouble in paradise?"

Fuck. Me.

"Well, things get crazy, and schedules are frustrating, so…" Chris was looking for a way to deflect this, hoping that they would drop it or that his time on-air would run out.

"Hey, man, we don't mean to pry…"

"Yes, we do," another one interrupted.

The third chimed in with, "We *totally* mean to pry."

Laughing, the first one said, "Okay, yes, we do. We're prying. Are you guys on the outs? Inquiring minds want to know, Chris."

Chris said, "Guys, I've got my mind wrapped around hockey. Looking forward to the next game. And the game after that. And hopefully lots of games after that. So, that's where my head is right now."

They relented. "All right, sounds like we're just relegated strictly to hockey talk with Chris right now, and we're up against a break. Hope things are going okay, pal, and we'll talk to you next week."

"Everything's good. Thanks for having me on, guys. It's a pleasure talking to you."

Chris hung up the phone, put his head in his

hands, with his elbows on his knees, and just stared at the floor for a few minutes. *I don't fucking need to be reminded of what I'm missing and have it broadcast to the entire DC area.*

***

The next Monday when Paige walked into her classroom, there was a vase on her desk with two red roses. The card read:

The blue and the dim and the dark cloths
Of night and light and the half light,

Paige sighed, wiped a small tear, and tucked the card into her wallet with the first one. He had not contacted her in any other way than this, these roses, since telling her she could have all the time she needed.

***

Zee knew what had happened between them, although Chris had tried not to make it too widely known. Too many questions, and he wanted to keep his head in the game as much as he could, but it had been impossible to keep it from Zee, considering how close they had all become.

Zee, for his part, was being admirably discreet and doing his best not to disrupt things in the locker room. Well, at least not in *that* way. Pranks always made people feel better. Laughter was great medicine.

Chris did his best to keep his personal life from affecting his game, and he succeeded on the ice, but off the ice, even just in the locker room, was a different story. Everything just felt…off.

***

By the third Monday, she wasn't surprised to see the vase with three red roses and knew what the card would say before she read it:

I would spread the cloths under your feet:

***

Life was going on as before; Liz watched games and sometimes met with Zee and/or Chris when they were in town. Paige graded papers and worried about her students' test scores.

And Chris…well, Chris played hockey and forced himself to do no more than send Paige roses every week. When he saw Liz, they usually didn't talk about Paige or the relationship or anything of importance. The concern showed on her face and in how hard she hugged him when they saw each other.

After one of their coffee dates, however, Liz started to leave but turned back to the table and sat down again.

"She's been taking skating lessons."

Chris was clearly startled.

"Really?" His look was mixed—part happiness, but with a clear thread of disappointment.

"What's wrong?" Liz reached out and put her hand on his arm. "I'm sorry, Chris, I thought knowing that would make you happy."

"It does. It should. I just…" Chris rubbed his hand on the back of his neck and looked up at the ceiling for a moment, gathering himself before continuing. "I just thought I would be the one to teach her."

Liz laughed and said, "No way, Chris. That would never happen."

He looked confused and a little hurt.

"You've gotta trust me on this one, Chris. Even if you guys weren't…even if you were together, she never would have let you teach her. Too much pressure. She'd rather learn on her own or from a neutral third party."

He still looked unsure, so she continued, "Don't be offended, at all, truly. That's just the way she is. She has her own style of learning new things, and she almost always prefers it to be by herself, at least at first. Once she's feeling more confident, she can handle the group dynamic better."

Chris stared at her, one eyebrow raised, and she stared back for a moment, wheels turning in her head.

Finally, Liz said, "Huh. Yeah, she definitely needs space to learn lessons. Even about herself."

Chris finally gave her a smile that looked a little more hopeful.

***

229

Monday. Four red roses, and the card:

But I, being poor, have only my dreams;

Paige snorted. *You're hardly poor, Chris.* She immediately felt a pang of regret at the slightly snide thought. He had never flaunted his salary, never made her feel "less than" because she wasn't in a high-paying, high-power job. He seemed to be genuinely impressed with her passion for teaching and supportive of her career, understanding how much it meant to her.

***

The playoffs were rapidly approaching, and the Guardians had just clinched their playoff spot—they had one more road trip, and then they were back in DC for the last game before the first round of the playoffs started.

Chris was going to put his head back and try to catch a little sleep on the flight, but Zee slid into a seat beside him shortly after takeoff.

"Hey, Becks." Zee was speaking uncharacteristically quietly. "I just wanted to check in. Any changes? How are you doing?"

While initially irritated by the interruption of his planned solitude, Chris found himself grateful for the concern.

"Nothing new. I send her roses every Monday, but other than that, I'm just trying to give her space."

"Shit. Sorry, man." He moved as if he were

going to get up but then asked, "Really, though, you okay? I mean, you're playing well, but you're definitely not the same. I don't think anyone else notices as much, but I do." With a much more characteristic little smirk, he added, "I need you to be on your 'A' game to make me look good, ya know."

Chris thought for a moment about how to answer. "I'm dealing. Hockey for me, roses for her. After the season is over, I can think about what more to do, but until then, I'm just trying to focus on us playing hockey as far into June as possible."

Zee clapped him on the shoulder as he got up to return to his seat.

"Sounds good, man. Hang in there."

***

Another Monday, with five red roses, and another card to tuck into her wallet:

I have spread my dreams under your feet;

Well, that was certainly true. Chris had worn his heart on his sleeve from day one. Gentle, sweet, unguarded, and vulnerable. Paige sniffled and wiped away a few tears, trying to get ready for her first class of the day.

There was only one more line in the poem. *What's going to happen after that?*

Chapter Twenty-Nine

"What's up?" Liz asked after hearing Paige cursing at her laptop.

"What? Oh, sorry. I didn't even realize that I had said anything out loud." She took a deep breath and blew it back out again. "Just an email from my mom. I seriously don't understand why Becca even taught her how to use the computer sometimes."

Liz walked closer to Paige and leaned against the wall, drinking a beer.

"I swear, Paige, sometimes I hate your mother so much I don't know how to handle it. I know that you have worked so hard on personal stuff, and the changes in you have been amazing over the years," she took a drink before continuing, "but she still makes me furious. She still intentionally pushes every one of your buttons. She does everything in her power to undermine your confidence."

Paige grimaced. "Yeah. But I am really proud of myself for where I am, you know?"

"God yes." Liz sat down at the kitchen island barstool and leaned on the counter. "As you should

be. But…"

Paige leaned on the other side of the counter. "I'll bite, but what?"

"You still don't appreciate yourself."

The answer surprised Paige, and her face showed it. "What do you mean?"

Liz thought for a moment, trying to put together the best way to describe what she was thinking. "I'm having a hard time coming up with the right way to get this across, so please bear with me and don't get upset, but I'm talking about self-worth."

"Oh, I don't think that's fair. I know my worth. I know that I'm good at my job, and I don't allow myself to be treated badly."

"Yes, that's true. But…" Fishing around a bit more, she said, "But that's just it, Paige. You know your worth *as a teacher.* You know your worth *as a friend*—shit, at least I hope you do—you know your worth *as a sister.* But you measure your worth by what you give to others. I'm not sure you really understand that you, just *you,* have worth separate and apart from what you contribute. That just you, standing here, right now, deserve good things for yourself. Not because you have done anything. Just *because.*"

Paige was quiet for several long moments and then simply said, softly, "Keep going."

Liz paused another moment, a bit nervous to broach the subject that they had avoided all this time.

"If one of your teacher friends came to you and told you that she was dating someone amazing…someone like Chris…you would be thrilled for her. You would never *for one second* doubt that your friend deserved to be happy. Never."

Paige flinched, visibly affected by what Liz was saying.

"You would tell your friend that she deserved every minute of happiness; you would do everything possible to convince her to believe in herself." Liz touched her arm gently to get Paige to focus on her. "Wouldn't you?"

Paige's eyes were bright.

Liz repeated quietly, "Wouldn't you tell your friend to believe that she deserves every sliver of happiness that life is offering her?"

Paige gave her a little smile but said, "I need some time to think, okay?"

"Of course, Paige." She walked around the counter and hugged Paige. "I love you like crazy. You know that."

"Love you too."

Liz walked down the hallway to her bedroom but stopped suddenly and turned around, looking intently back at Paige.

"What?" Paige asked.

Liz stared at Paige until she asked again, "What, Liz? You look like you've just solved a puzzle or something."

"Chris can take care of you."

Paige's eyes got wide—she very briefly looked like a deer in headlights—but after a pause she said, "I'm not sure what you mean."

"You have spent your entire life being the one who takes care of other people. And yet this man has every means at his disposal, and the desire, to take care of *you.*"

Paige's face was almost an unreadable mask as she looked at Liz.

"I just want you to realize, Paige, that just because he can take care of you doesn't mean that all of the horrible things your mom says are true. It doesn't mean you're taking advantage of him. It doesn't mean you're not able to take care of yourself or that you are somehow a failure. *You deserve happiness, and you are worthy of love.*"

"I need time," Paige whispered. "Let me think about this."

"I will. Sorry. I just realized that, and it caught me off guard."

As Liz disappeared into her room, Paige whispered, "Me too."

Chapter Thirty

Chris moved robotically through pre-game preparations and the on-ice warm-up. Nothing had been quite right with him since Paige broke things off, but the team had just gotten back in town from the last road trip of the season, and with the time change and travel schedule, he had been feeling more fatigued than usual and a bit irritable. And sometime over the last two days he had managed to tweak an ab muscle.

"Becks, you okay? You're looking kinda gray, man. That is not a good color for you."

"I'm fine," Chris snapped back at Navee. Derek Navikov played center and was normally the third forward on the line with Chris and Zee. Chris softened his tone and added, "Sorry, man. I have some fucked-up pre-game jitters tonight. I just puked like a rookie. I'll get my shit together before the puck drops."

"No worries." Navee slapped Chris on the back of the head. "We expect this shit from you. Everyone knows you're a slacker, asshole."

Chris managed a grin at the jibe.

The first period passed without incident. With no score, no penalties, and only ten total shots on goal between the two teams, there were very few play stoppages other than the TV time-outs. Both teams were moving fast, and the lines were rapidly cycling on and off the ice as each team tried to break through the other's defense to get to the net. At the first intermission, players were breathing hard in the locker room, trying to catch their breath and get their legs ready to keep up the pace in the second period.

Chris leaned on his stick with his head down as he sat on the bench in the locker room, trying to listen to the coaches and *not* think about his personal life. He rehydrated, hoping that would help with the headache that had started pressing behind his eyes, and joined the team back on the ice as the second period started.

The two teams were very evenly matched, and the blazing pace continued through the first ten minutes of the second period. The tide finally started to turn with a hooking penalty against the Winnipeg Rockets, putting the Guardians on the first power play of the game.

Dmitry sent a rocket of a slapshot top shelf over the goalie's glove and into the net, and the arena exploded with lights and sound. Every Guards fan was on their feet cheering as the big right-winger glided over the ice and pumped his arm in his "just scored a goal" move. His teammates swarmed him on the ice, and he skated over to tap gloves with everyone on the bench.

The Rockets needed to win this game to make it into the playoffs, and tempers were starting to fray as the second period wound down with the score still one-nothing in favor of the Guardians. Play was becoming increasingly more physical, and as the Rockets got frustrated, it was pretty clear there would probably be at least one fight before the game was over.

Chris took a cross-ice pass from Zee and was zooming up the rink when he was caught by a Rockets defenseman in a huge open-ice hit. With a shoulder to his right-hand mid-section, Chris was knocked up off his skates and went down, sprawling across the ice.

He started to get up, managing to get one skate under him before he simply fell face first onto the ice.

And stopped moving.

***

Paige was sitting in her room, spending a bit of quiet time reading for pleasure rather than grading papers or prepping for class. As usual, she could hear the occasional exclamation from the living room as Liz watched yet another hockey game. She felt her heart catch for a moment thinking about Chris as she heard Liz shout, "Yes! Goal! Hot damn!" She pushed the twinge down, determined to ignore the lump in her throat that happened when she imagined his smile.

She had just finished a chapter and was closing her book when she heard Liz calling her.

"Paige!"

She started to get up to go to the living room to see what was happening.

"Paige!"

Liz sounded worried, not excited.

"Paige! Hurry!"

Paige raced down the short hallway, alarmed by the fear in Liz's voice, and arrived in the living room to see Liz standing in front of the couch, staring at the TV.

"What? What's going on?"

Liz pointed to the television, and Paige turned to see that there was a player down on the ice. One of the Guardians.

"Oh no! Who is that?"

Liz looked at Paige, who felt her stomach plummet to the floor. Her breath caught, and it felt like her heart stopped as she looked back at the screen.

Paige shook her head slowly and whispered, "No."

It was Chris, the number fourteen on his jersey unmistakable as he was lying almost entirely face down.

"No. No. He's not moving." Paige turned to Liz, her face ashen. "What happened?" Her voice was wavering, rising as the fear spread. "No, no, no, *why isn't he moving?*"

"He got hit." Liz looked back at Paige, wide-eyed, for a split second before returning her gaze to the screen. "He got hit," she repeated. "It was hard, but it wasn't dirty."

The trainers were on the ice with a stretcher

when they saw Chris move his arms and legs, like he was trying to get up.

Paige felt her heart start beating again, but the panic wasn't going away.

"He started to get up after the hit, but then I think he passed out." Liz turned her attention back to Paige when Chris was wheeled off the ice on the stretcher, and the coverage cut to commercial.

Paige was standing stock-still, eyes wide, heart racing.

"Oh God. Oh my God." She turned to Liz. "What's going on? What's wrong with him? Is he going to be okay?" She put her face in her hands. "This can't be happening." *No no no no no no.*

Liz took her hand and looked her in the eye.

"Paige. Look at me." When she had Paige's focus, she added, "Listen. Go to your room and get a bag. Put in a sweatshirt, socks, underwear, deodorant, your toothbrush, and your phone charger. Then come back here. We're going to the hospital."

Paige nodded mutely and scurried to her room, following the simple instructions without question, relieved to have directions. When she got back to the living room a few minutes later, she found Liz waiting with her own bag, and she dutifully followed Liz to the garage and got in her car. Distantly, she thought, *Am I in shock? Maybe I'm in shock. Is this what shock feels like?*

There's one line of the poem left.

She sat quietly in the passenger seat as Liz drove out of the garage and onto the main road but snapped out of her zombie-like state when Liz turned on the radio and tuned it to the station broadcasting the game play-by-play.

"What?" Paige was stunned, suddenly furious. *"What the hell, Liz?* How can you care about the score of the game? Chris is hurt! He was unconscious! He wasn't moving! I can't believe you care who wins!"

"Paige," Liz said in a soothing voice. "Every fan is worried about Chris. The announcers are going to give an update on his condition as soon as they hear. We might find out from the radio before we can find out from the hospital."

"Oh." Paige's anger evaporated, realizing that of course Liz was worried about Chris. But now that one emotion had broken through her veneer of shock, the rest were following, and she was starting to cry. "I'm sorry." She was shaking again. "Oh my God, I'm so scared."

"I know, Paige. I know."

"He has to be okay. He has to." She turned to Liz, pleading, "He *has to.*"

I have to get the last line of the poem.

Liz took Paige's hand and squeezed it for a moment. "He will have the best possible care. Maybe it was nothing. Maybe he was just dehydrated or something really simple like that."

But neither of them believed that it was something simple. Pro-athletes are more careful than that. *Chris* was more careful than that.

"Okay," said Liz, taking a breath. "Let's think positive for a minute. We know that he was conscious and moving all his limbs before he left the ice. So there's that." She briefly looked over at

241

Paige to see that she was listening.

"Yes. That's good." *Please let him be all right. Please let him be all right. I need the last line. He can't leave me before the last line.* Paige tried to keep the waver out of her voice, asking, "What could have happened, do you think?"

"I'm really not sure. It was a big hit—highlight reel material—but it didn't look like it would knock him out. I mean, he even started to get up again before he lost consciousness."

They rode a few minutes without speaking, listening to the radio. The third period had just begun, and while the announcers confirmed that Chris had been taken to the hospital, there was still no word on what was wrong.

"How do you know where he is?" asked Paige, realizing suddenly that there were several major hospitals in DC itself, not to mention in the immediate suburbs.

"I asked Zee once where they would be taken if something happened on the ice. I was just curious."

Paige managed to snort out a small laugh. "Of course you did. Because you 'like to know stuff.'"

Liz smiled and added, "'About things. Lots of stuff about lots of things.'"

It was a catch phrase that Liz used to describe herself, with her penchant for asking tons of questions about almost anything. The normalcy of the quip helped Paige to relax just a bit.

"We'll be there soon, Paige. They will have taken him to Washington Hospital Center. It's going to take us a bit of time to find out where he is and what's going on, but as soon as the game is over,

I'll be able to talk to Zee to find out more information." She took Paige's hand again for a moment. "He's going to be okay."

Paige started to cry again. "I hope so." And then added, almost too quietly for Liz to hear, "He has to be." *Please, please, please...*

Chapter Thirty-One

Paige was pacing. She had called and made arrangements to miss work for the next few days. She had talked to Chris's mom to make sure she knew the latest. The team had already contacted his mom, but Paige felt she needed to talk with Emily directly. To make sure that his mom knew that she was at the hospital.

That Chris wouldn't be alone when he woke up.

That Paige hadn't abandoned him.

Except *he* didn't know that, because he was still in surgery. He was unconscious, having emergency surgery for a ruptured appendix, and he didn't know she was waiting for him, her heart twisting in her chest.

And so she paced, having nothing more of substance that she could do.

"Paige, sit." Liz patted the seat beside her. "Just for a minute."

Paige focused on her friend and then walked over and slumped into the chair. "I don't know what to do." Her breath caught. "Why did he play when he was sick? He must have known he was sick. How the hell can a person *not* know that they have appendicitis?"

She knew she was repeating herself—she had asked this same question out loud several times already and too many times to count in her head—but she was stuck in a loop, and until Chris was safely out of surgery, she didn't think she could break out of it.

Liz put her arm around Paige's shoulders and gave her a sideways hug.

"Hockey players play through minor stuff all the time," she said. "It's possible that he had only minor symptoms, not enough for him to think twice about it." At Paige's wry look, she added, "Or he was a big fucking idiot and wouldn't take himself out of the lineup because guys are dumbasses."

Paige barked out a small laugh and then sighed. "He's been in there a long time, Liz. I don't think that a normal appendectomy takes this long, even with a rupture." She stood up and started pacing again, unaware that she had done so.

"I'm sure they're taking extra time to make certain they have cleaned out all of the infection," Liz said, and Paige's face blanched.

"Oh God, what if he ends up with peritonitis? Or sepsis?" Her eyes welled again as her stomach clenched.

"Paige, breathe." Liz stood up and walked over to her. "He'll be out of surgery soon. It's going to be okay."

Zee came down the hall, carrying a tray with coffee for all of them, and asked, "Any word yet?"

"No," Paige replied, accepting the coffee with thanks and sitting down again, wrapping her hands around the warm cup.

Zee told her, "I've sent the other guys home and told Coach that I would keep him informed. No need for there to be a whole entourage here."

Just then a nurse came out, asking, "Christopher Beckman?"

Paige sprang up, almost spilling her coffee, and rushed over.

"Yes, I'm here for Chris. How is he? Is he okay? Can I see him?"

The nurse smiled and said, "He's out of surgery and in recovery. Please come with me and you can speak to the doctor."

Air flooded back into Paige's lungs. He had made it through surgery. She felt a little wobbly.

The news was good—the surgeon felt confident that they had managed to clean up everything, but it had been a longer than normal surgery due to the trauma. Piecing together what they could based on information from Zee and other players, Chris had probably been suffering from appendicitis for several days prior to the game. The on-ice hit had been hard enough to cause a rupture, and that pain had been severe enough to make him pass out.

The prognosis was excellent, and Paige felt a bit like she was going to ooze to the floor as the weight of that worry lifted from her.

"He's still coming out of anesthesia, but we will be transferring him to a regular room within the next half hour. We're going to keep him pretty heavily sedated through the night, and of course he's going to be on IV antibiotics for several days. We want to make sure there are no complications."

The doctor smiled reassuringly at Paige and added, "He's not going to be aware of anyone until tomorrow morning at least, but you will be able to sit with him as soon as he's admitted and in a regular room."

Paige started crying from relief, and Zee and Liz walked her back to the waiting room to sit down.

"I've gotta make some phone calls," Zee said, looking at Paige and Liz. "You two gonna be okay for a few minutes?"

"Yes," Paige replied. "Of course." She sniffed and sat up straighter. "I need to call his mom right away and let her know."

***

It was the wee hours of the morning before everything was settled, with Chris in a regular room. There was a small couch that folded down into a single bed and a recliner that pushed back almost flat.

Liz had grabbed the extra sheet, blanket, and pillow from the closet and was making up the couch in the hopes that Paige would get some sleep. Paige was currently sitting in a chair at Chris's side, holding his hand. He was, as the doctor had said, heavily sedated.

Paige got up and retrieved her sweatshirt from her bag, and Liz took the opportunity to encourage her to get some rest.

"This is going to be kind of a long haul, Paige.

You should grab some sleep now, while you can."

Paige sighed and responded, "I don't think I can sleep. I would rather sit next to him, you know? I just want to be near him."

She put the sweatshirt on and added, "Thank you for having me bring a bag. How did you know what...oh," she interrupted herself. "Of course, your parents. I'm sorry, I should have remembered."

Liz had lost both her parents, one to long term illness, the other to a heart attack. She had spent a large amount of time in hospital rooms as a result.

"Don't apologize," Liz responded. "It's nice to be able to put that knowledge to some good use. I don't know why, but I always seemed to get chilly in the hospital rooms. And it's really quite amazing how far clean socks, underwear, and deodorant can go toward making you feel human again. Not to mention clean teeth."

"Thank you." Paige started to tear up.

"Don't you start," warned Liz, feeling her eyes prickle. "We're both overtired, and if you start, then I'm going to. So cut it out."

Paige laughed softly and rolled her eyes, then took her seat again next to the bed.

Chapter Thirty-Two

Chris opened his eyes. He was groggy and confused and so very, very tired. *Hospital room?* He caught sight of brown hair. Someone had their head down on the side of the bed near his hand. He blinked his eyes, or thought he did, but there was more light coming in from the window when he opened them again.

He felt slightly clearer. *Definitely a hospital room. What the hell happened?*

He tried to sit up but felt a sharp pain in his right side and stopped.

The movement woke Paige. She squeezed his hand and raised her head from the bed. "Hey, you. How are you feeling?"

Chris just looked confused. "Paige?" His voice croaked and his throat hurt. *Why does my throat hurt?*

Liz stood up from the couch and walked over to him, saying, "Hi, Chris, nice to see you awake. I'll let the nurse know." She moved out of the doorway, heading to the nurse's station.

249

Chris blinked and looked around more, coming out of the fog slightly. Paige talked softly to Chris, briefly explaining what happened. He simply said, "Okay," and closed his eyes again. She was pretty sure he didn't retain any of the information. She smiled and sat back down, still holding his hand.

He woke up again a few minutes later when the nurse came in to check on him.

"Good morning!" she said brightly. "Nice to see you awake, Mr. Beckman."

"Chris." His head was slowly clearing, but his voice was very rough. "Call me Chris."

Paige got up and walked to the door as the nurse went through all the important rituals of hospital care, vital signs, pain levels, medications, etcetera.

The surgeon came by on his rounds while the nurse was there, so it was a good ten minutes before Paige and Liz went back into his room. The nurse had adjusted the bed, so Chris was sitting up, awake, but haggard.

He smiled when he saw Liz but was then visibly shaken when he caught sight of Paige.

"You're here." He shook his head slightly. "I thought I had dreamed that."

"I'm here, Chris." She took his hand and sat in the chair by the bed again. "I'm not going anywhere." Her voice sounded a little rough, and her eyes were bright.

Liz quietly left the room to find Zee.

Chris felt his chest tighten and closed his hand around hers, pulling gently to urge her up out of her chair. She stroked his face, moving her fingers through his hair, and he pulled her hand to draw her closer still. She rested her cheek against his, kissed the tender skin at the corner of his eye, and then kissed his lips briefly.

Paige straightened up and looked at him, and he lifted his left arm slightly in an invitation to join him on the bed. She smiled and said, "Are you sure?"

"Yes," Chris replied, his voice a little stronger. "The IVs and stuff are on the other side, and you are tiny." His eyes were getting heavy; they had given him another dose of pain medication, and he was going to fall asleep again soon. "Please, Paige." It was a whispered plea.

Paige tucked herself up on the bed with him, her head on his chest and shoulder, his left arm around her. She closed her eyes, sighed, and felt him relax, resting his cheek on the top of her head.

***

Zee caught the nurse's eye as she was about to enter the room and gestured in to where Paige was curled on the bed with Chris.

"Is it possible to let her stay that way?" he asked. "Because what you're looking at right there will heal him faster than any medication."

The nurse smiled. "I'll see what I can do. I think I can manage what I need to without moving her."

When Zee turned around, he saw Liz looking at him with a little smirky grin on her face.

"What?" he asked, smiling in return.

"You're a closet romantic." She was grinning broadly now, and Zee was shaking his head. "Don't try to deny it. I saw that. You," she poked him in the chest, "are all squishy inside."

"Whatever, Williams." But he grabbed her in a hug.

***

Before Chris even opened his eyes, he felt Paige next to him, tucked under his arm. He felt her breathing, the warmth of her body, the softness of her skin. His heart tightened in his chest, and he kissed her head, burying his nose in her hair for a long moment, breathing her in. *God, I have missed her so much.*

He was almost afraid to wake her, afraid that this was temporary. That when she awoke and found him coherent and stable, she would leave. The thought was enough to cause his arm to twitch in an instinctual, unconscious effort to hold her tighter.

As luck would have it, the movement woke her.

She pushed up from his chest to look at him, smiled, and then pushed away to try to stretch and get up.

He tried not to panic.

"Please, don't get up," he said, trying not to sound desperate, not certain that he succeeded. "I don't want you to get up."

"I need to stretch," Paige replied, moving off the bed. As she stood up, she added, "And to pee. Yikes." She scooted off to the in-room restroom and shut the door.

Chris put his head back and closed his eyes for a moment, shaking his head.

"She'll be back in a minute, Chris."

It was Liz. He hadn't noticed her sitting on the couch in the room. To be fair, he hadn't noticed anything except Paige.

"Hey, Liz."

"Hey, yourself. You gave us a scare. How are you feeling?"

He smiled a little. "Not too bad, considering I'm hooked up to all of this." He looked at the monitor and IV stand. "So, things are still fuzzy, but if I remember correctly, the nurse said I had a ruptured appendix? Is that right?"

"Yes." It was Paige who replied, coming out of the restroom drying her hands.

"The last thing I remember is being on the ice. Second period. Did we win?" He addressed this question to Liz.

"Yes, you guys won," she replied. "Rockets are out of the playoffs. They were pissed."

"You had appendicitis. The hit you took ruptured it." Paige ignored the conversation about the game. She hadn't moved her gaze from him since emerging from the restroom. "The pain was so bad you passed out. They took you off the ice on a gurney. You had emergency surgery. That's why you don't remember anything else." Her voice sounded strained.

"Oh. I guess that makes sense." Chris spoke cautiously, not sure what was happening between them. Or if anything was happening between them.

Liz took the opportunity to slip out of the room.

"No!" Paige's response was sharp, and Chris flinched slightly. "No, it doesn't make sense. You were sick. You had *appendicitis,* for God's sake!" She gasped a little, and Chris realized with a start that she was fighting back tears. "Why did you play when you were sick?"

"I didn't realize that I was."

Paige gaped at him.

"I swear, Paige."

She shook her head. There were definitely a few tears that were trying to sneak out. He held out his hand, and after a moment she walked to the side of the bed and took it.

"I didn't realize I was sick," he said softly. "I thought I was jet lagged from the trip and had pulled a muscle." He grimaced for a moment and added, "Although I guess I should have questioned it more when I puked before the game. I haven't done that since I was a rookie."

"You could have died." She barely whispered it, and Chris just stayed quiet. Paige took a ragged breath; she was losing composure. "I thought I had lost you."

"Baby." He pulled her close and held her in a hug, murmuring into her hair, "I'm okay. I'm going to be fine."

"I thought I wouldn't get the last line of our poem." She whispered it almost too quietly for him to hear.

She called it "our" poem.

He felt her take a shuddering breath, and then she sobbed quietly against his chest for a few minutes as she gave in and allowed the feelings to overwhelm her.

She pulled back to look at him, eyes bright, but

composed and stroked his hair gently.

"You can't play sick, Chris."

"I know, baby. It won't happen again."

"If I'm going to marry you, then you can't play sick. Ever."

"I know, baby, I swear…" He paused for a second while his brain caught up. "Wait, what?"

Paige smiled at him. "You heard me. You can't ever play sick again."

Chris was holding his breath.

She cupped his face in her hand. "Not if you still want me to marry you."

He pulled her into him so quickly that he dislodged some of the sensors, setting off alarm sounds and bringing a nurse to check and see what was going on. The nurse walked in on a rather passionate kiss. Paige still had her hands cupping his face; Chris had his one unencumbered arm snug around her waist. Neither noticed the arrival of the nurse until she cleared her throat.

They separated, and Chris did his best to turn his attention to the nurse, but he couldn't stop looking at Paige, and the nurse had to repeat things several times. Once she figured out that all was well and reattached all the sensors, she smiled and said, "As you were," as she left the room.

Paige leaned her forehead against Chris's and whispered, "I've missed you so much."

Chapter Thirty-Three

Chris was pretty sure there was a permanent grin on his face. Paige was downstairs getting some good coffee, and Liz was hanging out with him in the room. He had spoken with his mom, and he thought he had managed to convince her that he would be fine and that she didn't need to fly to DC. She might do it anyway.

Coach and the doctors had told him that he was out for the rest of the season, no matter how deep a playoff run they made. Even that frustrating bad news had to struggle to dim the joy that came from knowing that Paige was just downstairs and would be coming back to him soon. His face hurt from smiling.

Liz chuckled out loud, drawing his attention.

"What?"

"Really, Chris? You. And that grin." She was smiling at him, her eyes bright, sharing his joy.

"Hey, Liz, can I ask you to do me a big favor?"

"Of course, sweetie. Anything." Liz walked to his bedside. "What's up?"

***

Liz located the desk in Chris's apartment and opened the top drawer as instructed. He hadn't told her what she was supposed to bring to him; he had simply said, "You'll know it when you see it."

Her suspicions were confirmed when she saw the small velvet box.

Peeking inside, she couldn't help smiling—the ring set was perfect. Sparkly. Large, but not the least bit gaudy. It would look just right on Paige's hand.

Elegant, with substance. Just like Paige.

***

Liz managed to hand the box off to Chris when Paige was otherwise occupied. She gave him a kiss on the cheek and whispered, "Welcome to the family, Chris," before ducking back out of the room, where she met Zee on his way in.

Taking his elbow, she managed to maneuver them both so that they could watch through the doorway.

***

"Baby, I need to ask you something." Chris was sitting on the edge of the bed, and Paige walked over to join him.

"What's up?"

"I need to do this right." He got up from the bed

and settled carefully down on one knee.

Paige felt her heart start to race, and she whispered, "What are you doing?"

Opening the small box, Chris took her hand and said, "Paige Smith, will you marry me?"

She stared at him, wide-eyed, speechless.

After a moment, he said quietly, *"Tread softly because you tread on my dreams."*

She sank down to her knees next to him, tears in her eyes, and said, "Yes. Yes, Chris. I will marry you."

He took the engagement ring from the box and put it on her finger, and she just stared at it for a moment. Looking back up into his eyes, she asked, "When? When did you get this?"

Taking her face in his hands, he said, "Baby, you probably don't want to know."

Paige laughingly said, "You're probably right," and kissed him.

Liz, Zee, and the nurses who had gathered at the doorway cheered and clapped and filed into the room to congratulate them both. Holding Paige in a tight hug, Liz whispered, "I am *so damn happy* for you, Paige."

She whispered back, "Thank you," and gave Liz an extra squeeze. Pushing back, she said, "Oh my God, I've got to make some phone calls." Looking wide-eyed at Liz, she whispered again, "Holy shit, this is really happening!" Liz just laughed at her and then headed out the door toward the garage, on her way home.

"Liz." Zee hurried to catch up with her as she turned the corner of the hallway toward the elevators. "Liz!"

She turned and said, "Hey, what's up?" but her voice and her face were a little strained. Zee put his hands on her shoulders and looked her in the eye and saw her flinch slightly.

"Come here." He simply pulled her into his chest, and after the briefest moment of trying to stay strong, Liz let go and sobbed against his shoulder. Zee held her, not saying anything, and in a few minutes she breathed easier and pushed away.

Sniffling and wiping her eyes, she said quietly, "Please don't ever tell them."

"I promise."

"I love them both, and I am so happy for them."

Kissing her forehead, Zee said, "I know." Pushing her toward the elevator, he added, "Now get out of here. Go bring me a pizza or something."

***

After four days in the hospital, Chris was going stir crazy, beyond ready to go home. And to play hockey again. The Guards had won their first game of the series against the Philadelphia Liberty, and they were hoping to be up two games to none before they traveled to Pennsylvania for games three and four. Zee had swung by to say hi—he probably wouldn't be able to visit again until after they got back from the road trip.

They spent some time discussing the line changes that had been put in place to cover for Chris's absence; one of the young players that had been called up from the AHL team in Hershey was getting a chance playing left wing on the third line, and Andre Shifflin, the usual third line left winger, had been moved up to play with Navee and Zee.

"Shiffy's doing well. We've been taking some extra time in practice to work on our timing—I've gotten used to taking your slow-ass passes, so I've gotta adjust for his youth and speed."

"You're full of shit. And slow as fuck." Chris was up and sitting on the couch in the room, finally able to wear sweatpants and a t-shirt and walk around.

"Slower than you? I don't think so, Shuffleboard." He chuckled at his own joke. "So when are you getting out of here?"

"Today if I'm lucky," Chris replied and then grimaced as he moved too quickly to get up. "But hopefully tomorrow at the latest. This fucking sucks. I'm not even allowed to start any kind of rehab for at least another week."

Paige and Liz walked back into the room just then, and Paige said, "And so help me God, I will personally kill you if you start rehab even one day early."

Zee laughed out loud, shaking his head. "Already. It's started already." In an exaggerated stage whisper, he added, *"You're so screwed, Becks."*

Chris couldn't even hide the smile that happened when Paige walked into the room.

Zee moved toward the door, saying, "I need to get out of here. I've gotta get to the rink early."

Chris immediately looked suspicious. "Early? Why?"

Zee got a look on his face and paused before answering. "There was…an incident." The corner of his mouth twitched up. "I think it would be better to make sure I'm at the rink before anyone else."

"Jesus, Zee, what the hell did you do this time?" Chris was shaking his head and rolling his eyes.

"Nothing that can be proven."

No one responded; they all stared at Zee.

"What?"

The silence stretched, until he finally said, *"Allegedly* something happened involving Navee's water bottle." His eyes twinkled. "And a frog."

Liz burst out laughing, and Paige quietly murmured, "What am I getting myself into?"

Chris was chuckling to himself, still shaking his head.

Taking a breath, Liz said, "Okay, but please tell me that no frogs were harmed in the execution of this prank."

"Incident," Zee corrected. *"Alleged* incident."

"Fine. *Alleged incident.*" She poked Zee in the chest. "Please tell me that all *alleged* frogs are safe and released to their natural habitat."

"If there were any so-called frogs, they would have been well cared for." Zee was having a hard time not laughing. "I'm not a monster, Liz. Geez."

Chapter Thirty-Four

Once Chris was finally back at his apartment and settled in, Paige started back at work. But she was basically living at his apartment, only coming home to grab clothes occasionally, and she and Liz didn't see each other often in passing over the next few weeks.

During one of those rare times, Liz caught her and said, "Hey, I've talked to the landlord. They've got a waiting list for two-bedroom apartments, but they have a one-bedroom currently available. They're going to let us break the lease on this one at the end of the month if I move into the one-bedroom—since they've already got folks waiting, it's a win-win for them."

Paige sat down heavily on the couch.

"You don't have to do this, Liz. I'm sorry I haven't been here, but…"

"Paige," Liz interrupted her. "It's time. For both of us." She sat down next to Paige and took her hand. "You are looking at the next, amazing chapter of your life. And I'm going to be fine." Paige

looked concerned. "I promise, Paige. It's been almost two years. I can be on my own again. But I will never, ever stop being grateful to you for making this happen, us living together, you know…after Jimmy died."

There were tears in both of their eyes.

"You know I've been getting help, seeing a therapist, this whole time. It's made such a huge difference. I really will be fine on my own. But I will miss seeing you every day."

Paige had started crying. "You have to come over. A lot. Okay?"

"Definitely."

"Promise me."

Liz wiped the tears off her own cheeks and said, "You're an idiot. Your new house has a pool. You won't be able to get rid of me."

***

Chris was thrilled; the house was almost completely ready, and they could both move in at the same time. He made her pick out all the bedroom furniture, though.

"I saved that for last, just in case you decided to join me by the time I moved in." He still got a goofy smile on his face whenever he talked about them getting married, or moving in together, or really anything about her.

She couldn't help but smile back. "Let's go together to pick that out. It will keep your mind off other things. You're going completely nuts not being able to play."

"God, that's the truth. I mean, I know that I'm going to get back to a hundred percent, so I'm not worried, but this process is so damn frustrating, especially with the team playing without me." He mumbled a few choice words under his breath; the Guards were down three games to two in the second round of the playoffs. They were playing Pittsburgh, which made the frustration that much worse.

"Well, soon it will be June, and school will be out, and you will be feeling much better." She stood closer to him, sliding her hand along the side of his leg, around to squeeze his butt. "And then I will be able to work on much better methods of distraction than furniture shopping."

"I'm feeling much better now," Chris said quickly. "Like, right now." He cupped his hands around her breasts and squeezed gently in return.

"Mmm. Apparently so," she purred, moving her other hand to the front of his khaki pants and sliding it along the fly. "There is definitely something going on here."

"Paige…" His voice was full of hunger and longing, and he growled, "Go put on one of my dress shirts. And nothing else."

She felt the familiar flutter from the look in his eyes, and she gripped his shaft through his pants for a brief moment before turning to comply with his request.

When she came back to the living room, he was sitting in the big armchair, shirt untucked and unbuttoned, with the button and fly undone on his pants. He was just a little slouched and looked like sex personified.

Paige could feel her pulse speed up just looking at him and felt her body reacting, the flutters moving lower, arousal making her wet.

She said quietly, "My God, Chris, you are so handsome."

"Come here."

It was more an order than a request, and his voice was rough and low.

Paige complied, standing quietly in front of the chair. She had left the shirt she was wearing completely unbuttoned, but it was so large on her that it naturally fell closed in the front.

"Climb up."

Another order. He wasn't asking. His eyes were half-lidded, taking in every move she made. The flutters were becoming a low throb between her thighs.

She began to straddle him on the chair, and he released his very impressive erection from his pants.

He put his hands on her hips to position her and paused to ask, in a low growl, "Are you wet?"

Paige just nodded, unwilling to speak for fear of breaking this spell, this silent electricity between them. Her pulse was racing.

Chris guided her as she descended, and she was unable to keep back a soft moan of pleasure as he pressed his length inside her, slowly, taking his time to ensure she felt no discomfort, until he was as deep as possible.

He held there for a moment and then began to move her.

Slowly.

A small grinding motion.

Forward and backward.

Steady pace.

The movement was subtle, barely shifting. She was getting wetter by the moment, feeling him deep inside, the small shifts teasing her, making her want more. But he controlled the movement and didn't change tempo. Just that slow, shifting pressure of him, pressing against her, moving against her inner walls, the base of his cock teasing her clit.

He was staring at her, eyes pure lust, watching her. Paige flushed and gasped, surprised by how much these small movements were affecting her. She felt her muscles tensing, pressure increasing.

Her first climax gripped her, and she moaned as she held his shoulders, feeling her body contract around his erection, gripping him in waves.

The only change from Chris was in his eyes, a fleeting look of victory, followed by a darker look of lust. But his tempo didn't change. Slow movements. Subtle. Steady.

She struggled against him a bit, wanting speed and friction, but he gripped her hips more tightly, not allowing her to dictate pace. Forcing Paige to accept his control of this situation.

Paige felt a second climax building.

Slowly.

Slowly.

Her thighs started to quiver as she teetered on the precipice of orgasm and then was swept over in a rush, muscles contracting in pleasure as she came undone on his lap a second time, her moans pulsing in time with her body.

Chris was beginning to sweat, the only sign of how affected he was by this. His hands stayed firmly on her hips; his tempo remained maddeningly steady.

Paige felt her unsteady aftershocks, breathing hard.

She was so wet by this point that there was practically no friction between them, just the hot, slick sliding of his large body inside hers.

His pace became slightly erratic, not quite as steady, and Paige pressed herself harder against him. The continuing aftershocks were starting to feel like precursors, and she felt herself building again, gasping, until she unraveled one more time. The waves overtook her, and she cried out his name as she tightened around him.

At the sound of his name, Chris relented, closed his eyes, and gave in, grinding hard and fast, until he groaned low and long as he pulsed his release into her.

Paige collapsed against his chest, and Chris put his head back on the chair, shifting his hands from her hips up to her back to hold her against him, stroking her skin gently under his shirt.

He said, very quietly, "God, I needed that."

With a small sigh, Paige whispered back, "Me too."

Chapter Thirty-Five

Paige eventually called her mother to tell her about the engagement. Becca had offered to do it for her, but she didn't see how that would be any better, so she thanked Becca but said she would do it herself.

The conversation consisted of the predictable exhortations to get a prenuptial agreement, instructions to absolutely *not* return the ring if he changes his mind, and other words of advice regarding making him pay for the wedding ("I'm on a fixed income, I hope you don't expect anything from me") and not gaining weight now that she's "caught" him ("You don't want him to lose interest before you seal the deal").

Paige gritted her teeth through it.

In the end, though, she agreed to something, even though she didn't think it was a particularly good idea.

She agreed to come to Pennsylvania with Chris for a weekend to have dinner at her mom's house.

Chris was happy to do this; Paige tried to warn

him about the reality, but it was clear to her that he simply didn't have any frame of reference that would allow him to understand.

***

They checked into the hotel before going to her mom's house.

"I don't want to get there too early," Paige explained. "I want to make sure Becca is there first, with Margot and Jose, before we show up." She was pacing around the hotel room, trying to dispel some of the nervous energy.

"Paige, it's going to be fine." Chris stood in front of her and took her hands.

She huffed a little as she said, "You have no idea how badly this could go tonight."

He put his hands on her shoulders to hold her still and said, "You're right. But I'm going to be there with you, baby."

She wrapped her arms around him and pressed her face into his chest, seeking the comfort and reassurance she found in his arms, but the anxiety still squeezed her chest in a vise.

***

When they arrived at her mom's house, everyone came out to greet them, and things started out very well. Rose Smith, Paige's mother, was on her best behavior, being gracious and welcoming to Chris and Paige.

269

Once they were inside and Becca was helping her mom in the kitchen, Chris said very quietly, "This seems okay so far."

Paige sighed and responded, "Yes. But you need to remember that she has always been adept and controlling how things are seen from the outside."

Jose and Chris spent some time talking hockey—predictably, Jose was a Philadelphia Liberty fan, but they had a lively conversation while Margot listened in, occasionally commenting. She enjoyed watching hockey too, and Chris made a point of inviting her to a game the next time she was in DC, or the next time the Guardians played in Philly. Along with Becca and Jose, of course. Margot was thrilled.

Dinner passed relatively uneventfully, but Paige's mother was pushing wine on everyone, including Margot, and it had become obvious that she was intoxicated.

"Mom, Margot is fourteen," Becca said, removing the bottle from her mother's hands as she was starting to pour into Margot's glass.

"So what? Americans are too uptight about that. If we were in Europe, no one would care." She reached for the bottle again, saying, "Since when did you become so dull, Becca? You used to be the wild child. You weren't that much older than Margot when you got pregnant."

Paige interrupted to change the subject. "Margot, how about you help me clear the plates and we'll start the coffee and get ready for dessert?"

"Sure, Aunt Paige."

Once they were in the kitchen, Margot said,

"Aunt Paige, it's okay. Grammy says dumb stuff like that all the time. I just ignore it."

Paige smiled at her. "You're a smart kid. Honestly, you're helping me get away from the conversation as much as I was trying to get you away from it. So, thanks."

Margot hugged her.

Just then Rose came in the kitchen, followed by Becca. Becca was carrying plates, and Rose was instructing the men to stay behind and "talk about man things."

Paige glanced at Becca and flinched, bracing herself.

She knew what was coming.

"Well, Paige, he certainly seems like a very nice man."

"Thanks, Mom. He really is. I'm glad you like him."

"Well, it seems a little bit pointless to *like* him when he won't be around very long." Rose poured herself another glass and sat at the kitchen table while Becca, Margot, and Paige were starting the dishes.

Paige stiffened, her back toward her mother, and didn't respond.

"Have you gotten that prenup yet, like I told you?"

Paige didn't answer, and her mother just continued. "He's going to try to screw you out of money, you know. Just like your father. I'll have my lawyer draw up some papers for you."

Paige felt her shoulders slump. "Please don't, Mom."

Becca said, "I'm sure Paige will be able to find her own lawyer if she needs one."

"*If* she needs one? *If?* You mean *when.*" The next drink was being poured, and the slur was starting. "She won't look like that forever, you know."

Becca looked at Margot and said quietly, "Head out, kiddo."

Margot nodded, turned, and walked back toward where Jose and Chris were waiting.

"What?" Rose was getting agitated. "Why are you sending her away? She needs to know this stuff too." She called after Margot, "You need to know this too, Margot."

"No, she doesn't." Paige had finally turned away from the sink.

"Oh, she speaks. Please," Rose said, gesturing to Paige, "enlighten me as to what it takes to raise a daughter. As if you'd know. Twenty-eight years old and just *now* getting married. And you'd lose that hot little body if you ever got pregnant. He'd have no reason to want you then."

***

Jose looked up when Margot entered the room, his concern showing.

"It's that time," she said to him, and Jose handed her the car keys without question.

"I'll be out in a minute, kiddo."

Margot nodded and walked out the front door.

Chris was confused and concerned, as Jose got up to follow her.

"Go in there," he said. "This means things are getting bad. Becca sent Margot away because Rose is getting out of control. You need to check on Paige."

Chris got up hurriedly, worry creasing his face.

He was just outside the kitchen in time to hear, "Your looks are the only thing he wants. He wants you on his arm for people to see. And right now he wants you in his bed, but once your looks fade and your ass gets bigger, he'll be wanting to fuck someone else. You wait and see." The slurring was obvious and pronounced.

His anger was immediate and almost enough to overpower his sensibilities.

Chris managed to stride into the kitchen and put his arm around Paige so quickly that Rose barely registered his arrival.

"Ms. Smith," he said, managing to speak respectfully, but in a commanding tone that left no room for argument, "I want to spend the rest of my life with your daughter, and I don't appreciate your efforts to make her doubt that."

Rose was taken aback by this forthright comment and for a brief moment was unsure how to respond. She found her footing, though, and acid dripped from her voice as she spat back, "Sure, you want her now. She's a hot little trophy for you. But just wait until she gets older and loses some of those good looks."

Chris didn't even glance down at Paige before saying, in the same commanding tone, "Paige is the smartest woman I have ever met, with the kindest heart. She has a gift for teaching and a passion for service. I'm very sorry that you can't see that about her, but I assure you that I'm the luckiest man in the world that she has agreed to be my wife, and that has nothing to do with her looks."

Rose's face registered shock, and before she could open her mouth to retort, Chris finished with, "We will be leaving now. Thank you for dinner."

He took Paige's hand and walked them out the front door. Paige was too stunned to respond. Becca came running after them with Paige's purse. She said nothing but gave Chris a hug before going back into the house.

They got in the car, and Paige could see Chris's hands shaking as he started the car. As he backed out of the driveway, he had a death grip on the steering wheel. A glance at his face showed tensed jaw muscles. They rode for a few minutes in silence before Chris said, "Is there a park or something like that near here? I need to get out and walk. Or something." His voice was as tense as his jaw.

"Yes, turn right at the next light. There's a park with a lake a few miles away."

They continued to ride in silence, apart from Paige's directions, until they reached the park. Chris got out, opened the door for Paige, took her hand, and started walking rapidly along the path by the water's edge. Paige had to rush to keep up with his long strides.

About ten minutes later, Chris slowed the pace, finally stopping at a bench along the pathway where he sat down, looking out at the water. Paige sat next to him, putting her hand on his.

"Thank you," she said quietly.

He was silent for a moment longer. Still looking at the water, he said, "I have never been so angry in my entire life." He turned to look at her, his face still almost unreadable. "I don't even know what to say to you."

"What do you mean?"

"How is it possible that you grew up to be...you?" Cracks formed in his armor, and Paige saw the warring emotions playing across his features. "How on earth could you grow up with...*that*...and be *you?*"

She sighed and said, "Becca and I stuck together. She was the rebellious one, so of course I was the 'good' daughter, but we were always there for each other."

Shaking his head slightly, Chris said, "That doesn't explain how either of you could have grown up in that toxic cesspool and become decent human beings."

"It wasn't always that bad."

He just looked at her.

"Yeah, okay, never mind. It was always pretty bad." Sitting back on the bench, she said, "Some of the best people in my life were my teachers. Ones that cared about their students. That noticed really low self-esteem, for instance, and subtly went about trying to help. That kind of thing."

Chris pulled her in and kissed her forehead. "And so you became a teacher. God, Paige, I don't deserve you."

She laughed out loud and said, "Are you kidding me, Chris? You're the best thing that has ever happened to me." Her eyes welled up. *"And* you

275

just stood up for me to my mother, in a completely calm and rational way, without causing a scene, but without letting her get away with trying to tear me down." She shook her head. "I don't even know how you did that. I have never been able to respond without ending up in hysterics of some form or another."

"Baby, I don't even know how that happened, because I saw red the minute she started insulting you. Us. What we have." He sat up and took a deep breath. "Part of me was ready to tear the entire house apart."

"I've realized that I go into 'fight or flight' mode when I'm there." Paige leaned into his shoulder, and he put his arm around her. "My brain actually treats visits with my mother as literal life-or-death situations." Looking up into his eyes, she said, "And you, Chris, just swooped in with your shining armor and your white horse and saved me. Pretty impressive."

"I don't want you to ever see her again, Paige. I know that's not completely reasonable to ask of you, but my God, I am still so angry."

"I get it. But you know what?" She started smiling. "For the first time, *ever,* I do not feel guilty about leaving. This is the first time that I have left like this where I don't feel a kind of pull, some form of obligation, to turn around and try to apologize or smooth things over. This feels like a new start, Chris, and I am so grateful."

***

They met up with Becca, Margot, and Jose for breakfast the next morning. Chris had offered to drive them straight home the night before, but Paige had decided she wanted to show him some of the area where she grew up, to share some of the happier memories.

To leave the area on her terms, in her time, and not because she needed to escape.

To spend happy quality time with her sister and her niece, so they could get to know Chris better without interference.

As they were leaving the diner, Becca pulled Paige a little to the side, gesturing for Jose and Margot to head to the car, but motioning for Chris to stay.

"It's over, Paige. I'm done. After you left last night, I told her I wouldn't see her again until she got help. That I wouldn't accept any phone calls unless they were coming from an in-patient rehab facility. I can't tell you what to do," she continued with a small smile, "but I would strongly suggest that you do the same."

Paige looked stunned, and Chris took her hand as Becca turned to address him.

"Thank you, Chris." She smiled warmly, but her eyes were bright. "Thank you for taking care of my little sister. I should have been doing that all this time."

Paige started to protest, but Becca stopped her.

"Don't, Paige. Don't make excuses for me. I had my own reasons, and my own damage, but that doesn't mean what I said isn't true. I know you don't need anyone to help you, but I can't tell you

277

how happy it makes me to see you two together."

Paige asked, "How does Margot feel about this?"

Becca gave a wry laugh. "She's so much smarter than we ever were, Paige. She said, and I quote, 'Grammy has been making you unhappy for a long time, Mom. Don't worry about me. She's sick and needs help.'"

"Wow." The one word was inadequate to convey how impressed she was by this, but her face and tone showed it.

"Right?" Becca said. "Seriously, I should have done this a long time ago. I apologized to Jose last night, because I have let Mom say the most horrible things about him, and to him, without taking this stand. Like I said," she hugged Paige and then Chris, "this was long overdue."

Chapter Thirty-Six

Liz was waiting on the sidewalk outside of her office building; Paige was supposed to be meeting her to go to lunch to celebrate the end of the school year. She wasn't even looking at the car that pulled up in front of the building until Paige rolled the passenger window down and called her.

"Liz! Come on, get in!"

"What's this?" Liz asked as she got into the car. "I thought we were just meeting for lunch. I figured we were going to walk down the street or grab something from a food truck, and I expected you to show up by Metro. Where are we going? And why?" She laughed for a moment and then added, "Not that I'm complaining. I haven't gone *away* from the office for lunch in a hundred forevers."

"I got a wild hair and wanted to do something fun and different. I called your boss to make sure it would be all right for you to take a really long lunch."

"Really? You called Jason?" Liz turned in her seat to look at Paige. "What did he say?" She started to look suspicious and said, "What's really going on?"

"We're going to Old Town for lunch!" Paige chirped. "Chris is going to join us, and we have a reservation at DiNatali Brothers."

"Ooh, really? I'm suddenly very hungry."

Paige laughed, and they spent some time discussing the menu and then moved on to other topics, chatting until they pulled up in the middle of Old Town Alexandria, on King Street, where Paige maneuvered the car into a parking garage.

"I thought the restaurant was further down toward the waterfront," Liz commented as they reached street level.

"It is," said Paige, "But parking is easier here, and I've got a quick errand to run after lunch. We have a little bit of time until the reservation, and it's not a long walk."

Chris was waiting for them outside of the garage, looking as handsome as ever in suit pants and a crisp white shirt, sleeves rolled to the elbows and top buttons undone.

"Damn, Paige, the guy could be a model if he wanted to," Liz whispered to Paige, nudging her with her elbow.

"I know, right?" Paige whispered back, surprising Liz, who had expected some type of half-hearted admonishment.

"Hey, two beautiful women! Must be my lucky day."

Chris greeted Liz with a hug and Paige with a sweet lingering kiss, and Liz paused a moment to take in the happiness that practically glowed between them.

"You two are so damn cute together," she said with a grin. "But let's get this lunch show on the road, because now I'm dying for pasta!"

The three of them strolled the few blocks to the restaurant, chatting about nothing in particular and enjoying the lovely weather. There was uncharacteristically low humidity, and the light breeze kept the sun from feeling uncomfortably hot. Once they arrived, they enjoyed a leisurely lunch that fulfilled all of Liz's expectations.

The three of them took their time afterward as well, walking slowly back toward the parking garage, chatting and window-shopping. They stopped when Paige said, "We still have an errand to run, so come on, Liz, while we duck in here. Shouldn't take too long, and don't worry, Jason was very nice when I asked him to borrow you for such a long time today."

"What's the errand?" Liz asked. She looked up at the building as they were walking toward it, stopped suddenly, and her eyes got wide. "No," she whispered and looked over at Chris and Paige, who were grinning at her. "Really?"

"Really."

"Oh my God oh my God oh my God, *no way!*" Liz was beside herself, practically dancing on the sidewalk, and Chris and Paige had started laughing. *"What are you waiting for?* Come on! *You're getting married!"* She squeezed between them, grabbing them both and dragging them to the doorway of the courthouse.

***

Vows were said, the bride was kissed, paperwork was signed. Laughter, tears, and hugs.

Liz whispered, "I love you both so much," as she squeezed them tightly. "Thank you for including me."

"So you wanna house-sit for a few weeks?" Paige asked, dangling keys in front of her.

"What? Are you kidding?" Liz snatched the keys from her, making Chris laugh. "Damn right! A pool…mmm…and a full liquor cabinet…"

"Hey, hang on there…" Chris teased.

"Ample space for a keg party…"

"Wait a minute." Chris nudged her. "We want to get the house back in the same condition as when we left. Just to make that clear."

"So where are you going?"

Paige raised her eyebrows and looked to Chris. "Well, that's a good question, isn't it? All I know is that there's a beach involved, which he only grudgingly told me so that I could pack properly. Everything else has been a tightly kept secret."

Chris was grinning. "Well, baby, how about if I tell you when we're in the limo on the way to the airport?" He put his hand around Paige's waist, leading her out the front doors where an enormous black stretch limo was waiting for them.

Liz gave a low whistle. "Holy crap, Chris! You went all out."

Paige was staring and said, "But my car is here…"

Liz answered, "Just give me your car keys too.

I'll take care of it, Paige. No worries." She gave Chris a kiss on the cheek and one more hug to Paige. "Text me when you get there. And have an amazing time." She snapped a quick picture of them next to the limo and then went back to the garage for Paige's car to head back to work.

"Do you like it, Mrs. Beckman?" Chris whispered in her ear.

Giving a start, Paige turned to him, wide-eyed. "I love it." She giggled and added, "Mr. Beckman."

The driver held the door open, and Paige, feeling like she was floating on air, stepped inside.

Chris followed, and when they were sitting together, Chris said, "How does Hawaii sound to you?"

Paige put her head back against the seat and sighed, smiling. "Like a dream come true."

***

"Hey, Micky!"

"Becks! How's life? How's rehab going?"

Chris shifted the phone to his other ear and turned to look at Paige. He grinned and gave her a wink. "Well, for the next two weeks, rehab is going to consist of lying on a beach in Hawaii and banging my wife, so I'd say it's going just fine."

Micky started laughing but stopped short when his brain caught up to all of the words Chris had actually said.

"Ha! Wait, what? Your *what?* Your *wife?* Are you fucking kidding me?"

"Dead serious, my friend."

Paige could clearly hear the shouts of laughter through the phone, loud enough that Chris held the phone away from his ear.

"Holy shit, Becks!" More laughter. "Oh my God, I can't believe it. That is fantastic, my brother. Congratulations, Becks. My mom will be thrilled. She loves Paige already. Wait, when did this happen?"

"Like twenty minutes ago. We're in the limo."

Chris could not stop grinning. It was adorable.

They chatted for a few minutes, trying to figure out a time to get together…Chris and Paige had already decided to host a house warming/pool party at the end of July, but Micky would be in Rome with his parents and youngest sister to celebrate her graduation.

"I think we're going to come to Minnesota for a while in August. You going to be around then?"

Micky thought for a minute and said, "Yeah, I think that will work out. Let's touch base later and figure details. I've barely had a day to get to know your *wife."* Chris heard him chuckle to himself. *"Wife.* Shit, Becks. That's a helluva thing."

"Do you want to talk to her?"

"Yes! Put her on the phone!" Chris passed the phone to Paige.

"Hi, Micky!"

"I have a new sister-in-law! Congrats, Paige. I'm really happy for you guys." Micky's voice was joyful.

"Thank you! I'm pretty damn happy, myself."

"I am looking forward to getting to know you better. We'll figure out times to get together. It's a pain trying to work around schedules, but we will make it happen."

"Absolutely. Looking forward to it."

Micky got quiet for a moment and then said, "Paige?" in a voice that was far more serious.

"Yes, Micky?"

Micky paused again and then, quietly, with a bit of a rasp, said, "Be good to him, okay? Please. He deserves it."

Paige blinked back a tear at the raw emotion she heard in his voice and replied, "I will, Micky. I promise."

She handed the phone back to Chris, and the two men finished up their conversation. Chris hung up, tossed the phone on the seat next to him, and turned to Paige.

"That's it, baby. Obligations fulfilled. Everyone knows that needs to know, and now it's just you and me. For two weeks."

He put his hand on her knee and dropped his gaze to watch as he drew his hand ever so slowly up the inside of her leg.

Her breath hitched slightly, and she said, "Chris!" in a voice that was a little surprised and a little turned on.

"Mmm?" Chris hummed his question back to her, still watching his hand slowly push up the skirt of her sundress.

She gasped a little as he reached mid-thigh and was unable to keep from relaxing her legs, allowing them to part slightly to afford him room.

"What about the driver?" The question sounded breathy, and Chris looked up in time to see her put her head back and close her eyes.

He smiled, shifted his hand higher still, and said, "There's a privacy barrier. I asked him to keep it in place until we get to the airport." Moving his lips to her throat, he dragged his mouth up to her ear and said, "And I told him to drive around wherever he needed to be sure we had at least two hours alone together in the back of this limo."

Paige's lips were parted, and her cheeks were flushed. Chris watched her eyelashes flutter against her cheeks as he moved his hand further up her thigh, coming closer to her panties, and felt her legs part further for him.

"I've been thinking about this. About you." He had reached the edge of her satiny underwear and moved his finger to graze against it with the briefest of touches.

A quiet, breathy, "Oh," escaped her lips, and she opened her legs to him completely. He smiled against her cheek and, with just barely more pressure, dragged three fingers along the soft fabric from her entrance to her clit, allowing his thumb and pinky to run along the edges of her panties, along the sensitive skin there.

The flush had spread down her neck, turning the skin of her upper chest a beautiful pink.

Chris dragged his fingers back and forth along her crotch, teasing through the silky fabric, and Paige squirmed. He felt her heat through her panties and whispered in her ear, "Baby, you're getting wet. I can feel it."

She whimpered.

"I've been thinking about what I would say to

you, my beautiful word junkie." He used his middle finger to apply more pressure, drawing it slowly up through the valley of her labia as he continued to whisper to her. "I thought that maybe you would like it if I talked dirty to you too." He moved up over her clit with a little more pressure, hearing her gasp.

"But then I thought…" he said, reaching the top of her underwear and slowly sliding his fingers in reverse, down inside her panties. "I thought that maybe…" He had reached her clit again, and she moaned. "Maybe it would turn you on even more…" He reached her entrance and said, "…if I told you what it feels like when I slide inside you," as he pushed his finger slowly into her depths.

"Oh God." She was panting. "Chris…"

"It's like heaven, Paige." His voice was rough and soft at the same time, and he pressed into her and began moving slowly in and out. "It's like sliding into a soft, hot, wet, velvet glove."

Paige was breathing hard, moving against his hand, eyes closed, drowning in his words.

"When I slide deep inside you, when I feel your slick heat holding me so tight…" He pressed a second finger into her, and she moaned again. "When I'm as deep in you as it's possible to be…" He moved his thumb to her clit, and she cried out, shifting her hips against his hand. "Baby, it feels like I'm home."

"Oh God, Chris!" She no longer cared if the driver could hear her.

"I don't want to move, because it feels so good to have you pressed around me, and I don't want it to end." He brought her earlobe into his mouth and briefly sucked and nibbled on it before continuing.

"But it's impossible not to move with you, to move in you, to feel that satin friction between us. To feel the tension building." He increased the speed of his movements, rocking his fingers into her faster as she rocked her body against him.

"And, baby, watching you come is the most exquisitely beautiful sight I have ever seen." Paige gripped his shirt, grinding against him as he sped up again.

He leaned into her ear and said, "Come for me, Paige. Come for me."

Paige shuddered, and spasmed, and screamed, and Chris captured her scream with a hard kiss, holding her to him with one arm as she rode through her orgasm on his hand, then slowly sliding his fingers from her when the spasms were finally done.

"Oh God, Chris." Paige looked over to see him smiling at her. She felt almost unhinged, disconnected. She chuckled for a moment and then said, "I didn't know that you would say...stuff. And that I would like it."

Chris brought his fingers up and put them in his mouth, tasting her. He closed his eyes and made a sound of desire.

"I was torn between doing that and going down on you," he said, eyes dark with lust. "God, I love going down on you." His voice was getting lower, and he started fondling her breast with one hand. "I just couldn't figure out a way to talk to you at the same time."

He was circling her nipple; Paige was beginning to pant again.

"I love teasing you with my tongue. I love having my head between your thighs. I love feeling you grind against my face." His voice was rough, and he shifted to be able to use both hands on her breasts. "It makes me so hard. The smell of you; I came so fucking hard when you left your panties for me."

One hand still on her breast, the other reached under her dress. He grabbed her panties at one hip, bunching the fabric.

"Goddamn, Paige." He gave her nipple one last quick pinch before moving his hand to take hold of her panties by the other hip. He moved to kneel on the floor of the limo between her feet. "Goddamn. I can't…" He gritted his teeth. "Fucking…" He curled his hands into fists around the fabric. "Wait."

Chris flexed his arms and pulled to the sides, the panties shredding under his strength, and Paige gasped.

"Oh my God, Chris…" Her voice was breathy, and she cried out as Chris looped her legs over his shoulders and buried his face between her thighs.

She twined her fingers through his hair and moved against his hot tongue as he reached his hands to her rear to pull her closer.

He kept his tongue moving on her clit, tracing patterns with the tip, then switching to flattened licking, then circling, then back to fluttering patterns back and forth across, until she bucked against his mouth.

"Chris! Oh God, oh my God…" And then her

voice failed as her thighs clamped around his head, pushing against his mouth, muscles vibrating, toes curling. She finally pushed him away.

"Chris, I need you. Now, now, please I need you inside me."

She sat up and fumbled with his belt and pants, pushing his clothing down to wrap her hands around his throbbing erection as he pressed her down on the bench seat. One knee on the seat, the other foot on the floor, he pushed inside her with a grunt.

"Yes, yes, yes, oh yes…" she was whispering along with his thrusting. He almost immediately lost himself in the rhythm of their joining, his hands braced on the backrest and seat.

"Gonna come so hard, Paige." His voice was strained as he continued pumping. "Fuck, gonna come so hard."

"Faster…" It was a breathy whisper. "Harder…" And Chris sped up, pounding into her until just a few moments later Paige grabbed his ass with both hands and screamed his name.

White hot pleasure shot through him, the feeling so intense it was as if he were turning inside out in his body's effort to push himself into every part of her, every pulsing contraction making his whole body spasm. It went on for what felt like an eternity.

Chris managed to have the presence of mind to hold Paige and roll them both over, so that she was lying on top of him when he finally collapsed onto the seat, completely spent.

They lay together for a few minutes in satiated silence before Paige said quietly, "Holy crap."

Chris started laughing quietly, his torso shaking

Paige until she started laughing too. She finally pushed herself up and looked at him, her face flushed and her hair mussed, as beautiful as he had ever seen her.

The limo intercom clicked on, and they heard the driver say, "Mr. Beckman, we will be arriving at the airport in twenty minutes."

Chris acknowledged the message and then turned to his wife.

"God, baby. I thought sex was amazing *before.*"

Paige blushed and said, "Me too. That was…well, I think that was the actual definition of ecstasy."

Chris found a few bottles of water for them, and they began the process of putting themselves back together enough to be able to walk out of the limo. They spent the last few minutes quietly snuggling together.

"I don't know about you, but I suspect I will spend some time sleeping on the flight," Chris said, turning his head to look down at his wife. "I feel like a bag of Jell-O."

"Mmmm. Me too. Turns out married sex is pretty great. Who knew?" She sighed and snuggled closer.

"Two weeks of this, baby. Two weeks before I have to share you with anyone."

"Two weeks to start the rest of our lives."

Epilogue

Chris stood by the sliding glass doors with his arm around Paige, looking out toward their backyard and the pool, where Zee was hamming it up for a bunch of kids. There were about twelve families in attendance at their housewarming/pool party, and Zee had been the life of the party for the children, keeping them entertained in the pool ever since Liz shoved him in when he wasn't looking.

To be fair, he had dumped a large glass of ice water over her head earlier, so retaliation was to be expected.

Paige turned to put her arms around him and buried her face in his chest, sighing in contentment.

"Thank you, Chris."

He smiled, looking down at her.

"What for?"

"For this." She waved her hand across, gesturing at the backyard. "And this," she said, waving toward the house. "And this," she said finally, taking his hands and holding them out to the side, gesturing at him with her head. "For you." Her voice got quieter. "For us."

Chris tucked her hair behind her ear and held her cheek in his hand.

"Of course, baby."

"No, truly." She wanted him to understand. "Thank you for not giving up on me. On us." Her eyes were tearing. "Thank you for believing."

"Always." He leaned down and kissed her gently. "I will never stop chasing you, Paige."

About the Author

Law firm office cog by day.
Writer of steamy romance by night.
Hockey fan all the time.

Ellen lives in the Northern Virginia area with her husband and two sons, along with various furry and scaly creatures.
Life is good.

Facebook:
https://www.facebook.com/ellen.devlin.5494

Twitter:
https://twitter.com/ellendev_author

Website:
http://www.ellendevlin.com/

Join our Reader Group on Facebook and don't miss out on meeting our authors and entering epic giveaways!

Limitless Reading

Where reading a book
is your first step to becoming
limitless...

LIMITLESS PUBLISHING Reader Group

Join today! *"Where reading a book is your first step to becoming limitless..."*

https://www.facebook.com/groups/Limitless Reading/